It was a moonscape of desolation, destruction and death.

Where rockets had blazed into the hill, craters smoked; where MG-tracer and cannon-fire had lashed the ground, grass was seared and blackened, bushes shredded. Earth had been churned up by grenade blasts, redistributed by exploding rockets, further flayed by automatic fire. Before it had been dry earth. Now it was soggy. Now mixed in with it was blood, a lot of blood. And other body fluids. The area around the hill and on its slopes was like an open-air slaughter-house.

Bodies lay all around. Some were unrecognizable even as corpses, the result of direct or near-direct hits from the lashing firestorm that had savaged them from the sky.

There was a smell of burning in the air, and the strong and steely stench of death.

Other books by the same author in Star:

GUNSHIPS 4: SKY FIRE

Jack Hamilton Teed

A STAR BOOK

published by
the Paperback Division of
W.H. ALLEN & CO. PLC

A Star Book
Published in 1986
by the Paperback Division of
W.H. Allen & Co. PLC
44 Hill Street, London W1X 8LB

Copyright © Jack Hamilton Teed, 1986

Typeset in Plantin by Fleet Graphics, Enfield, Middlesex

Printed in Great Britain by
Hunt Barnard Printing Ltd., Aylesbury, Bucks.

ISBN 0 352 31577 6

PROLOGUE

The second man took just under a minute to die.

By the stopwatch, fifty-three seconds. There was some small change but the watchers weren't much interested in the fine detail, what happened too far beyond the decimal point. Fifty-three seconds said it all.

Fifty-three seconds was the cut-off point. Life had departed. The man was clinically dead. Now the rot, literally, set in.

One of the watchers – under more normal circumstances a dapper little man with a liking for fine wines, French women and coarse cheroots (not necessarily in that order) – closed his eyes behind the huge lenses of his face-mask. He was hot and sticky, and this worried him because the cumbersome overgarment he was wearing was supposed to allow for sweat-evaporation. Clearly the system wasn't working too well and the thought that preyed on his mind was that if it wasn't working one way, in an emergency could it be guaranteed to work the other?

Of course, *they* said it would. *They* had assured everybody that the protective suits and face-cowls had been tested under the most severe conditions. But what did *they* really know. How severe was severe? In any case, could you ever really believe anything *they* said? It would be just like *them* to supply the watchers with faulty suits, or suits that had not been tested properly, simply to see what would happen if a disaster occurred.

7

The dapper little man opened his eyes again and shifted slightly where he stood, his movements clumsy in the heavy suit. He deliberately did not glance at the thick plateglass set into the solid ferro-concrete wall facing him. He'd seen what had happened to the first man – the one who'd taken over five minutes to reach that stage where he could, with absolute certainty, be pronounced clinically dead. What had happened to the first man after that point had been in many ways worse, far more hideous and stomach-churning, than what had gone before. The dapper little man needed no reminder now; the sight would probably remain with him for the rest of his days. He closed his eyes again – and as though a switch had been thrown he was back in time twenty-four hours, in exactly the same place, with exactly the same monstrously-garbed companions, watching . . . watching . . .

The scientist was unusually tall for one of his race. The dapper little man guessed somewhere around the five foot ten or eleven mark. Possibly even six foot. He wore steel-rimmed glasses and, though gaunt of face, had a jolly smile. His colleague was stockier, running to fat. He too smiled a lot, but there was little warmth in the expression. The tall scientist on the other hand seemed genuinely cheerful. The dapper little man thought that if the tests were successful he had every reason to be.

'Please,' said the tall scientist. 'If we could all now put on our suits? There is of course no danger. The suits are merely a precautionary measure.' He chuckled as he gestured at the bulky garments lying on benches to one side. His stocky colleague smiled with his mouth only.

The dapper little man climbed into the padded boot-extremities, glancing at the rest of his companions. All looked slightly apprehensive, as well as mildly embarrassed that they should have to dress in front of other people, even though their undergarments were military coveralls that enclosed everything from wrists to ankles.

The dapper little man heaved at the bulky mass of material and shrugged himself into it, leaving the cowl hanging down his back while he zipped up various fasteners. The tall scientist was demonstrating how to slip the cowl over the head into the most comfortable position. He did this slickly, flipping the cowl over his head in one swift movement and masking his face completely, then flipping it back again. The dapper little man was reminded of an airline hostess demonstrating survival equipment. An apt analogy, he thought gloomily.

'Please note the breathing filter. It not only contains activated charcoal to absorb vapour but also paper filters to block particle-entry. The charcoal is impregnated with copper compounds, and is completely effective against any tiny molecule agent such as, say, hydrogen cyanide. Not,' he chuckled, 'that we need worry about that for this particular test.'

No indeed, thought the dapper little man glumly. This new agent made cyanide gas seem like the invention of ignorant barbarians.

'Note the voicemitters,' went on the unusually tall scientist, tapping at the bulbous snout beneath the two large eye-pieces. 'We will be able to hear each other and communicate with ease, although the voice quality is somewhat fuzzy. The ear-pieces are protected, of course. We have already developed a more sophisticated version with internal transceivers but it was not thought necessary to utilize that version for this particular series of tests.'

The dapper little man pulled the cowl over his head, clipped and zipped it into place. His fingers felt like sausages, even though the Butyl rubber gloves which encased them were skintight.

The wide lenses gave him plenty of vision. Even so he was already beginning to feel claustrophobic in the bulky garment. He coughed, and the sound seemed to reverberate around his head. He felt he could do with a drink.

Now suited up, his companions were all experimentally coughing and sniffing and snorting, as though for something to do. There was much shuffling around and subdued muttering. As the tall scientist had said, sound was by no means distinct. The dapper little man swivelled slowly round, taking in the rest of the room.

It was bare, concrete-walled; a utility room, nothing else.

Narrow benches lined two walls but that was all. There were no tables, no chairs. In one wall was a narrow oblong of reinforced glass through which the shuffling men in their cumbrous garments could see into the next room. It was as bare as this one, but with white-washed walls; in it a large clock was set into the wall, high up, opposite the viewing window. They could also see that the walls, as well as the glass panel, were extremely thick. Below the glass, on their side, a shelf was set into the wall; on it sat a single telephone, and above this a small instrument panel.

'The over-large eye-pieces have been specially designed,' the tall scientist said, his voice rasping foggily, 'to accommodate sighting a rifle or even using a missile-launcher. None of these functions need worry any of us here.' He laughed.

The dapper little man was suddenly reminded of one of his professors at the Sorbonne, years ago, a tall, vulture-like man who laughed a lot and was a great back-slapper, full of *bonhomie*. He was also, the dapper little man remembered, a profoundly unpleasant man behind his jovial mask, a shit of the first water. He suspected that the tall scientist, whom he had only met a few days before, was built along the same ugly lines. He too, the dapper little man was willing to bet, could be a monster if provoked.

'We are ready to begin!' the tall scientist's stocky companion barked suddenly. The dapper little man wondered which was the most senior, which had the most power. The unusually tall scientist, of course. It had to be him. That was why he was so jovial. He could afford to play any part he wanted to play, could afford to act the clown whenever it pleased him. The stocky man did not have so much power, and thus lacked that option.

The group crowded clumsily towards the viewing window. The dapper little man noted that the floor of the next-door room was white-washed concrete. Here there were not even any benches. There was nothing in it at all. It was just a white-walled, white-floored box. He glanced at the ceiling and saw that it was unpainted, then he noticed a tiny grille in the corner-angle high up on the right. That, presumably, was the inlet. He looked at the door, which was similar to the door in a

10

bank-vault, circular and heavy, ponderous. It now swung slowly open.

A naked man stumbled through the round steel-lined opening. Tall, Caucasian, powerfully-built, he looked in the best of health, the peak of condition. This surprised the dapper little man for a moment, before it occurred to him that the subject would have to be in good health and strong for the test to have any value. The door swung shut.

As though he had been reading the dapper little man's thoughts the unusually tall scientist said, 'Please to note the subject's condition, gentlemen. He is, as you can see, fit and healthy, which I assure you was by no means the case when we chose him. For two months we have been building him up. He has received the best medical attention we can provide, and the best food. T-bone steaks, salads, fresh vegetables. He is also, incidentally, perhaps because of this two-month regime, extremely virile. As well as good nourishing food we have been feeding him a diet of playful young ladies.' He laughed again. 'I use the word "feeding" metaphorically, of course. He may be likened to a young bull ready for the slaughter.'

There was an obedient group chuckle.

'May I ask a question?'

It was one of the dapper little man's colleagues who spoke. The dapper little man turned slightly in an effort to identify the questioner but it was impossible.

'Certainly.'

'Does he understand . . . ' the voice stopped, then carried on uncertainly. 'I mean, why does he think he is getting such treatment? Under the circumstances.'

'Ah. Yes. He was under the impression that an amnesty had been arranged by the Red Cross organization and that he was to have been released. What he thinks now I have no idea. He was given a special sedative last night, which I imagine will have worn off by now.'

This was clearly an attempt at irony. It was obvious to all those present that any drug that might have been administered to the man had long since ceased to be effective.

The dapper little man gazed at the subject, who was clearly puzzled and not a little frightened. The dapper little man

11

noted that the subject's penis was shrunken and the scrotum underneath was tight and wrinkled, though whether this was due to fear or the room's temperature was hard to say. Probably the latter. It would be cold in there.

He stood in the centre of the room staring around him. He licked his lips. His eyes swivelled this way and that. He turned slowly, saw the clock. A frown of puzzlement crossed his face. He went towards the clock and raised one hand, but it was out of reach. He turned again, facing the watchers. His face did not register any particular emotion.

'Can he see us?'

'No. At the moment the window is one-way, although it can be altered into a two-way mode. He is looking at himself.'

'Are we able to communicate with him in any way?'

'Yes, there is a transmitter system, but it is not necessary for this experiment.'

The man prowled around the room, slapping at the concrete walls with an open palm. He reached the door and felt round the steel fascia, but there was no handle or bar or release-button on the inside and he slammed his fist against the steel in frustration, then winced with pain. He started to shout, but the room was sound-proofed and the watchers could not hear what he was shouting. All they saw was his mouth opening and shutting, opening and shutting, lines of exertion furrowing his cheeks. He began pummelling the door with his fists, then fell back from it, breathing heavily and angrily.

The dapper little man turned his head and looked at the tall scientist, who was standing to his left. From this position he could not see the tall man's face at all, and he wondered idly if his expression was one of gloating pleasure or scientific detachment. Not that it made much difference either way.

Inside the next room the subject was now standing underneath the clock. The dapper little man noted that although it was set into the wall, a metal rim ran right round the clock's face, protruding slightly. The second hand jerked inexorably round; the time was 16:56.38.

Suddenly the naked man bent at the knees and sprang high, his hands outstretched. He clutched at the rim and the dapper little man stiffened with surprise as there was a fork-lightning

12

spark and the subject was thrown back through the air as though he had been punched by an invisible fist. He slammed down onto the concrete floor, yelling silently, his face twisted in agony, his arms held crossways over his chest, fists clenched under his armpits.

'A mild but salutary warning,' said the unusually tall scientist, chuckling throatily.

The naked man got heavily to his feet, shaking his hands, his face screwed up in a rictus of shock and pain. The clock now said 16:59.15.

The stocky scientist reached forward and picked up the telephone hand-set. He barked, 'Forty-five seconds!' He turned to the watchers, gesturing at the small instrument panel. 'We are able to control the experiment from here as well as from outside. This particular experiment will be set off from outside.'

The tall scientist now had a large stopwatch in his gloved hand.

He said, 'Please to note the grille, gentlemen.'

The dapper little man's eyes turned to the tiny grille. He could hear the stocky scientist counting off the seconds into the hand-set. 'Twenty. Fifteen. Ten . . . nine . . . eight . . . '

The naked man in the white box was shouting angrily at the door.

' . . . Three . . . two . . . one . . . *now*!'

The dapper little man saw a puff of red vapour surround the bars of the grille, but that was all. One second it was there, the next it had gone. All things considered, not very impressive. He had been expecting a great gout or spray of something, and in any case . . .

'Now observe the subject, please,' said the tall scientist.

Someone said, 'Is that all?' in a surprised tone of voice.

'*The subject!*'

The tall scientist's voice was a harsh snap of command. There was no jollity there at all now.

The naked man had suddenly stopped shouting.

He was coughing slightly, as though to clear his throat. One hand went up to his chest, the fingers lying splayed out across the mat of black hair there. Then he wiped his nose across the

13

back of his wrist. The dapper little man could see that quite suddenly there was a good deal of mucus running down from the nostrils. It was almost pouring out. The subject began coughing again, wiping his nose, coughing. His left hand came up and it was as though he was reaching out for something that only he could see. He looked bewildered. The hand was shaking quite violently. He took a step forward, then another. Then he began to turn towards the viewing window. The dapper little man noted mechanically that the pupils of the subject's eyes were expanding rapidly, visibly, until it looked as though there were no irises at all. Then the pupils contracted, just as suddenly, into tiny pinpoints. The clock said 17:1.03.

'Note the eye-activity,' said the tall scientist. 'Rapid expansion, equally rapid contraction. A curious effect. We have no explanation for it at the moment.'

The naked man suddenly gripped his stomach. Fluid was still running out of his nostrils and his eyes too were now weeping profusely. He bent over in an abrupt jack-knife motion, his face contorted. Fluid flooded down from his eyes, nose and mouth. In fact, fluid seemed to be gushing out of every orifice. The dapper little man winced in mild embarrassment as he realized that the subject was involuntarily urinating. The man clutched at his penis but it was only a feeble gesture; urine splashed off his twitching fingers, sprayed over the floor. The clock said 17:1.48.

The naked man vomited explosively. At the same moment, it seemed, he defecated in a great rush of diarrhoea that was more red than brown. It was as though a plug had been pulled. The dark mess gushed down the whiteness of his legs, flooded across the floor. Still clutching at his stomach the man fell forward onto the concrete. The clock said 17:2.16.

'Notice the complete breakdown and liquefaction of all bodily waste-matter,' rasped the tall scientist. 'This breakdown is almost instantaneous with the agent's introduction into the system. For the past month – indeed, up until yesterday – the subject's stools have been solid and perfectly normal. Now, within microseconds, the faeces have become liquid. Notice too how much blood there is. This is due to the rapid decom-

14

position of the stomach lining.'

The man staggered to his feet. He appeared dazed. It was clear that he was reaching the point where not only would he not know where he was and what was happening to him, but that this information, were it given to him, would mean nothing at all. He could be conscious of nothing now but the agony that was racking him internally. He stumbled a few paces and reeled into the wall. He clutched at the white-washed concrete surface with his fingers, swaying. He looked to the dapper little man as though he were on the top of a very tall building trying to hold himself up against a strong wind. He tottered round, his back now against the wall. His mouth was slack and drooling. His pupils had almost vanished. The clock said 17:3.39.

Abruptly he jumped forward towards the viewing-window as though pitchforked. He fell to his knees, then staggered back up onto his feet again. His arms and legs began to twitch in dreadful spasms. His chest heaved. His head jerked backwards, forwards, sideways. Uncontrollably. The dapper little man was reminded of a very old film he had once seen, a primitive science fiction movie made in the 1920s. Something to do with robots trying to destroy their human masters. Something had gone wrong and the robots had all gone crazy. The robots had been actors dressed up, of course, and their spastic twitchings and jerkings (rather like the crowds of blacked-up white actors in *Birth of a Nation*, which the dapper little man had also seen years ago) had merely looked embarrassing and absurd to the sophisticated art-house audience, who had all howled with laughter. The naked man's spasms looked exactly like the ludicrous antics of the spurious robots. It occurred to the dapper little man that that audience of movie buffs would not have laughed at this sight, the sight he was looking at now. He certainly did not feel like laughing. In fact, he was beginning to feel sick. The clock said 17:4.52.

At that moment blood spouted from the naked man's eyes.

Also from his ears and nostrils. He was vomiting blood, too. Pissing it. Blood was sluicing from between his buttocks. The clock said 17:4.57.

15

There was a sussuration of sound in the dapper little man's ears, the shocked gasps of his colleagues watching the scene. He realized that his own mouth was open, that he was adding to the sound himself.

'The subject,' said the unusually tall scientist, 'is now experiencing what can only be described as traumatic internal haemorrhaging. This will continue for some seconds.'

Something else was happening. Wide-eyed, the dapper little man saw that there were angry red blotches on the naked man's skin. At first he thought these were blood-splashes from the various orifices out of which scarlet fluid was still spouting, but then he noticed that they were turning darker red before his eyes. To carmine. To purple. To black. The clock said 17:5.04.

'You will all have noted,' continued the tall scientist, 'the marks of unusually rapid necrosis already in evidence. An essential feature of this particular agent.'

The naked man stumbled forward towards the viewing-window, still twitching in gross spastic spasms, still gushing blood. Then he lost his balance completely, keeling over to one side and crashing to the concrete floor. This time he didn't even attempt to get up. By now the white floor seemed awash with blood and liquid shit. The man's hands and feet continued to jerk convulsively but the spasms were growing feebler. The clock said 17:5.18.

The dapper little man wanted desperately to mop his brow and drink a glass of ice-cold water. Several glasses in fact. That would deal with the sweat-loss. Then a triple, or even quadruple, brandy. That might – but only might – deal with the horror he felt, and the threat to his grip on reality. He tried to swallow, but it was difficult.

The naked man no longer seemed naked. He seemed to be clothed in a ghastly red and black wet-suit. Feeble spasms still rocked his body in an undulating motion. Then even these ceased. The blood-flow was slower now; dark liquid oozed from the ugly shape in a sluggish, thickening seep. The clock said 17:5.29.

The tall scientist abruptly snapped at his stopwatch and turned away from the viewing-window.

16

'The subject is now clinically dead. However, the process of dissolution will continue for another ninety seconds.' He paused, then chuckled. 'That of course is an approximate figure. I would not want you to quote me on it.'

No one laughed with him.

The naked man's flesh was now all-over black. It looked as though he had been in a fire and was charred from head to toe. The dapper little man wanted to turn away but could not. He was mesmerized by the sight. Beneath the blood-slick that covered it the flesh was sinking in hollows, caving in. The dapper little man endeavoured to rationalize this. What it could only mean was that the bone, gristle and cartilege was actually crumbling, that the body itself was quite literally rotting away as he watched.

But that was impossible.

Except – it was happening. It was happening right there, on the fouled floor of the white-box chamber next door. What six minutes before had been a healthy human being in the peak of condition was decomposing in the time it took to extract a cheroot from its box and light it.

The dapper little man turned away. He'd had enough. He noticed that his colleagues had had their fill too. Only the tall scientist's stocky companion remained, face-cowl pressed to the glass, gloating over the last oozings.

The tall scientist went to the door and the rest clumped after him. They had been told not to take their suits off. Just in case. With this kind of scientific breakthrough you could never be entirely sure of the safety margin. Under his face-cowl the dapper little man's expression was bleak.

They were herded into another, larger chamber. This contained cubicles where each man was subjected to a number of high-pressure, high-temperature detergent sprays angled down from walls and ceilings, as well as upwards from the floor. The force of the sprays was such that the men had to cling to special hand-grips set into the wall or be bowled over by the intense detergent bombardment, which lasted for nearly ten minutes.

In his cubicle the dapper little man breathed a long, heavy sigh as the sprays ceased. He unzipped, then pulled off the face-cowl and climbed out of the overgarments. He put on a pair of white boots and paddled across the soapy floor to a locker in which were hanging several pairs of sterile whites, jackets and trousers. He dressed. He followed his colleagues into a starkly furnished lecture room. He still needed a very large brandy – but first . . .

The very tall scientist was rolling himself a cigarette. His long fingers packed and dabbed at the tobacco, expertly twirling the paper around it into a neat thin cylinder. He flicked along its length with his tongue, gave it one more twirl, put it between his lips. The dapper little man leaned forward and offered the flame of his lighter.

'Ahh. Thank you.'

The tall scientist sucked smoke into his lungs, nodding gratefully. He spat shreds of tobacco at the floor.

'A triumph,' said the dapper little man enthusiastically.

The unusually tall scientist's smile was, for once, self-deprecatory, although the dapper little man wasn't fooled for a moment.

'A modest one only, I regret to say.'

'No, no. A quite brilliant achievement. You may count on my whole-hearted support in this enterprise.'

The tall scientist gave him a shrewd look.

'Your enthusiasm is worth much, my friend. As is also your support. You may be sure I will not forget it.'

The dapper little man gave a slight bow of the head. Others of his colleagues now crowded round the tall scientist, jabbering excitedly, but he had got there first and that was all that mattered. His name was known anyway; now his face had been registered, his 'enthusiasm' noted.

The stocky scientist entered the room and clapped his hands.

'Places, please!'

The dapper little man and his companions dutifully sat down behind small tables equipped with pads and pencils. At the front of the room the tall scientist beamed at them. He was still smoking his cigarette.

'You are privileged, gentlemen. You are the first to witness this historic demonstration. My colleagues and I have been

18

toiling for many years and the agent whose effects you have just witnessed is the end-product of much research, much labour. The work has been arduous; at times the problems seemed intractable. But the goal we set ourselves was a worthy one, and as . . . my leader once said, the worthy aim demands the hardest sweat.'

He went on in this vein for some time. The dapper little man heard him with only half an ear. He had noted with some amusement the barely perceptible pause before the word 'my'. The unusually tall scientist had been on the very brink of alienating the whole lot of them, destroying all the fruits of his 'arduous' effects (which had most likely been made by a horde of underlings anyhow) by saying '*our* leader'.

That, thought the dapper little man wryly, would certainly have put the cat among the pigeons!

Remembering that now, twenty-four hours later, caused another twitch of amusement. The dapper little man smiled dourly at the thought as he stood for the second time in front of the viewing-window in his bulky overgarments and goggle-eyed face-mask. He still did not raise his eyes to look inside the chamber. It had been bad enough watching the original process repeat itself with another subject – seeing the horrifying five-minute sequence compacted into fifty-three seconds. It had been like watching a speeded-up film. The dose for the first experiment had been five-tenths of a milligram. The dose for this second demonstration had been ten milligrams. It had taken the original subject four minutes and fifty-two seconds to reach the point where he started haemorrhaging. The second subject had erupted in a bloody explosion in just forty-eight seconds.

It appalled the dapper little man, who had always believed his horror-threshold was extremely high. So much for that.

He decontaminated, managed to get in first with some effusive congratulations once more, listened to the tall scientist explaining in graphic detail what they had all just seen, joined in a half-hour back-slapping session with his colleagues, and at last found his way back to the office he had been assigned in the complex.

He poured himself a strong slug of brandy, gulped at it, and lit one of his favourite thin coarse-leaf cheroots. He sat back in the utility-style swivel-chair and stared at the bare and depressingly-coloured wall in the cheerless room. The door opened, shut. He didn't bother to turn round. His chief aide, a man who had been with him for nearly twenty years and whose fierce, almost fanatical, loyalty was the one solid fixture in an increasingly fluid world, came round the desk and stood silently beside the visitor's chair. The dapper little man nodded. His aide, another unusually tall man with an oddly wizened face, sat down.

'Another glorious fucking triumph for our brothers-in-arms?' His accent was thick, provincial. He had never lost that touch of peasant his master had deliberately shuffled off decades before. Although master could often be as coarse-tongued as servant; as now.

'Don't give me that shit,' said the dapper little man.

'What sort of shit d'you want?'

The dapper little man reached forward and spun the dial of the desk telephone a couple of notches. He stuck a pencil in one of the number-slots, jamming the dial. He knew the room was safe – his aide had spent two hours on it when they'd arrived, checking out everything: desk, chairs, electric ceiling fan, ceiling itself, floor, phone, walls, filing cabinet – but you could never be too careful.

'I've just seen the death of the human race.'

'So you said yesterday.'

'I don't like it.'

'You said that too.'

'And I don't like *them*.'

The man with the wizened face laughed. He said, 'Have I your permission?'

'Yes, yes.' The dapper little man waved a hand irritably. The aide lit a cigarette.

'I don't like the way things are going.'

'You keep repeating yourself.'

'At this rate the bastards'll be taking over completely.'

'Not much you can do about it.'

The dapper little man pondered this. He nodded slowly.

'There's certainly not much I personally, or the people who think as I do, can do about it,' he agreed.

'Well, there's fuck-all anyone else can do.'

The dapper little man delicately picked his nose and flicked what came out into the waste-bin by the side of his desk. He sucked at the cheroot and let the smoke curl lazily out of his mouth and nostrils. With the cheroot between his fingers he leaned forward on the desk with his elbows and pyramided his hands, staring through the drift of smoke at the man with the wizened face.

'That's not entirely true,' he said.

I

It was a moonscape of desolation, destruction and death.

Where rockets had blazed into the hill, craters smoked; where MG-tracer and cannon-fire had lashed the ground, grass was seared and blackened, bushes shredded. Earth had been churned up by grenade blasts, redistributed by exploding rockets, further flayed by automatic fire. Before it had been dry earth. Now it was soggy. Now mixed in with it was blood, a lot of blood. And other body fluids. The area around the hill and on its slopes was like an open-air slaughter-house.

Bodies lay all around. Some in jumbled, twisted heaps, some in spreadeagled isolation. Some were whole with red MG stitch marks criss-crossing them, others were missing limbs or heads, or both. Some were unrecognizable even as corpses, the result of direct or near-direct hits from the lashing firestorm that had savaged them from the sky.

There was a smell of burning in the air, and the strong and steely stench of death.

There was also the racketing roar of helicopter gunship rotors. Some of the birds hung high in the sky, their spotlights turning night into brilliant, hard-edged day. Others were squatting on the low land beside the river: nose-on they looked like giant bugs about to pounce. Men milled about, picking over the debris of bodies, small-arms hardware and spent rounds, shouting at each other over the noise of the choppers.

An officer wandered around holding a clipboard, puffing at a short stub of cigar jutting out of his mouth as he made rapid notes with a pencil. A black sergeant hurried up to him.

'Ninety-nine poin' nine-niner, sir. That theirs.'

The officer nodded, speaking round the cigar.

'What's our score?'

'Only one, sir. Far as we can tell. That check out with what the colonel say.'

'Right. Always best to make sure, sergeant.'

'Sir.'

'Get all documentation, weaponry, any other hardware. List it. The usual.'

'Sir. What about the one?'

'Bag 'im an' tag 'im, sergeant. Get 'im out.'

The sergeant snapped a salute and doubled off, yelling at a small group of grunts who were lighting cigarettes by one of the choppers.

'C'mon, girls! Put those fuckin' things out or yo' ass is grass an' I gonna mow it! This ain't fuckin' Coney Island!'

The officer – a major – was black too. He watched the grunts galloping after the sergeant for a moment, then went back to his note-taking. He wrote fast, in shorthand. The paper in front of him was easy to discern; there were no shadows under the powerful glare of the spots from high above.

He moved slowly towards the cratered hill, writing as he walked. It was not a straight path he trod. Every other step was a side-shift to avoid a sprawled figure or a disembodied head with staring eyes or a for-the-moment-unidentifiable something that had once been an integral part of a man. He moved nimbly, like a ballet-dancer.

Colonel John Hardin of the US Special Forces watched the black major zig-zagging slowly in his direction. Hardin had finished cleaning his Kalashnikov AK-47 and now he was reassembling the weapon. There was a light film of oil on the parts and on his fingers, and every now and then he used a piece of rag to wipe his hands dry. He checked the banana-shaped mag for the third or fourth time, then slid it smoothly up into the weapon. He aimed the assault-rifle at a body slumped some way down the hill and idly snapped off a phantom shot.

He was tired. This was not surprising. Only a half-hour before, he and his rag-tag squad had been defending the hill against possibly as many as ten times their strength. At the end it had been hand-to-hand, a desperate and ferocious battle for survival with what seemed like an unstoppable horde of kill-crazy EnVees.

Now it was over. The gunships of the SSG – that very special force within the Special Forces – had been alerted via a last-ditch SOS and had made it just in time. Quite literally only seconds before Hardin and his men would have been cut down and shredded by the seemingly blood-maddened Vietnamese, whose honcho, in his frantic effort to get his hands on a fortune in pure mega-grade heroin, had been willing to sacrifice any number of EnVees to overwhelm the position.

Hardin's gaunt mud-and-blood-smeared features creased up into a bleak smile at the irony of it. The heroin itself – ten keys of No. 4, 'croak-dope' so pure that on street level it had to be cut one part genuine to fifteen parts flour-and-talcum because if you hit intravenously without cutting, your heart exploded and your brains blew out – had already been destroyed long before the EnVees came screaming up the slopes of the hill from all sides. It had gone up in a blazing spout of flame in the crashing destruction of an Air Cav Huey piloted by a crazed Remington Raider from Saigon who was taking payola from the Corsican Mafia. Maybe as much as ten million bucks worth of scag fried out to nothing in probably the most expensive funeral pyre in the whole fucking war.*

Hardin shook his head briefly. It was a crazy world and a crazy war. At times it seemed like the only thing you could do about the insanity of Vietnam was shake your head, mutter 'fuck it,' and drive on.

He noticed that the black major had been joined by a lieutenant who also had a clipboard in his hands. They were comparing notes. Hardin put a cigarette in his mouth and Zippoed it alight.

He had a long report to make to General Lewis J. Halderling, boss of the SSG, about the whole heroin business

* See *Needlepoint* by J.H. Teed

and Mafia links with the US forces in Vietnam. He wasn't looking forward to it. There was a hell of a lot of work in prospect, a lot of dictating, and reading, and checking and re-checking, and sitting around in un-airconditioned offices waiting to testify at military tribunals. Stupid work that at the same time had to be done, *needed* to be done. In Hardin's heart was a cold blaze of anger at the rot of organized crime that had spread like a vile cancer through certain parts of the most powerful army the world had ever seen. And what galled him – what brought a bile of sour bitterness seeping up into the back of his throat – was that even after a hundred tribunals much of the rot would still be there, somewhere, in some ugly form or other.

He sucked at the cigarette, inhaled deeply, blew a plume of smoke out into the spotlit darkness.

Still, he thought, something would be achieved. And Halderling would have fun with it, if nothing else. The canker of Mafia-dominated heroin-running had spread into areas for which Halderling had no use whatever. There was a CIA involvement somewhere and Halderling would love that. He got off on trying conclusions with the Company, and more often than not the battle went his way – or at least, not entirely the Company's way. Not losing, in this game, was often as good as winning.

Hardin too had immense grudges, some of them going back years, against those wackos emanating out of Langley. The Company owed him; certain senior operatives would like nothing more than to see him six foot under. That was a fact. And the feeling was mutual. It was the Company, in one way or another, that had got him into his present bizarre predica-ment, a position in which he was supposed to be on an extended R-and-R because of the weird things that had been happening to him over the past few months.

A rogue general had been shifting top-level secrets to the EnVees. Hardin had iced him. Some of the general's personal files, however, were discovered to be not merely hot but actively incandescent: they fingered not only high-ups in MACVee, but men who were tight with South Vietnam's President Thieu himself. That had stirred the pot. And then

Hardin had broken up an army of renegades in a near-impregnable valley in Cambodia backed by a small bunch of CIA lunatics who'd been hot for throwing nukes at China. Just to stir the shit around a little.

And now this, he thought moodily, staring at the bloody battlefield in front of him. Corsican and Sicilian Mafiosi in a to-the-death war for the multi-million dollar Laos-Saigon dope-trail, and it looked like a Company element were hedging their bets and supporting both sides at once to cream off the profits from whoever won. Not to mention Charlie Cong, who'd also muscled in on the act; jumped onto the bandwagon to subsidize arms-and-matériel-buying with all that moola.

'Hey! Sir!'

Hardin didn't bother to turn round. He knew who it was. Charlie Garrett, one-time private, then corporal who'd been busted back down to private again for some misdemeanour or other. Oh yeah, and who was currently supposed to be dead-by-firing-squad on account of he'd murdered some fat-cat EssVee, having been put up to the job by the EssVee's son. Not forgetting why he'd joined up in the first place, which was because he'd been a Murder Inc hitman who'd pissed off some high-up in the Mob and been placed on a squelch-list himself.

Garrett stomped up and squatted down beside Hardin. He was a solid man, not yet run to fat; if you ran into him head-first in the dark it'd be akin to butting a brick wall.

He pulled off his helmet, ran a hand through his close-cropped reddish hair. He shot a grin at Hardin that was almost too fast to note.

'Hey, ya think they'll pull us out now, give us ribbons, honourable discharges? Send us back to the World? Huh? Sir?'

Hardin shrugged and stubbed out his cigarette.

'That's the sixty-four thousand dollar question, Garrett. I don't have the answer. I already told you that.'

'Yeah, but, you know, we been muscular for MACVee, for fuck's sake. They gotta give us something. Shit!'

'Last I heard, you ought to have been stuck up in front of a wall with an eight-man rifle party waving at you.'

Garrett scowled. His scowls generally stayed on his craggy face considerably longer than his smiles, which were notable for their rarity.

'Well, hell, I know *that*. But it ain't the fuckin' point. We done a lotta good work. Saved *your* shit a deal a times. Sir.'

Hardin chuckled. He couldn't help it. He pushed back his helmet, wiped the back of his hand across his brow. This took some of the sweat off but added to the grime.

'Jesus, Garrett. You are one cool sonofabitch.'

Garrett's expression shifted into neutral.

'There's the matter of those ten keys of happy powder to be discussed, Garrett. If you'd taken 'em to Lieutenant Comeraro like I told you to,' Hardin waved a hand at the scene of desolation in front of him, 'none of this would've happened ...'

'Well, I didn't know it was scag,' said Garrett defensively. 'It was that prick Renucci. He jumped me, took off with the bag. Wasn't my fault things tipped over the edge.'

'Crap,' said Hardin. 'You opened the bag, Garrett, and saw what was in it. It's the only explanation for what took you so long. You then got bounced by Renucci. And because you never got to Lieutenant Comeraro he and the rest of the squad were grabbed by the bad guys. You were gonna take it on the lam with all that dope, fade out, disappear. You thought it was Christmas Day four months early.'

'If that prick Renucci hadn't jumped me,' said Garrett moodily, 'you cocksuckers wouldn't't've seen me for dust.'

Hardin let a faint grin twitch at the corners of his mouth. There was no percentage in making a fuss. Garrett was Garrett, take him or leave him. There were very few things you could say in his favour, a hell of a lot against him. Even so it was difficult, under the circumstances of the general Vietnam madness, not to admit a sneaking and very small liking for this arrogant, thuggish, monumentally self-centred but by no means monumentally evil man. In an ordered society Garrett was the type of guy you'd automatically set the dogs onto if he came within a few hundred yards of your house. But this was not an ordered society. This was not the World. This was Disneyland. None of it was real.

He glanced to his left where Sergeant Olsen was organizing a weapons-clean with the remnants of the squad.

All things considered, it was not a squad whose sheer quality shone out like a good deed in a naughty world. That had to be admitted. Olsen, for instance. Fragged his own Loot in the field. Another candidate for that last cigarette at dawn. Doc Pepper, the medic. A dopestick of the first water, who'd been running junk out of Central Supplies and been tagged by the MPs in some seedy situation or other. Leroy Vogt. A kid who'd blown away his sarge in a firefight.

There'd been others: Colby, Meeker, O'Mara. They'd died. And then there were the guys he'd somehow picked up on the renegades assignment: Lieutenant Comeraro, Sergeant Fuller. They'd in fact done nothing wrong. There was no threat of execution hanging over them, nor the prospect of a five-to-ten in the brig. But somehow they'd been stuck on to him, and from what Phil Esteban had said back at SSG HQ at Do Thon, it was not going to be a simple matter to get rid of them. Not that Hardin wanted to, particularly. Both Comeraro and Fuller were Special Forces from Chuck Welland's base at Pen Kho, down south about a hundred klicks or so, and both were solid and dependable men. But all in all it was a scarecrow squad, and made more so at the moment by the presence of three men – Hallings, Rand and Laguna, if those were indeed their real names – who were not even enlisted men but, as far as he could gather, Mafia minions in stolen plumage.

Jesus, Hardin thought, the guy that tackles the paperwork on all this deserves a Silver Star. At least. He turned back to Garrett.

'You'd've been eaten by tigers, Garrett. You wouldn't have had a fucking chance.'

Garrett acknowledged the truth of this by changing the subject. Other matters had greater priority.

'We done what we fuckin' set out ta' do,' he grumbled. 'We been in some real shitstorms. The way I thought it was gonna be, we do the dirty work an' we get let off the hook. Well fuck it, we *done* the dirty work. Now they gotta let us go.'

In a way all this was true. Hardin had had the word of Lew Halderling himself on that, after the renegade business, and he'd worked for Halderling too loyally and for too long for the general to break that word. Even so, Halderling was a busy man. He had other priorities. And in any case the 'squad' was now inextricably linked with Hardin himself, and the way things were, that meant a good many strikes against them; all of them. At the moment Hardin was in bad odour at various levels of Command; anyone consorting with him, however loosely, automatically gathered some of those same black marks.

He said to Garrett. 'Maybe, maybe not. You know what this man's army's like, Garrett.'

'Yeah,' said the big man disgustedly, getting the message, 'a crock is what it's like.'

'You're still alive, Garrett,' said Hardin bleakly. 'Don't knock it.'

Garrett banged his helmet on and stalked off down the hill, and Hardin could almost discern the black cloud hovering over his head. He shrugged. Garrett would toe the line. He had to. If he didn't, he'd be thrown to the wolves – in the shape of the South Vietnamese authorities, hot for executing him – quicker than it took to spit.

Hardin glanced at his watch, yawned. It still needed an hour or so to dawn and there was still a hell of a lot of work to be done. But others could ramrod all that. He needed a shower and a bed, and food that wasn't just C-rats. The sooner he and his men got out of here and back down to Do Thon the better.

The black major had climbed the hill. He lifted an eyebrow at Hardin.

'You could do with some rack, sir.' It wasn't a question.

'You're not kidding.'

'Jesus.' The major gazed around at the carnage, a mildly perplexed expression on his face. 'Was a near thing. We have a rough body-count of forty-eight, but I guess there's more than that. We have nine seriously wounded, and another fifteen not so seriously. We have only two EnVees without a scratch.' He grinned. 'How come you missed 'em?'

Hardin grinned back.

'More to the point, how come they missed us?'

'Yeah, you only had . . . ' he consulted his clipboard, 'one KIA, far as I can make out.'

'Guy called Snell. If that really was his name.'

The major twitched his eyebrow again.

'You, uh . . . have some doubt about that, sir?'

Hardin shook his head. The intricacies of the situation would take about a week to figure out, another week to explain. He didn't feel up to telling the guy that Snell was a Mafia mobsman who'd gone wacko under fire.

'Forget it. It's a complex business. It'll all come out with the suds.'

The major shrugged, went back to his clipboard.

'Could be there are one or two still loose, Colonel.' He gestured at the hovering gunships. 'When we arrived they were all over you on top of the hill. We had the floods on and we lit up most of the area, but I wouldn't swear some of the Cong didn't make it to the trees.' He frowned. 'See, we haven't tagged anyone yet who had a high rank. With this muscular force I'd expect the equivalent of a major at least. Maybe even a colonel.' He shrugged again. 'But so far it's one big zero. These guys are all enlisted men, NCOs. That weight.'

Lieutenant Comeraro appeared at Hardin's side with a weary salute.

'You have any orders, Colonel?'

'Yeah. I think we'd better climb on the nearest chopper and get the fuck out. How are the Mafia-men making out?'

The black major's face registered cautious incomprehension. Comeraro gestured down the hill.

'Garrett's guarding them. Kicking them around some. He seems pissed off about something.'

'He is.'

Hardin wasn't entirely sure he liked the idea of Garrett, ex-Mobsman, mixing with the three Mafiosi. On the one hand, there wasn't much he could do with a couple of hundred grunts milling around. On the other, Garrett being Garrett . . .

'Tell Fuller to take over from Garrett. Garrett and those guys are too rich a cocktail. We'll move out soon.'

The young lieutenant with the clipboard scrambled up to the top of the hill. There was a head, unattached, lying in his path. Its eyes were open, staring sightlessly up into the night. The lieutenant casually kicked it and watched it bounce down the hill.

'Hey-yyy!' He grinned at Hardin. 'Real duck-shoot you had here, sir! Musta been tight as an asshole for a minute or two, till we came along. Real tight. Guess we saved your nuts, hah?'

Hardin's expression was about as friendly as rocks on Mars. A feeling of sudden rage surged through him. He leaned forward and stared into the man's eyes.

'*Salute, you sonofabitch!*' he hissed.

The lieutenant gulped, startled, and leaned away from him. His right hand began a rapid climb through the air.

But the extended fingers never reached his forehead.

The sound *Uggh!*, or something very close to it, came out of his open mouth and his left eye suddenly disappeared in a flare of blood. Dropping the clipboard, he reeled away from them in what seemed like some complicated dance-movement, then collapsed onto the ground, pitching over and over down the littered hill slope.

'*Down!*' yelled Hardin.

II

Lieutenant Arthur Comeraro swore as he dived into the earth, squirming round as he hit dirt. The shot had come from behind him, from the dense woods that spread away to the south. He stared at the trees. The thunderous clatter of the hovering gunships drowned the sounds of gunfire but he could see the muzzle-flashes quite clearly.

The crazy bastards, he thought. There's about a zillion weaponed-up US grunts here, but only a handful of EnVees. What are they trying to do? Commit suicide?

Sure, he thought. That's exactly what they're trying to do. They don't give a good goddamn. If they can take out ten or twenty of us it'll all have been worth it, even if we pulverize them. Even if we trample the shit out of the little fuckers they're going to die smiling. What the hell *could* you do in a situation like this? They simply didn't *care*!

More and more, Lieutenant Arthur Comeraro was coming round to the belief that this was a wasted war, that it was a conflict the US forces had no hope of winning. This wasn't defeatist, nor was it political; neither did it have much to do with the anti-war whoopings of the media worldwide or chanting students back in America. It was on-the-ground knowledge coming from the closeness of combat and the gut-feelings it generated. From the psychic awareness of the man who actually, physically, had to walk through rice-paddies, prowl the jungle, sift through a thousand hootch-villes, as

33

opposed to the game-plans and guesses of those who sat in offices and briefing-rooms and tapped wallmaps with pointers. What the fuck did *they* know? Even if the intelligence garnered by Command from all kinds of sources, straight as well as tricky, was an optimum 80 per cent correct (and it never was; never could be, for a million reasons) it did not give you anywhere near the true picture of what was going on out here, the real score. It was as different as an oil painting was to a sharply-defined photograph. And even the sharply-defined photograph could be wrong. Face it, the thought tumbled through Comeraro's mind, the camera too can lie.

But his eyes now took in a fact that was true in every sense of the word and yet one which simply would not be believed by the average civilian.

Not many guys seemed to be aware that they were being fired at.

A weird, weird fact.

Below, to his left, a detail were carting away bodies towards the river. To his immediate right men were making piles of discarded rifles. Further away to his right, nearer the river on that side of the hill, two or three choppers were sinking down to land, guided by a couple of guys waving their arms. It was only in front of him, below, that men were in a flap – diving for the ground, rolling desperately towards the nearest cover, jumping for rocket-craters.

Comeraro flicked his M-16 selector to 'Automatic' and squeezed a four-round burst at the muzzle-flash fireflies. Six seconds had elapsed since he'd hit the ground.

Hardin, nearby, grabbed at the black major's shoulder and yelled, 'Get your wireman. Warn the choppers off. Any moment now some clown up there's gonna see what's going on and panic and rocket the trees. I want as many as I can get down there alive.'

The major snapped 'Rodge!' and rolled away, off the hill-top. He'd instantly grasped Hardin's thought-processes. No En Vee high-rankers amongst the dead. Therefore (as he, the major, had suggested) the high-rankers had skipped as soon as the gunships had appeared. They'd probably been watching all this time, waiting for the optimum moment to strike. High-rankers would have important documentation on them: identity-cards, maps, troop-movement orders, maybe even forward-planning papers. Gold dust.

Two or three rockets, from above, well-placed, would destroy the men: good. But they'd also destroy all that beautiful intelligence: bad. Very bad. *Goddamn bad.* The major scrambled down the hill, yelling for his radio-operator.

Hardin wriggled round to Comarero.

'Get down there to the front, keep up firelines. Send Olsen and Vogt over. I'm gonna flank the fuckers, flush 'em out. Stop firing in five.'

Comeraro slid away from the lip of the hill, disappearing over the edge that faced the river.

Hardin squirmed off the hill the way the black major had gone, his AK-47 gripped in his right hand. All trace of his former weariness had vanished; it was as though he were a slate that had been almost wiped clean. All that remained was a fluidity of movement and thought. He was now like a well-oiled machine.

He reached the bottom of the hill, avoiding the tumble of bodies that still littered its slopes. He began to run at a wide angle for the nearby trees, noting, out of the corner of his eyes, the figures of Sergeant Olsen and Leroy Vogt galloping towards him.

They made it to the trees, dived into cover. This was not true jungle but forestation, much of it cultivated. There was a tangle of undergrowth and thick brush, but it was relatively dry, relatively easy to slide through. Also, there were paths; animal tracks and those made by humans, the Montagnards from the village not far away.

Hardin could now detect a new note to the gunships' rotor-clatter. Those still in hover were pulling off, rising higher, out of rifle-range. Light still poured down, however, transforming the forest interior into a strange kind of lime-lit landscape. There was a stark, unnatural quality to everyday objects like tree-boles, branches, bushes, men's faces. The shadows were deeper, too, blacker, almost ebony in colour.

Olsen whispered, 'What's the plan, sir? Kick ass, take no names?'

'We're looking for honchos,' muttered Hardin. 'And we're looking to take 'em alive.'

'Uh-huh.' Olsen nodded. He reached out and pulled at Vogt's shoulder, dragging him close. 'You hear that? Kick-ass, but kick the high-ups to disable.'

Leroy Vogt nodded, dry-mouthed.

'What about their grunts?' he said.

Olsen didn't need to check with Hardin.

'Kill 'em.'

'But how do we distinguish who's who?'

There was a faintly desperate note in Vogt's voice which was triggered not so much by fear as by sheer bewilderment. He knew it was a stupid question almost as soon as the words came out.

Although he had been in Nam now for over six months his experience of the conflict had not been at all a normal one. Less than a month in, he had shot his sergeant, under the impression the guy had been about to murder an EssVee kid. Actually the EssVee kid, a little girl, had been carrying a primed grenade which would have blown Vogt, the sergeant and most of the rest of the squad into bloody chunks. The sarge had known this, Vogt hadn't. Vogt had been court-martialled, slung in the brig. That was bad enough, but worse was to follow. After a series of bizarre and extremely unmilitary manoeuvres he'd become attached to Colonel Hardin. From that moment on, he figured he'd been in more desperate encounters than just about anyone else in Nam, Special Forces included. It'd been one terrible dose of blazing combat after another, intermingled with scenes of stark slaughter and madness. He knew, because he'd gathered as much from Olsen and Sergeant Fuller, both lifers, that Nam was crazy, but for the average grunt not nearly as flat-out insane as the wild and ferocious madness encountered on these strictly unofficial missions with Colonel John Hardin.

And the point was, Vogt had never had time to learn, had never had time to get used to a war situation. No one had given him the ground-rules, told him the do's and don'ts, fed him battle and survival lore. He'd had to pick it all up as best he could.

'Look,' said Olsen patiently, 'even EnVee honchos got

36

flashes. You know that, Vogt. Any case, they'll frankly be the ones yellin' and screamin' and wavin' handguns. It's the grunts who'll be doin' the shootin'. Hit the guys doin' the shootin' and we'll frankly be A-OK.' A friendly grin split his lumpy features. 'Okay?'

'Yeah, sarge. I guess.'

'Sure. See, I gotta tell ya, Vogt. The trouble is, you ain't been broken in.'

'Yeah, sarge. I know.'

'It's a friggin' fact. With you, it's frankly been instant OJT.'

Vogt shot him a puzzled look.

'OJT?'

'Yeah,' said Olsen darkly. 'On-the-job training. Now let's count meat, right?'

'Right,' muttered Leroy Vogt.

Hardin could hear the crackle of small-arms fire. He'd already pinpointed the muzzle-flashes on the hill-top, knew where he was going. Charlie would most likely be moving around in the area he was holding, wanting to create as much mayhem as possible but fearful of getting fingered by mortars from the ground or rocket-fire from above before that objective had been achieved. So he'd be popping off shots here, popping them off there, popping them off fucking everywhere, and constantly shifting ground. Even so Charlie would not be moving too far from where he'd started firing. It was a good position. Hardin had recognized that as soon as he'd spotted the firing. In war, you tried not to lose a good position.

Hardin gestured to his right, to the south.

'Far back as we can. Olsen, you take the side. Lay it on. Vogt, with me. We'll hit the bastards from the rear.'

They had moved out of the blaze of light from the chopper spots. Here it was twilight. Olsen ducked low and merged into the thick shrubbery without a sound. It was like smoke dissipating. Leroy Vogt watched him disappear and shivered slightly. He remembered what you were always told in Vietnam, from the time you got off the troop transports, whether boat or lumbering plane; what was drummed into you again and again: 'The jungle belongs to Charlie.' It was one of the few things he'd managed to learn. That and 'the night belongs

37

to Charlie'. Every goddamn thing in this goddamn country seemed to belong to Charlie.

The EnVees seemed to be able to use the jungle to its best advantage, in a way most Americans simply could not. But then they, or their parents, or their goddamn grandparents, had been using it for generations. To get anywhere you had to retake the jungle and it seemed incredible to Vogt sometimes that someone like Olsen, big, burly, seemingly clumsy and ungainly, could just vanish like that, without a sound, in the flicker of an eyelid. It meant Olsen had geared himself to meeting the EnVees on their own terms, fighting them with their own weapons. It was survival.

He looked back at Hardin. The tall colonel had vanished too. A flutter of nervous apprehension caught at Vogt's stomach, then he swallowed, shook his head, dived towards more shrubbery in the direction Hardin ought to have taken. *Must* have taken.

Survival.

He breathed again. Hardin was waiting for him, beckoning urgently, just visible beyond the thick foliage.

Here there was less undergrowth, which meant you could see more easily where you were; more important, where the bad guys were. But less undergrowth also meant less cover. The bad guys, if they were looking, could see you.

Hardin was crouched beside a tangle of thorn. Vogt crawled to him, peered round. To his right vague figures were moving in the darkness, how many he could not make out. It looked to be a lot. Christ, maybe a whole fucking platoon.

'They got a mortar,' muttered Hardin. 'Bad news. We can take it out easy, but they can zero in on us, blow us away.'

'Grenades?' said Vogt, wondering why Hardin didn't simply hurl a couple and finish the mortar-team off. And surely there were more guys than . . .

'It'll panic 'em. They'll be figuring anyway that someone's gonna start flanking them both sides any moment. We have to hit 'em before they start throwing out men, extending their lines. I want the head-men and I want 'em alive. Apart from all the documentation they could have, they know a hell of a lot about all that heroin. But I don't want any noise.'

To his left Vogt could hear concentrated firing from the EnVees nearer the edge of the woods, the harsh high-pitched chatter of Kalashnikovs. He wondered where Olsen was, what he was doing. What he was thinking.

Hardin said, 'Here. Take this. Do it fast. Keep doing it.'

Vogt gulped as his right hand was taken and something cold and heavy pressed into it. A knife-haft.

'Jesus!'

'Don't let me down, Vogt. We're gonna jump right in among these fuckers.'

Vogt peered at the knife in the dim twilight. It looked to his startled gaze to be about a foot long, a goddamn *bayonet*! But of course it wasn't. The blade was thickish and about seven inches in length, the haft ribbed and shorter, stubbier.

'Hold it like a sword, use it like a carver. Upwards, sideways. Some of these guys, they see you waving a knife, they'll shit themselves and surrender anyway. A blade in the guts is worse than a magful of rounds.' Hardin's voice dropped. 'Believe it.'

Vogt nodded, swallowed. He'd picked up on Hardin saying 'Don't let me down'. Other guys would've snarled, 'don't fuck up, you little prick'.

There was a big – a vast – difference in approach: Hardin might lead you into all kinds of hair-raising and horrendous shit but you always felt like giving of your best for him. Vogt had noticed that. Intuitively, you trusted him. And you wanted him to trust you.

'Go for the stomach. Don't be fancy. Don't go for the head because you'll miss it. Forget about the heart because you could get stuck in bones and rib-cage. Go low. All the time, go low.'

Vogt started into the darkness. He could see vague movement, shadowy forms, a deeper black than the surrounding darkness. Hardin was talking quickly but coolly. That helped.

'There are six of them. They won't shoot. Remember that. They shoot and they'll waste their own guys as well. Remember too, they won't know what the hell is happening. It'll be like a couple of madmen've dropped out of the sky. So act crazy, but don't yell. That's the only direct order I'm gonna give you. *Don't* for fuck's sake yell.'

By now Vogt could feel himself trembling with anticipation. His breathing was shallow, light. He could feel adrenalin pumping into his bloodstream. He wanted to move. Now. He wanted to jump.

'Four fucking big strides and we're there. Vogt. Count of three. One, two, let's go.'

The last two words weren't even emphasized. Vogt noticed that as though he were someone else listening in on the conversation. Nevertheless, as Hardin murmured them he found himself catapulted forward as though that someone else had kicked him.

Four strides and a man loomed up. Vogt thrust hard at him, felt the knife thump in. It was like hitting a sandbag. He heard a squeezed-out grunt and smelled a gust of rancid breath, then a head slumped forward onto his left shoulder and he found himself supporting a dead man. Or at least a man who wasn't going to be hitting back at him. Vogt almost didn't know how it had happened.

He heaved at the weight, panicking slightly, and then his blade was free again and the man was falling soundlessly away from him. He swept his knife-hand round in a wild semi-circle and it sliced into something else, somebody else. He knew it couldn't be Hardin because Hardin was somewhere to his left. He sprang at the obstruction, suddenly aware of more grunts and gasps and high-pitched squeals that were cut off before they got really shrill. He jammed his knife forward, closed with the figure. A splayed-out hand slammed into his face, something thumped into his back, something else banged into his legs. If anything, all this heaving and jostling drove him into a deeper frenzy. He grabbed at clothes, maybe a linen or cotton shirt, tugged at it to keep his balance and at the same time jammed the knife into the bulk of the man, anywhere he could find, jabbing and pulling and jabbing again. All he could hear was a terrible choking, gargling sound that seemed to be directed into his left ear. Vogt overbalanced, fell on his victim, tried to get up again but the knife wasn't in his hand any more and in any case his right leg seemed to be trapped under some

40

heavy weight. Panic started to flood through him.

'*Lie still!*'

Hardin. A hissed whisper.

Suddenly, M-16 fire clattered away, short solid bursts. Not near, but not too far either. Probably Olsen. Almost certainly Olsen. And now he could hear shouted orders in Vietnamese, cries of pain.

Hardin said, 'It's okay. It's over. You got a body on you. Wait.'

The weight disappeared from Vogt's legs and he scrambled to his feet. In fact he couldn't get away from the man he was lying on fast enough. He found he was trembling again, but not violently.

'I lost the knife, sir.'

'Forget it. We'll find it later. Come on.'

'What about . . .' Vogt gestured helplessly.

'These guys are either offed or outed. You did a good job. But one of 'em moved too damn fast, got away.'

Vogt was suddenly aware that it was not as dark as it had been. Dawn was on its way. It seemed like only seconds before that the darkness had almost been something you could reach out for and feel. Now a wan light was filtering through the trees. He was able to make out a jumble of bodies in the area, and a knocked-over US 81mm mortar, its bipod sticking up into the air.

Shells were scattered around, kicked over in the intense scuffle of a few minutes ago. Or was it more? Suddenly Vogt felt that the fight had taken place hours ago.

'Move!' snapped Hardin, who didn't want Vogt thinking too much or too deeply at this stage about what had just happened. Time enough for reflection afterwards. Preferably long afterwards.

Vogt unslung his rifle and jumped after Hardin. Bushes were dim objects that suddenly he felt he could dodge with ease. They were following a path but it was mostly short grass and they made almost no sound at all as they ran. But someone was making a hell of a row: crashing through brush headlong, snapping twigs, ploughing into undergrowth. There was desperation in that frenzied flight.

41

Then, suddenly, silence. Hardin slid to a halt, flung an arm out to stop his companion.

Vogt too halted, peered around. They were close to a massive barrier of undergrowth with large flower-heads sagging down from it. Here it was danker than before. There was a faint sewer-smell of rot and decay. All at once Vogt could hear scuffling sounds, and the harsh gasps of someone breathing heavily.

Hardin gestured to his front, turned, and began to catfoot it round the foliage. Vogt followed, easing to Hardin's right so as not to be directly behind the tall man. Rounding the shrubbery he saw the EnVee first – a little man, on his knees, clawing at the earth like a frantic dog after a bone he'd buried. Or – no, thought Vogt – trying to *bury* something before his pursuers caught up with him.

Hardin stepped forward, his AK-47 levelled. The man glanced round, saw them. Vogt noticed that the guy did not register fear, or surprise, or terror, but rage. His right hand snapped out and he grabbed at a round object – and instantly Vogt was back in the past with Sarge Morelli, the big friendly Italian with the extravagant moustaches, because the object was a grenade and the guy was going to throw it and they'd be liberally plastered all over the landscape in about two seconds flat.

He screamed '*Grenade*!' – and then a steel bar thudded into his chest. Hardin's arm, slamming him over backwards. He hit the ground and the ground then rose up, or maybe the very air itself was suddenly transformed into a vast scoop which drove into his flailing legs and flipped him right over – a backwards somersault he could never have perfected even if he'd practised for six months. He tumbled over and over, deafened by the bang that seemed as big as the world.

He lay half in a bush, half on a bed of disturbed leaves, and shook his head dazedly. His ears were popping and he slapped at them irritably. Beyond, Hardin was on his feet, cursing in a cold, controlled manner. Vogt climbed to his feet and staggered towards him.

Where the EnVee honcho had been was a mess of blood and body-chunks. It looked like someone had tipped the contents

42

of a butcher's block on to the ground. For a moment Vogt couldn't understand what had happened.

'He drop the egg?' he asked wonderingly. 'It slipped out of his fingers?'

'No!' snapped Hardin. 'The fucker blew himself away deliberately!' He pointed at scraps of charred paper scattered around. 'Goddamn fucking asshole bastard!'

Vogt stared at Hardin. He'd never seen the tall man like this before, so angry, so venomous. He'd never heard him spill out so much profanity either.

'Jesus-*fucker*. The guy must've had some sweet secrets on him. He was gonna bury something, then we came up and he figured out split-second fast that he might not hit the both of us with the grenade so the best thing was to hit his own Goddamn sweet ass. I should've blown his legs off.' He swung round on Vogt, rasped, 'Would you've done that? Iced yourself?'

'I, uh . . . ' Vogt was pretty certain he wouldn't.

'Of course you fucking wouldn't!' Hardin spat out. 'And that's precisely fucking why we don't have a hope in hell of holding this goddamn asshole country!'

Vogt had no answer to that but he realized that this was sheer frustration speaking now, because he'd been with Hardin long enough to know that the tall man's true feelings for Vietnam were deep and abiding. Not hate at all but love. What he hated was what the war was doing to the country. More particularly, what his own countrymen were doing to the country. Vogt kept his mouth tight shut.

Hardin kicked bits of debris around, peering down at the blood-splashed leaves and churned-up dirt. He suddenly stopped, grabbed at something.

'What the hell is this?'

It was a piece of greyish-white plastic, clearly part of a separate accoutrement, machine-moulded. Vogt couldn't identify it.

'Webbing?'

'No webbing I've ever seen.'

Hardin frowned, then began to pick through the disturbed dirt. He came up with what looked to be a piece of tubing that

43

seemed to have perished, although that was obviously blast-effect. That too was greyish in colour, as was a scrap of what felt like thin canvas material, almost gauzy in texture.

At that moment Comeraro appeared and Vogt was suddenly aware that he hadn't heard firing for a while.

Comeraro said, 'Cleaned 'em, sir. Took most of 'em prisoner. Got a lieutenant and a guy who's got no tabs. Probably political officer, but could be higher than that. You can never tell with these guys.' He stared at Vogt, raised both eyebrows.

Garrett's voice could be heard, coming closer. He shambled into view with Sergeant Fuller, who was rolling a cigarette and glaring at him.

'Tell ya, Sarge,' said Garrett loudly, 'we need R-'n'-R and that's the fuckin' truth. An' I want to know if we're gettin' paid for all this bullshit pissin' around we're doin'. I didn't sign up to take part in no private fuckin' war, lemme tell ya.'

'One of these days, Garrett, I'm gonna square you away real good,' growled Fuller. 'Fact I'm gonna fucking *cube* ya.'

Garrett let a wolfish smirk play across his craggy features for as long as it took the average flamenco dancer to snap her fingers once. Then he spotted Vogt.

'Hey, shitstick, you gonna . . . ' His voice trailed away. He stared at Vogt open-mouthed. 'Christ on a crappin' cross. You look like ya been in a fuckin' stockyard, Vogt.'

Vogt glanced down at himself. And froze. He felt his stomach turn over, his gorge begin to rise. Events over the past quarter-hour or so had happened too swiftly for him to do more than move fast, register orders and do what he was told. It suddenly occurred to him that when you stick people with a knife, blood tends to flow.

Or, to be more accurate, spout. He stared down at the front of his battle-fatigues, which had changed colour from olive-drab to deep carmine. Right down to his boots.

Captain Frank Marco said, 'Okay, let's crank.'

He threw the cigarette he was smoking to the ground, tromped on it with his boot, stared disgustedly at a bevy of grunts who were unconcernedly pissing into the river, and turned towards the Huey UH-1D that for now was his and his alone and the hell with Command.

Hardin, amused, watched the tall, skinny black as he slapped the chopper's nose with his right hand, then his left.

'Superstition, Marco. Mere superstition.'

'Fuckin'-A,' said Marco. 'That come reet down from mah monkey-men ancestors, Whitey. S'why I never belly-flop in the Big Green.' He paused thoughtfully. 'Well, like the man say, hardly ever. This voodoo shit don't work so good out here. Alien fuckin' territory, man.'

Marco was East Coast with a Master's degree in social anthropology: He'd had an academic career all mapped out but flying had intervened. Then the war. Academe or war-flying: those had been the options. The decision had not, for Marco, been too much of a tough tussle. He was a superlative flyer.

He climbed into his seat. The first thing he did was check the small canvas holdall beside his chair, into which he now never failed to stuff a .45 automatic. This was in case of emergencies and dated back to when a Marine Loot had wigged out and turned a gun on him, forcing him to take off from a hot LZ on which the Marine's men had all been left to die. In turn, this had led Marco into a wild confrontation with danger and near-disaster during which he'd met up with Hardin.

But all that was centuries ago. Now he strapped in, checked relays and circuit-breakers, his long fingers briefly grazing each button and knob and handle-lock.

Hardin sat in the co-pilot's seat, already strapped and flight-helmet fitted. He glanced behind him at the Huey's cargo hold, mentally checking off those who were there: Comeraro, Olsen, Fuller, Garrett, Vogt, Doc Pepper and the three Mafiosi, Hallings, Rand and Laguna. Those three looked unsettled, miserable. No wonder. Difficult to know what would happen to them at Do Thon. The best they could hope for was some kind of intensive plea-bargaining if they decided to blow the whistle on the whole heroin-trail business. And even then they'd be in deep shit with Mafia honchos outside who'd be wanting to deep-six them fast to stop them gabbing. Any way you looked at it these guys were in a whole heap of trouble.

45

Hardin grinned sourly. Tough, he thought.

Marco pulled his flight-helmet on and linked up. He squeezed the radio-trigger on his cyclic and said 'You on?' into his mouthpiece.

Hardin made an O with his forefinger and thumb.

The tall black yawned and sniffed. He looked round. His normal co-pilot for this run, Foxley, was acting as crew-chief and port MG-gunner in the back. By rights Hardin should not be up front, but Marco welcomed him and Foxley, a tough-looking kid from Washington State, didn't give a shit either way. Port-gunner meant he had a chance to use the Mini – Mean Mini, the meat-grinder. They were a man short anyhow. The starboard gunner was a guy called Veips, well-known for the deadly accuracy of his firelines.

Marco rolled the throttle open and triggered the starter on his collective. The electric motor whined, the rotors turned lazily. There was a loud hissing noise and then the turbine caught with a throaty cough which suddenly exploded into an ear-splitting bellow of sound. Marco eyed the EGT gauge.

'Everything OK?' he asked over the intercom.

'All secure,' Foxley said.

Marco opened the throttle to the operating position and pushed the cyclic around some. He slowly pulled up on the collective and the rotors, invisible now, clawed air. Grunts, their clothes flapping in the downdraught, dropped away below at an angle as the bird rose.

'Do Thon, tray-bon,' muttered Marco.

The east was a blaze of intense, almost blinding blue-and-white irradiation. Hardin reached for a pair of aviator's sunspex and put them on. He too yawned. He was tired again, weary, faintly depressed. He'd been running on adrenalin, pure blood-jolt, for too long. It was rich fuel. He needed rest, a drink, a hit. He leaned over to his left and gazed down at the scene of destruction disappearing below. He sourly wondered what came next in the Disneyland carnival.

What came next started happening after only ten minutes flying time.

They were racing through clear, clean air, low, thirty feet above the jungle topgrowth. Hardin, hunched in his seat, glasses off again, was gazing to his left, through the open door, at the blur of green that sped past. It seemed to him as though it must go on for ever. He was so tired he was becoming mesmerized by the sight. In his mind the forest was beckoning to him, sending out psychic signals. There were times when he wanted to be nowhere else in the world.

'Shit,' said Marco in his ear. 'Someone got a problem.'

Hardin snapped out of his daze and stared ahead. Smoke drifted from the jungle about two miles away. Even as his eyes took in the sight there was an eruption, an orange-cored flash, more smoke.

'Take a look-see,' he told the pilot.

'You a real muth'fuck,' complained Marco. 'Your momma, she musta been real disappointed in you.'

'She was, she was.'

Marco swung the Huey away from the smoke, dropping speed, turning in a wide low semi.

'Hang on to yo' nuts,' he intercommed.

Hardin half-turned in his chair, saw Foxley jabbing fingers at Comeraro and Comeraro yelling at the rest of the men to cling on to whatever they could, just in case Marco took her too steep and someone took a flier out the door. It had happened.

Marco sent the chopper drifting round at an angle, port side down, around what was now clearly identifiable as a clearing in the jungle – or, as Hardin could now see, a complex of inter-locking clearings, mostly overgrown with elephant grass, the smaller ones linked to the main one where a firefight was taking place. You couldn't mistake the sight. Puffs of smoke, muzzle-flashes, and now, as they dipped closer, movement in the bushes. He glimpsed running figures but couldn't identify them. He saw a kaleidoscope of muzzle-flashes across one side of the larger clearing, then the chopper was easing away again, Marco taking her professionally around in another wide semi.

This time the fight below leapt into clear focus for Hardin as he saw a US grunt running for bush-cover and not making it, suddenly being punched over by invisible fists in mid-stride, his M-16 flying from his grasp.

'Got 'em. There's a group to the north, in the heavy foliage.

Must be bandits. Our guys are to the south.' He suddenly noted masonry blocks, creeper-choked. 'Yeah, some kind of building. Temple probably. Looks like they're holed up there.'

'The south?' said Marco, easing on the cyclic.

'Affirmative.'

'Okay, let's hit 'em. Fire at will. Fox, give 'em a taste of Mean Mini on the next pass.'

Foxley rodged. On the other side of the cabin area Veips the hot-shot gave a sour, tight grin. The M-134 Mini-Gun, electrically operated, could blaze out a devastating 6000 rounds per minute, maximum firepower. It could shred big trees, homogenize human beings. For that reason it did not appeal to Veips, who preferred to lay down neat, precise lines of tracer, professional and utterly dispassionate. Mean Mini was overkill, as far as Veips was concerned. Any dingbat could blow a guy apart, or even several guys, by wasting a million rounds of ammo. Very few could pull the same trick with a couple of icily directed squirts. Veips was one of the few.

Marco had sent the chopper in another wide circle and now sailed across the main clearing west to east. The Mini-Gun racketed thunderously, even above the roar of the rotors. Hardin, peering left, watched the jungle curtain being literally torn apart by the withering stream of rounds.

They circled again, pouring more blazing destruction into the jungle.

Hardin said, 'We'll land.'

'Rodge. Jus' give the mothers a couple of pods.'

Hardin unclipped and scrambled back into the rear. He grabbed Fuller and Comeraro, bawled orders.

'Fuller, keep an eye on the Mafia. They get restless, shoot 'em in the legs. Comeraro, we're going in. Take Olsen and Vogt round to the top of the clearing, infiltrate the trees.'

He went back to his seat as Marco thumbed a 2.75" rocket from each of the Huey's side-mounted pods. The rockets streaked into the trees and green turned white then red as they both erupted. Smoke billowed out and gusted upwards, blackening the sky.

'Stop the fuckers laughing in church,' muttered Marco. 'Fox, give it another grind 'swe settle.' He turned to Hardin. 'Our

48

guys, they don' seem to be on the net. I been tryin' coordinates.'

Hardin shrugged.

The Huey sank down towards stubby grass, almost like a lawn, and as they neared the ground Hardin could see other buildings hidden in the trees, piles of collapsed masonry. They looked to have been collapsed for a long time, but you could never tell out here. The jungle was a swift invader of derelict real estate.

As Marco settled the chopper, Foxley cut loose with the Mini again, and as the rotor-roar died the sound became overpowering, terrifying, an eardrum-blasting cacophony. When that too died the silence was truly overwhelming.

'I think we did 'em,' said Marco. 'Least, ain' no one shootin' back.'

Hardin watched Comeraro and his two-man team disappear to his left, galloping for the treeline. Above him the rotors idled, but there was no other sound to be heard. He jumped down from the chopper and lay on the ground, AK-47 thrust out, his eyes sweeping the torn and devastated jungle curtain.

'More fuckin' work,' grumbled Garrett, still in the chopper behind him. 'What are we, knights in fuckin' armour?'

Garrett's tone of voice was such that anyone who did not know him and could not at that moment see him would imagine that he was right now lighting a cigarette, or pulling out a pack of cards, or getting down to rack out on the cargo area floor. But Hardin did not need to look round or check this out. The point about Garrett was that he bitched almost continuously, but his eyes too would be alert, responsive to any unnatural movement. His M-16, rock-steady in his lumpy hands, would be following his eyes; his firing-finger crooked for the first squeeze.

'Nah,' Garrett went on, 'looks like we crapped on em' good. Them two rockets did the trick all right. Betcha there ain't enough left of them gooners to stuff into a C-rat can.'

Hardin agreed. He knew Charlie. Firing would have broken out by now if many of the enemy force had survived. There might be one or two left alive but they'd already be beating a retreat into deeper forest to lick their wounds.

49

He climbed to his feet and walked round the chopper's nose, staring at the scenery. Here, on the ground, he wondered why he had not seen more of the buildings that could now be clearly discerned amongst the thinning trees on the south side of the clearing. They were gigantic, even though most were in ruins; tumbled blocks of stone lying around in heaps. But those buildings that remained reasonably intact reared high into the forest, alien-looking, monolithic. To his left, wide stone steps rose to a massive doorspace guarded by looming statues. The faces were grotesque, pop-eyed; mouths curved down in a glower of sullen rage. Demons of some kind, by the look of them – and where there were demons in South East Asia there had to be gods.

As he moved toward the crumbling stairway a Marine captain appeared, followed by a half-dozen grunts. They clattered down the steps and the captain strode across. He was medium-sized, stocky, but with a face, Hardin thought, as dark and lowering as that of any one of the demons that towered above him. He saluted.

'Captain Reisman, sir. You, uh . . . came none too soon. It was getting kind of hairy for the moment.'

Hardin said, 'What gives, Captain?'

Reisman looked faintly uneasy.

'Well, uh . . . it's kind of difficult to say, sir . . .'

Hardin felt tension building up inside him. Not to mention a lurking suspicion that everything here was not exactly squared away. Why hadn't they answered when Marco had tried to contact them? Who were these guys, and what were they doing in the middle of goddamn nowhere?

'What d'you mean, difficult. Who're you with? What the fuck goes on here, Captain?'

'He was protecting us . . .'

Hardin's head lifted. Standing at the top of the steps, as though suddenly conjured up out of nowhere, maybe even by one of the demons of the temple, was a girl.

III

She was tall, maybe five-ten, and dressed in neat dark green fatigues that did not at all look as though they had been shoved across the counter at the quartermaster's stores by a grouchy corporal. In fact, they looked like they'd been bought at Sak's. Her face was long, with high cheekbones; the nose too was long, with a slight curve, but nothing pronounced. Black hair, probably long, was pushed up beneath a green baseball cap. Her mouth, full-lipped and wide, seemed out of proportion to the rest of her face. Hardin felt instant attraction.

He said curtly, 'And you are . . . ?'

He noted, out of the corner of his eye, Reisman's face, deadpan. The man's eyes gave him away, though: dark and angry. He was truly pissed off about something. Hardin's brief glance at Reisman's grunts seemed on the surface casual, but he was taking in everything about them. They looked, all of them, to be what they purported to be, including Reisman himself. But who could tell? The men sent out by the Corsican Mafia on the heroin deal had all dressed correctly, had all seemed on the face of it to be what they'd said they were. It was only when Hardin and his men had been in close proximity for some time that they started smelling a rat. It was easy enough – if you had the money and the clout to go with it – to pick up the right clothes, badges, flashes, webbing and hardware (especially hardware in the Saigon Black Market) anywhere in Nam. All you had to do then was act mean and you were instantly indistinguishable from just about everyone who had a legitimate reason to be there.

But Hardin was smelling something bad here and his sixth sense rarely let him down. There was something about Reisman and his men that was not genuine. Something he could not put his finger on. Something . . .

The girl said, 'Kate Berry, Captain.'

She half-turned, an oddly graceful movement that caught at Hardin, and gestured. Two men were behind her now at the top of the steps, one humping a heavy camera on his shoulder, the other with a network of smaller cameras, light-meters, film cans and the like hanging from an assortment of straps and neck-bands, like roses on a trellis. Both were dressed in safari jackets and denims, olive-drab in colour. Though again, definitely not army issue.

'Max Ryfield, Harry Verblosky. We're on assignment. *Pix Magazine*. MACVee very kindly gave us some assistance.' She glanced at Reisman. 'Very fine assistance. Only trouble is, not enough. I have to say we were getting kind of worried till you showed up.'

Hardin stared at her.

'This is bandit country,' he said tightly.

The girl shrugged.

'Well, that's why we had Captain Reisman and his men along.'

'You have documentation?'

She frowned, clearly slightly puzzled.

'Sure. Harry?'

The man with the cameras slung across his chest fished into an inside pocket of his natty jacket and handed a bundle of papers to Hardin. They checked out. The passes all had the correct dates and the correct places of origin and the correct signatures. But then of course they would. Hardin had only asked for them as a matter of form. He was beginning to get the picture. Little wonder Reisman was extravagantly pissed off; in his place Hardin himself would have been murderous by now. He handed the papers back.

'Everything okay, Captain?'

'Uh, lady . . . ' Marco had ambled across from the chopper. He stooped slightly beside her and hooked a thumb at himself. 'I a captain.' He pointed at Reisman. 'He a captain.' He pointed at Hardin. 'He a colonel. See, lady, if you look, the flashes ain' the same.'

The girl threw Hardin a smile that on the surface was one of sheer embarrassment, but lurking in her eyes was an amusement that showed she was not at all put out.

'Why, I'm sorry, Colonel, uh . . . ?'

'Hardin. John Hardin.'

He felt rather than saw Reisman stiffen slightly and another wave of anger surge through him. Hardin's reputation was a badge he didn't care for, had never cared for. It was something he could well do without.

'I'm really sorry, Colonel Hardin. You must think I'm very stupid. It's the first time we've been in South East Asia, and the first time we've been this close to the military. Usually I . . .'

Hardin turned to Reisman, cutting her off. He could now detect a definite thread of mockery in her tone. He found her powerfully attractive, but right at that moment he felt like socking her.

'You realize one of your men is either dead or seriously wounded.'

Reisman was standing stiffly to one side.

'Yessir. He got it in the chest. We pulled him in. He'll be fine, soon as we can medevac him out.' He turned to Hardin. 'Could I see you, sir?'

Hardin, tight-lipped, nodded. The two men moved away from the group and onto the steps, Reisman mounting them, then disappearing under the ponderous door lintel. Hardin followed. It was cool here and not simply because they were out of the sun. Hardin felt the chill of ages inside this ruined temple. A vast room extended away from him, piles of rubble dotting the stone floor. Sunlight blazed down in narrow, dazzling columns through holes in the roof, high above. Debris was strewn everywhere. Bushes grew through cracks in the floor and one wall was thick with creeper. A bird suddenly flew across his line of vision, shrieking, and disappeared out the door. From crumbling niches in the walls that were clear of vine, gods – or maybe demons – stared at eternity, faint smiles on their time-and weather-ravaged faces.

Hardin and Reisman walked slowly down the hall. There were doorways leading off to other rooms, each as big as the one they were now in; yet more doorways in those, yet more rooms beyond. The place was like a huge maze. More rubble, more debris. And shadows; thick impenetrable shadows where the sun had not reached in centuries.

Reisman said, 'I guess you're wondering . . .'

'No, I get the picture, Captain. You got the shitty detail, right?'

Reisman looked confused.

Hardin said, 'This has happened before. Couple of years ago. Some big magazine sent some goddamn newshound with a whole pack of photogs to snap pix of a temple down in the Delta. Only trouble was, Charlie got there first. In fact he owned the area. We had to send in a muscular force to retake it. Banged in everything. They finally shifted Charlie's butt and sent the photogs in. Charlie counter-attacked. So did we. They came back again. So did we. Then they hit us a third time and did it good. Command had to send in another force and back 'em with arty and gunships and fucking Phantoms. It was a goddamn *war* for Chrissake, and all for a few snapshots for some sheet back in the World. MACVee said it was good for propaganda; they said the area was supposed to be clean anyway. They'd already said the place was sterile so they had to *make* it fucking sterile. I think we lost about eighty men, three choppers and a fuck of a lot of matériel. Soon as we'd got our pix and beat it, Charlie de-sterilized the place, took it right the fuck back again.' He stared angrily at Reisman, then relented and offered him a cigarette. Reisman nodded gratefully. 'I take it this is the same kind of deal?'

'Yeah. Right, sir. That's it. We, uh . . . got the shitty detail, like you said. We could've called in, uh . . . arty, but I dunno, it just didn't seem to be right. Christ,' he puffed greedily at the cigarette, not looking at Hardin, 'we got more important things to do than this.'

'You never said a truer word,' muttered Hardin.

He was thinking: That stupid goddamn bitch – don't these people know what's going on out here, for Christ's sake? Hardin had a high regard for real newshounds, photographers, cameramen. They risked a lot to get their stories, their pictures. Sometimes they died on the job. Command had other ideas about the Press; Command hated their guts, and for obvious reasons. But Command didn't see them in action. In any case Hardin's views on the war and Command's were often diametrically opposed.

But a civilian team doing a feature on some goddamn temple in the jungle was something else again. Whole different ball game, in fact.

Then Hardin backtracked. Sourly, he realized his anger was directed at the wrong target. It was the fuck-ups in Saigon who ought to be on the block, not this stupid asshole picture-team. It was Command who wanted to get over to the great US public that everything was fine, everything was secured, everything was A-OK. No problems, Mr and Mrs America. See, we can send a team out to snap this wonderful old temple. Been there a long time. And it proves two things, ladies and gentlemen: it proves that those damn Commies don't have it all their own way, because this temple is many, many klicks into the jungle; and it proves that we don't just get off on beating the shit out of the peasants, we got culture too.

Hardin often thought that when some of these three-star generals went to get their heads close-cropped the barber took their fucking brains out too.

He suddenly grinned at the thought. Reisman looked at him uncomfortably.

Hardin said, 'Okay, Captain, we'll get you and your men out of here. And the goddamn civilians.'

Reisman didn't move, didn't respond. He looked to Hardin as if his brain-relays were clicking into action, pondering alternatives, checking options.

'S'matter? You wanna finish the job?' Hardin chuckled. 'Commendable, Captain. Highly commendable. But forget it. The EnVees could be back, with a more muscular force. I don't intend to spend any more of Command's money, ammo and, getting right down to it, men on this piss-off job.'

He was suddenly aware that someone else had entered the temple. He glanced round and saw that it was the girl. She was carrying a shoulder-bag recorder with apparent ease, her boots ringing on the stone flags. Reisman stared at her.

She said, 'I think we're finished, Captain.'

Reisman continued staring at her for some seconds then turned and strode down the alleyway and out into the hot sunlight.

'You think you've finished, do you?' said Hardin. '*You* think.' He smiled with his teeth.

The girl plumped the recorder-bag onto a pile of rubble and sat down, one booted leg swinging free. A foot away from her a shaft of sunlight blazed down from a ragged hole in the roof, slightly blurring her outline, her face.

'You don't like me, Colonel.' The voice was cool and assured, reasonable in tone.

'Lady, I could probably like you a lot, but out here you're about as useful as a guy with no arms at a gymnasts' convention.'

'Or a one-legged man at an ass-kicking contest?'

Hardin chuckled.

'Yeah. Why not?'

She was powerfully attractive, no question about that. Coolness never failed to interest him. The woman who was self-assured, confident, able to make her own decisions about her life and who had the fairly unusual ability to make a way through the wood held a strong magnetism for him. He had a feeling that Kate Berry was just such a woman.

'You don't think MACVee should have let us in?'

'I think MACVee are a crock.'

'But surely,' she offered him a cigarette and, when he shook his head, lit one herself, her long slim fingers Zippoing it alight, 'it's fine propaganda. We're showing . . .'

'Ms Berry, you're showing nothing. As propaganda this effort isn't worth a pinch of shit.'

'Kate,' she said.

'What?'

'Kate. My name's Kate.'

'Why should I call you that?'

56

'Everyone does.'

'So?'

She said, musingly, 'John Hardin. I believe I've heard tell of you.'

'I doubt it. This is your first time in South East Asia, your first time close to the military.'

Now she was discomposed, very faintly at a loss.

'Hell of a memory you've got, Colonel. Still, you're wrong. I mean I'm sure I have heard your name mentioned. In Saigon, MACVee headquarters. It reminds me of . . . Ohh, wasn't there an American gunfighter or sheriff called Hardin?'

'Odd phrase,' said Hardin. 'Why not just say gunfighter? Aren't *you* American?'

She pulled at the cigarette, shot him a tight and chilly smile.

'As apple pie, buster.'

'There was a gunfighter. There was also a President, but name of Harding with a 'g'. I expect you're confusing me with the actor.'

She stared at him, head slightly bent down.

'The actor?' she said coldly.

'Yeah, Ty Hardin. Played in a lot of movies, TV Westerns. I expect that's who you're mistaking me for.' He smiled agreeably, shook his head. 'No relation.'

'Well, didn't I get it wrong,' she said, her tone now icy.

As she spoke Hardin tensed. He suddenly knew, without the slightest shadow of a doubt, that someone was listening in on their conversation. It was an instinct for imminent danger that he had long cultivated and one which, over a decade and a half, had never failed him yet.

His eyes travelled across and around the vast room but of course there was nothing, at least not near enough for his psychic alarm to have been triggered off so positively. He turned. A few feet away from him was another doorway. He moved towards it silently, waving an arm at the girl and at the same time saying, 'Looks like you did. You can't win 'em all. Even hot-shot photojournalists like you can . . . '

He jumped past the doorway, into the next room, his AK-47 held out. This was a smaller chamber; other doors led off from

57

it. There was a window-space along one of the walls through which the jungle had crept long since. Now there was a riot of greenery covering the sill and questing out towards the centre of the room, a tangled mass of bush and creeper. He wondered if someone might be outside, hidden under the window, stooping down below the sill and out of sight. Or perhaps concealed in the tangle of foliage actually inside the room itself.

His ears could detect nothing. Nothing alien to the jungle itself, anyhow. There was the subdued hum and saw of insects, the cries of birds; he could hear, as though through plate-glass, conversation from the clearing behind him, the crackle of Marco's chopper-radio on open channel.

He stood there like a statue carved from stone – like one of the statues that gazed dispassionately down at him from the wall-niches – but adrenalin was shooting into his bloodstream, seething through his system. His AK was on single-shot. He pumped two rounds into the mass of shrubbery that cascaded into the room, then sprinted across and jumped high and sideways, hurtling through the window-space and out into the jungle. As he hit the ground he spun round and sent another couple of rounds hammering into the stonework of the temple wall.

But there was nothing there. Nothing and no one. There were only bird-noises, rising to a frenzy of alarm, and human cries, equally frantic, echoing from the other side of the building.

He stared angrily round. No one. But there had been. Somewhere. He was never wrong, not about this. His psychic alarm-bell had saved his ass more times than he cared to count.

Marco appeared at the window, shoving at the tangle of branches, his shoulders bent as he leaned over the foliage inside, a .45 in his gloved hand.

'Don' shoot. I your buddy.'

Reisman and some of his grunts crowded behind him, waving M-16s.

'Did they sneak back round here, sir?'

Hardin shook his head.

'Someone got left behind. Maybe. I thought I caught something. Could've been some of the fauna.' He said to Marco, 'Where's Comeraro?'

'They still in the woods, far as I know. Maybe they havin' a fuckin' picnic.'

'We're moving out. Now. Get these guys onto the chopper. There's one WIA.'

'Captain Reisman here phoned for another bird,' Marco informed him. 'We take all these mothers, we never lift off. We got room for the wounded guy is all, but Captain Reisman want to keep his group together, right an' tight.'

Hardin gestured irritably. He climbed back over the sill, ploughed heavily through the massed green stuff. In the larger room the girl was still sitting on the rubble, still gently swinging her booted foot, still smoking. The eyes that now held his were dark and liquid pools, but by no means unreadable. All kinds of signals were there. They appraised him frankly, with something in them that was far more than idle interest. Perhaps, thought Hardin, she was the type of woman who was attracted to danger-zone men, attracted to the kind of guy who gave out that certain aura of violence and peril, the kind of guy who might just not be around tomorrow.

Marco and Reisman and the grunts were disappearing into the blinding sunlight outside, a clatter of boots and talk and shouted orders. The girl dropped her eyes, lazily shifted herself off the stone and hunched the recorder-bag onto her shoulder again.

'Were you wrong, Colonel Hardin?'

'Who knows?'

'You mind if I file a story on this – incident-in-the-jungle kind of thing?'

'You can do what the hell you like.'

'I can indeed, Colonel. And I do.'

'You know,' said Hardin equably, 'I have a feeling you probably fuck like a crazed weasel.'

Lieutenant Comeraro came running up the steps of the temple, a blurred dark shape in the hot light. He was holding something.

'Colonel. Weird thing. No EnVees but a lotta blood. They dragged off their dead, and damn fast. But they dropped this.'

Hardin stared at the object in Comeraro's hand. He now knew exactly what he'd found earlier after the firefight in the forest – the bits and pieces of something greyish-white, the unknown artifact that might be rubber or plastic or both.

A gas-mask.

The man did not move even when the sound of the two helicopters had faded to complete silence.

He waited five minutes, ten minutes. He waited twenty minutes. He waited a full half-hour and still did not move. He lay in an uncomfortable half-crouch up against the stone wall, entirely covered in creeper and dense vegetation.

He had sustained two hits in the right leg, both from ricocheting rounds which had ripped through the foliage, hit the stonework under the window at an angle and caromed off into him, one into the fleshy part at the back of the leg, the other into the heel of his foot. The pain had been enormous and he'd had to clench his teeth and fists to stop himself shrieking. His jaw now ached and there were wounds in the palms of his hands like the Stigmata, which, having been brought up by the French Fathers, he knew all about.

When the American had jumped back into the room through the window he'd missed hitting him by inches. Less. When the others had tramped into the hallway he'd risked frantically tying a strip of cloth, which they all carried for just such an emergency as this, round his leg just below the knee, twisting it as tight as he dared. There were no arterial wounds, but it was better to be safe than sorry. He was glad he'd done that because now he had to report back to his unit, tell them the bad news.

The gas-mask. The Americans now had one. But *that* wasn't the bad news. His unit would already know that because of course it was Major Han's mask and Major Han must be dead or the Americans would not have found it.

No, the bad news was the identity of the American who now had the mask. The American who had fired at him, although he could have sworn that he had made no noise at all. But then the American – this particular American – would have needed no noise to direct him to an enemy. The man had heard the

American's name spoken. It was a name well-known to Military Intelligence and the Political cadres.

Hardin. Colonel John Hardin.

And now Hardin had the mask.

Nothing, of course, could stop that mask reaching the hands of American Intelligence, barring a miracle. Despite his Catholic upbringing – or perhaps because of it – the man did not believe in miracles. But that no longer mattered. It was what they did with the mask that mattered.

Despite the extreme urgency of the situation the man lay back and fought the pain in his leg. He did not finally move until a full hour had passed from the time the helicopters had taken off. Only then was he certain the Americans had not left anyone behind.

IV

'Worrying,' said Colonel Phil Esteban. 'But it fits.'

'Fits?' said Hardin.

'Yeah, too well.'

Esteban was a tall, stringy man who wore rimless glasses and a perpetually preoccupied air. He looked like a college professor and often acted like one. Sometimes, however, he didn't act like a college professor at all.

Esteban was the statistics man, the logistics expert. He knew everything there was to know about the SSG in the matter of men and matériel. He knew where they'd been, where they were, where they were going. More often than not he knew the whys and wherefores too: why they'd been to wherever it was they'd been, why they were wherever they were, why they were heading towards whatever godforsaken destination was scored on their topo-maps.

Most of this priceless information was in his head. Sure, it was also on cards, in folders, in box-files, and if he wanted it he could always find it, despite his office looking like a waste-paper tip. But he rarely needed to check out the paper. His brain held it all, neatly filed and tabulated. To describe Phil Esteban's memory as phenomenal was the same as saying the World Trades Centre was quite tall.

Now he sat behind his desk, took off his glasses, and gently rubbed at the lenses with a tissue. He put his glasses back on again and sipped black coffee from a paper cup. He made a face.

'Jesus, this shit. Tastes like yak's piss.'

Hardin was interested. Most of Phil Esteban's comments were usually based on hard experience.

'You ever tasted yak's piss, Phil?'

A brief smile fluttered across the thin man's narrow, scholarly face. He didn't reply. The gas-mask lay in front of him, together with the bits and pieces Hardin had rescued from the grenade blast. Esteban tapped one of the pieces with a pencil.

'Part of the respirator.'

'I can see that now.'

'Yeah.'

Smoke curled from a cigarette in the heavy-duty glass ashtray on Esteban's desk. Behind him was a window facing east; another dawn was coming up fast. Esteban was at his best on the post-graveyard shift.

He said, 'It's sophisticated. Chinese manufacture. I had Harry look at it. He said we don't have anything like it. He was very excited, nearly wet himself. He said if the yellow men up north are manufacturing stuff like this they're way ahead. Way ahead of us *and* the Russians. The way he was acting you'd think I'd offered him the secret of multiple orgasms for men.'

Harry Schwemmer was the SSG's tame labman. He also liked the ladies.

Esteban said, 'The guy who fragged himself was the only one to have one of these. None of the other gooners had one. We've managed to identify what he was, just about. Equivalent of a colonel. That strikes me as very suggestive.'

Hardin nodded.

'Only upper echelons get gas-masks. Therefore, they're in short supply. Therefore they're new.'

'Right. Which might be taken to be good news, although it's the only good news there is. Harry's coming over sometime around now. He's managed to extrapolate, from the mask itself, some grim detail.' Esteban's mouth was a thin sour line. 'Some truly grim detail. But it ties in with – or at least could tie in with – some intelligence we've been getting in for the past six months or so.'

'Why are you telling me all this, Phil?'

Hardin was lying back in his chair tossing his Zippo up and down, up and down in his right hand. The compact weight of it, each time it slapped down on his extended palm, was oddly soothing. He felt vaguely light-headed, but this was not surprising as he'd been hitting the weed with Marco the night before.

'I'm telling you all this because Halderling wants you told.'

'Which means he wants me out there, sorting it out. Whatever the fuck it is.'

'You better ask him, John.' Esteban's face was impassive.

'I don't think I'll bother, Phil.' Hardin's was equally so.

There seemed little point. Hardin had a notion that he was being eased toward a situation from which it would not be easy to escape. Right now he felt like going with the flow.

'Some of our on-the-ground assets have been feeding us reports of activity north of the DeeEmZee, and not too damn far either. In between ten and fifty klicks. There's a lotta bustle up there but no one can find out what gives. Supply-movement, rail-movement, truck-movement, mucho air-activity. It's almost like a no-go zone but the zone itself is far too extended to pinpoint anything with any kind of accuracy.'

'X marks the spot, usually dead-centre,' Hardin commented.

Esteban made an assenting noise through his nose, then shook his head briefly.

'Not necessarily. You remember when Halderling sent you into Russia that time, the missile sites at Obresk?'

Hardin remembered. He'd been eight years younger then; it seemed like eighty.

'I was a callow youth,' he remarked.

'Same thing then,' Esteban went on. 'Huge no-go zone, maybe a hundred square miles. The U-2s were picking up nothing, absolute zero. In any case we had to be circumspect because of the Powers thing. But we ought to have hit pay-dirt somewhere. So you and, uh – the fat guy with the bald head, Fenner, that got knocked off in Athens couple of years later – you and him dropped in and found the sites right on the

64

eastern edge of the area. Smart thinking by the Russians. Our planes hadn't been anywhere near.'

'Getting out of that one was a fucker,' grumbled Hardin. 'We made it by the seat of our goddamn pants.' He stopped tossing the Zippo and used it in the manner its designer had originally intended. He blew smoke out of his mouth in a long plume and stowed the lighter in a pocket. 'Okay, so the EnVees are probably being smart too and what they're trying to hide almost certainly ain't where it ought to be. How solid is the information?'

'About as solid as cloud-wrack, but the sources themselves are A-1. None of it may fit in with this gas-mask, but something else does. Like I said, too well.' Esteban suddenly lifted his head and stared directly at Hardin. 'You ever hear of "sky-fire" or "fire from the sky"?'

Despite himself, Hardin could not suppress a trickle of cold chill into the base of his spine. He had no idea what Esteban was talking about, but the fact that Esteban thought it necessary to underscore it in his voice, the way he pronounced the words was enough to set psychic alarms sounding off silently but insistently throughout his system. Phil Esteban was not the man to over-dramatize anything.

'Jesus, Phil, now what?'

'Have you? Heard anything at all?' Esteban's voice was clipped with urgency. 'A fire from the sky?'

'No.'

Esteban pondered this for a few seconds, then nodded.

'No,' he agreed. 'You haven't been up in that part of Laos for a year or more.' He grinned suddenly, the tension dropping instantly in the room. 'That I know of, anyhow.'

Hardin acknowledged this with an old-fashioned look, but then the smile was wiped from Esteban's face and a taut chill was back in the air.

'We have three separate and distinct reports, all of which are unconfirmed, none of which are in any way as detailed as we'd like. But all three come from rock-solid reliables, men we feel we can trust implicitly who've never let us down yet.' Esteban leaned back in his chair and stared up at the ceiling. 'All, in one way or another, tell of something that came out of the sky and burned people, burned 'em bad. In each case it happened in the Highlands, way off the beaten track. In each case it happened to hill tribesmen, but the kind who didn't mix much with anybody, us or the enemy. Two reports speak of helicopters, the third doesn't, but that doesn't necessarily mean anything. That third report differs from the other two mainly in not mentioning "fire" from the sky, or anything from the sky – but the results of whatever took place definitely fit in with the other two reports. It's the same, only the third report is for various reasons more nebulous than the other two, which, Christ knows, are vague enough anyhow. All three incidents happened around six, seven months ago. Of course there could be more than just three, but if so we didn't catch 'em.'

He leaned forward, stubbed out the smouldering cigarette in the ashtray, tapped another out of his pack, lit it.

'I'll run through them in brief, because there's no particular need to go through every goddamn turn of the wheel like our Intelligence people had to. It's all written down and you can read it later. Basically, what seems to have happened is this: Dawn. First light. Lone chopper flying over remote hamlet. Red spray of vapour, very fast. Chopper gets out on the double. Later – maybe an hour, maybe a day, time doesn't mean much to those guys up there – people start vomiting, reeling around, falling over, going into spasms. They're throwing up blood mainly. Many die immediately. Those that don't break out in sores all over the exposed parts of their bodies – black blisters that swell and erupt. There are headaches, real bad headaches; loss of vision, slurring of speech, bloody diarrhoea, general sickness, mainly blood, and lethargy. Are you up on nerve or gas agents?'

'I'm not in Harry's league,' said Hardin quietly.

'No, neither am I. Like I said, he's coming in later. Okay, here's the way of it. What I've just told you is an amalgamation of all the reports. One report, the vaguest of the three, is from an asset who was told what happened maybe three or four times removed. That's the one that doesn't mention helicopters or anything coming down from the sky. We know there must have been a chopper, but it probably got lost in the telling. Second report is much tighter, although still not as tight as we'd like. Our man, different man, got it from someone he bumped into on an information trawl. The way he heard it, it happened to one of this guy's kin in a village way up in the hills. There was mention of a chopper and the red stuff. To our asset it seemed like just a story. He didn't take it too seriously, thought it was just some wacko exaggeration, until he got back to us and we told him to find out more. He tried to but couldn't locate his source.' He shrugged. 'It happens. He made some further enquiries but got nowhere. The latest report is the most detailed. Our man, different man again, heard the story first-hand. He was picking up material in a village and came across this very sick hillman. The hillman told him what had happened and where his village was, maybe fifty klicks to the north. At first it seemed the hill-man hadn't been badly hit by this shit. He'd got a few sores was all, and he'd then travelled to the village where our asset found him. But while he was travelling he was getting sicker and sicker until he got to the village and wham, that was it. Kept on spewing blood. But he described exactly – or as exactly as it was possible for him to describe – what had taken place. It was this guy who called the stuff "fire from the sky", but of course he didn't know it was vapour or what the fuck it was, except it burned like hell. We've figured all of this out by correlating the three stories. In each case, the symptoms caused by the vapour or gas are pretty much the same, given the different circumstances of each report.'

While he'd been talking Esteban had not been smoking. The cigarette, smouldering away, had been held in his right hand. The only drag he'd taken from it had been at the start, when he'd lit up. Now he stubbed it out and lit yet another.

Hardin said, 'Yeah, I see what you mean.'

'About it fitting too well with these gas masks?'

Hardin grunted in agreement. He was thinking that this looked to be a bad one, a very bad one. If the EnVees were using nerve agents – and this seemed to be on the cards – all hell could break loose. A good deal depended on how far the North Vietnamese wanted to take it – and then he thought: No, not the North Vietnamese, the Chinese. He doubted that the EnVees had reached a sufficiently high level of technology to produce a nerve agent, if that was what it really was, that could get Harry Schwemmer excited. In any case the mask itself was Chinese, and with the Chinese it was fogsville, militarily, diplomatically, even sociologically. In many ways the Bamboo Curtain was tougher, more tangible than the Iron Curtain. They were truly an unknown quantity; the only solid fact you could put at their door was that they didn't seem to mind chucking grenades around haphazardly – the Cultural Revolution proved that. On the face of it, they were capable of any degree of mayhem, seemingly just for the hell of it. And they certainly had the brains, and the skills.

He said, 'Christ, Phil, you're starting to get me worried.'

'Join the club.'

'Any other evidence . . . stories?'

Esteban shrugged.

'In fact, yes. But even more fuzzy than the ones I've just told you. As you were, *far* more fuzzy. Once we started to get this stuff together we sent all the agents we could out to try for more information, but it was hopeless. Yeah, people had heard of something, but it was always in a ville about twenty klicks away and when you got there it was some other place thirty klicks away again. Like that.' He took a sudden drag at the cigarette he was holding. 'But I haven't finished yet.'

'Uh-huh?' Hardin suddenly felt as though all the energy had been sucked out of him.

'No. The third story, the most detailed one. It was the last to come in and our guys were beginning to sniff real trouble. Our asset had left the hillman in the village he found him in. He'd given the guy some antibiotics and medication for his sores; told the headman to look after him good, then came back to us. He knew this was the real McCoy, the kind of information that was going to stir the shit around, give our guys the hots. It took him a couple of weeks to make it back down here, a week or so of de-briefing – I mean we really pulled him apart. Then we sent him out again with a back-up team which included a medic. But when they reached the ville no one wanted to know. The guy wasn't there. Disappeared. No one'd talk. Gave the impression he'd never been there in the first place.

The headman got very pissed off, refused to talk to our guys, became threatening. So okay, our asset still had the location of the hillman's own village, which the guy had given him. Our men hoofed it for fifty klicks or more right up into the mountains. They found the ville okay, but . . . '

'Lemme guess,' interrupted Hardin tiredly. 'Razed to the ground, stiffs everywhere, nobody left to talk.'

'You spoiled my story,' said Esteban. His voice was neutral. 'And you only got it half-right anyway. Yep, razed to the ground – and cleared. There was nothing – but *nothing*. No bodies, human or animal. Not even a dead fucking chicken. Everything had been burned. Where the ville had been was a hole in the jungle. They'd even used flamethrowers on the earth. It was sanitized, completely and utterly.'

'Jesus,' said Hardin. 'I don't like this shit one bit.' He thought about what Esteban had said. It was a chilling story, with chilling implications. 'Looks like these were some kind of trial runs.'

'Affirmative.'

'And the EnVees cleared up the mess afterwards so there'd be no evidence. Burned-out villes are a dime a dozen round here. It might have attracted attention from the air because it was so thorough, but it would still have been marked down as just one more atrocity. Atrocities are a dime a dozen too. Who gives a shit any more?'

'Not only that,' said Esteban bleakly, 'but they're travelling round the country knocking off witnesses and putting the fear of God into village honchos.'

Hardin pondered that, then shook his head.

'No. I doubt that.' He grinned suddenly, a dark flicker that held no humour. 'You're getting paranoid in your old age, Phil. No, I think the hillman's disappearance is a simple case of panicsville. He was mucho sick. The villagers didn't like the look of him, iced him, dumped him. Simple as that. They didn't want any trouble.'

'You're probably right,' said Esteban moodily. 'But it doesn't do any harm to get paranoid with a bastard like this.'

'What about this maybe-maybe-not building activity beyond the DeeEmZee?'

69

The intercom on Esteban's desk buzzed, and as he reached out and depressed a knob he said, 'No maybe about it. It's a fact. They're building something up there even if we don't know what or where. Whether it's relevant or not is the main question. I think it is – Yeah?'

'Major Schwemmer's here, sir.'

'Throw him in.'

Harry Schwemmer bustled in. He was in his late thirties, a fat little man with a close crew-cut and a superabundance of energy. A dew of sweat lay on his brow; dark patches could be seen under his arms. It was beginning to heat up outside. Even so he still moved like a manic ballet-dancer, hopping over unsteady file-piles, agilely avoiding books and briefcases that were like an obstacle course from the door to Esteban's desk. He was very light on his feet.

'Phil. Hi, John.' He flumped down in a chair, pulling up his trousers to preserve the crease. 'Jeeze, can you guys get me an interview with the mother who's behind all this? I gotta notion to kiss his fucking feet.'

'Very funny,' said Hardin darkly.

Schwemmer grinned a lop-sided grin.

'Yeah, I know, I know,' he said apologetically. 'Good old Harry. All he fucking cares about is the science of it. Death and destruction he don't give a screw about. Well, listen up, guys,' he slapped a card-file onto Esteban's desk, 'I do care but I gotta say this bastard, if I'm right and don't forget I'm only theorizing on what evidence we have, which is frankly screw-all in concrete terms, *except* for the mask, then this mother-raper's cracked what the Chem Corps wild men have been busting their nuts to crack since the end of World War Two.' He paused, then said slowly, 'And it may be horror city, but it is also fan-fuckin'-*tastic*!' He spat the final two syllables out from between gleaming teeth.

'I always loved the cool, objective way you look at life, Harry,' said Hardin, stretching himself.

He did not at all dislike Schwemmer; in fact there were times when he actively sought out the bouncy little man's company. Harry Schwemmer was openly sex-crazed and proud of it: he had a fund of wildly funny anecdotes to do with his experien-

70

·ces in quest of, as he invariably called it, the Perfect Screw. So far he had not found it. He'd come close on many occasions, he said, but the all-time high in, as he put it, fuckdom still eluded his eager grasp. But he persevered. The goal, he said, was worth the effort. Any amount of effort, in fact.

Most of Harry's stories were against himself; in Harry's Quest for the Perfect Screw there had been many disasters, although the sought-after short-term goal was usually attained in the end, perfect or not. That was what Hardin liked about him. A Don Juan he wasn't; he might lose sleep in calculating to a nicety some ingenious scheme to inveigle a particularly intractable chick into the sack, but he actually liked women; liked talking to them; liked being in their company. It was Hardin's theory that the average stud didn't much care for the female sex: conquest was all; cock-notching; the trophy syndrome. That was not Harry's bag.

He certainly had magnetism, and to spare. There was no denying that. He was a roly-poly guy and to look at him you wouldn't think he stood a cat in hell's chance against some burly six-foot jock with smouldering eyes and a marshmallow mouth. But whenever there was a contest it was invariably no-contest. Harry Schwemmer could charm a rattler whose tail had been stepped on.

And he was a hell of a chemist, too.

Now he pulled a stubby bulldog pipe out of his shirt pocket and lit it. He shot Hardin a mean, calculating look belied by the humour in his eyes.

'You sign an affidavit to back up that statement, Colonel?'

'Sure will, Major.'

'I need all the help I can get these days, what with one thing and another. I like the idea of cool and objective. Wouldja sign to dispassionate too?'

'Glad to.'

'Gee, that's swella ya. Halderling says I gotta clean up my act. He says my name's a byword for vice and sin and debauchery. I said I was trying my best but the cards weren't falling my way. All rightee!' He tapped the card-file precariously perched on the edge of Esteban's desk. 'You guys wanna lecture?'

71

'Make it short, Harry,' said Esteban. 'Or shortish at least.'

'Short as ya like.' Schwemmer puffed at his pipe, the jolliness suddenly gone from his expression and tone. 'Okay, this guy – I keep calling him this guy, and I'll still keep calling him this guy even though it may be two or three guys, or indeed gals, and he, she or they almost certainly have a raft of chemists and technics as back up – has, in my opinion, made a fuck of a breakthrough. We'll start with World War One.' He waved the pipe at Hardin. 'World War One, ya got poison gas. Basically this was invented accidentally by a Kraut who got the Nobel Prize for substantially reducing the threat of world famine and thus the sum-total of human misery. The chronic-irony-choke of that I'll leave you to deal with yourselves. But here's another wildey: you can trace the first manufacture of poison gas right down to the fact that this perverted genius, name of Fritz Haber, figured out how to make fertilizer cheaply and economically and some other guy, name forgotten for the moment, did the same with colour dye. That's grabbed you, right? Okay. Before Haber came along, fertilizer came out of nitrates which in turn came out of saltpetre. The single largest saltpetre deposits in the world lay in South America, in the Chilean deserts. That's a fuck of a way from civilization and it cost a fuck of a lot of dough to transport, so Haber invented a process for manufacturing nitrates without using saltpetre. Bingo! Now let's shift ass to dyes, more specifically indigo, or blue, dye. Only China had a source of indigo dye in any quantity. The Krauts controlled it, but they paid a deal of bread for it. So they put their beady little minds to it and came up with a synthetic indigo dye which they didn't need to pay a cent for. Bingo again! Now we get to World War One proper.'

It was clear Schwemmer was enjoying himself. He liked an audience, male or female (though preferably the latter), and he had a knack of keeping up a flow and maintaining interest at the same time. Before he'd been talent-spotted by Halderling he'd been with MIT.

'Okay.' He jabbed his pipe this time at Esteban. 'Now what else can you think of that depended on saltpetre? Don't shout all at once because I'm gonna tell you anyway. Gunpowder. In

1915 Germany damn near lost the fucking war because they were running out of gunpowder. Why were they running out of gunpowder? Because the British had blockaded them real good and they couldn't get to fucking Chile for the goddamn saltpetre deposits, that's why. They managed to send ships out into the South Atlantic but got bruised to hell, and no one could figure out what in God's sweet name they were doing there anyway. But the fact of the matter was, they had about six months' worth of bang-powder left and after that it was gonna be a case of break out the cutlasses, men, it's close-quarter work from now on. Basically, they were up shit creek. Enter the evil genius, Fritz Haber, who launched a crash programme to adapt manufacturing plants from fertilizer production to gunpowder production. I mean, if you can make artificial fertilizer it doesn't take too long to figure out a way to do likewise for gunpowder. Bingo yet again!'

He paused, grinned at the two men watching him. 'But where, I hear you thinking, does indigo dye come into it? I'll tell ya. Both in the production of artificial dyes and non-salt-petre-based gunpowder there were some real weird by-products. F'rinstance, they created synthetic indigo by the reduction of nitrobenzene – and just *one* of the by-products of this process was the generation of *forty fucking tons of liquid fucking chlorine per day*. And these guys, they didn't know what to do with the fucking stuff! – till Haber hadda light-bulb light up in his skull. *Chlorine gas.*'

Schwemmer leaned back in his chair with an air of triumph.

'Yeah, chlorine gas. Amongst others. Okay, swift rundown on some of the devil's brews both the Krauts and the Allies, who cottoned on fast when the first poison clouds rolled over their trenches, came up with. Phosgene, chlorine, mustard gas, chloropicrin, adamsite. Some were deadly, others were merely harassing agents. Phosgene was an asphyxiant, for instance: you choked to death on it. Chloropicrin made you throw up. Mustard was a vesicant, a blister agent. Also had a delayed effect. You felt okay for maybe twenty-four hours then, *bam*! Ingenious. Adamsite was a harassing agent, arsenic-based. The list goes on. Those, gentlemen, are what are known in the trade as the first generation gases. But let us move on. Far more fascinating ways of screwing your enemies are only just over the horizon.'

He coughed a few times, cleared his throat, then reached across the desk and grabbed up Esteban's discarded coffee, swallowing what remained in a single gulp. Esteban winced.

'Second generation,' said Schwemmer, 'Second World War. The Krauts are at it again. Not content with fooling around with straight poison gas they hadda go not just one better but about a thousand. They invented nerve gases, an awesome leap in toxicity. Chemical weapons of World War One killed in a matter of hours, if they killed at all. Many didn't, just left you a fucking wreck for twenty years. Nerve gases killed in minutes. They were a chemical stew of ferocious power. The chief ones were tabun, sarin, and the kingpin of them all, soman. Nerve gases basically play merry hell with the enzymes in the human nervous system. They stop certain parts of your body doing what comes naturally. The second generation gases made the first generation seem about as venomous as an over-dose of jellybeans. Now the weird thing is, the Nazis never *used* nerve gas, although they produced maybe 30,000 tons of the goddamn stuff before the end of the war. Main reason they never used it was they figured the Allies had shit that was twice as powerful. The fact of the matter was, the Allies weren't investigating nerve agents much at all. The British in particular were pissing around with biological and bacteriological weapons, biotoxins like anthrax and botulin. There's a theory too that Hitler, who was gassed himself on the Western Front, hated the stuff, although that didn't stop the fucker using it to get rid of a few million Jews. Whatever, they manufactured it but simply stockpiled it. When the Allied Command found all this crap and realized what it was, they nearly had forty blue fits apiece because they also realized the Nazis had actually had the capability of winning the war two or three years *before* the Normandy Landings.

'So okay,' Schwemmer gestured with his hands, 'what happened to all this shit? I'll tell ya. Souvenir-hunting is what happened to it. Each of the Allies grabbed as much as they could from whatever manufactory they over-ran in '44-'45. The British and US forces captured a hell of a lot of sarin, which was the second-deadliest agent. The Reds stumbled onto a factory in Poland which had been pumping out tabun but which had also been instrumental in discovering soman, the dirtiest agent of the lot. So the Reds, after the war, began boiling up vats of the goddamn stuff while we did likewise. Gradually . . . '

'Harry,' said Phil Esteban.

'Uh?'

'Get to the point.'

'Awright, awready.' Schwemmer looked pained. 'Jesus. You gotta have the background, for Christ's sake.'

'Give us some foreground.'

'Look, I gotta tell you about soman, I gotta give you some more about that. It's great stuff!' Schwemmer's eyes were alive with enthusiasm.

Esteban said, 'The trouble is, Harry, we really don't have much time. I like hearing you gab, John likes hearing you gab, but there's a time-factor here.'

Schwemmer grinned weakly.

'Well, okay, I can cut out soman. But it's so . . . so . . . *grisly*!' His voice went up into a squeak of ardour as he rubbed his hands with melodramatic glee. Even Hardin had to smile. 'But on the other hand,' Schwemmer went on, 'the stuff *based* on soman is even more gruesome, so, yeah, let's shift butt to that. Or at least,' he amended, 'let's shift to what you might call the stumbling-block scientists have been up against over the past twenty-five years. Speed. And I don't mean funny-pills either. I mean *speed*. What we like to call rate-of-death, mega-kill.'

'A pretty fucking gruesome concept in itself,' muttered Hardin.

'Sure. Herman Kahn's got a lot to answer for. See, for years both our guys and their guys have been looking for the fast kill, and . . . '

'You mean mere minutes is considered too slow,' said Hardin.

'Sure. You got it.'

'A bullet through the heart takes but a second.' Hardin was smiling grimly.

75

'Too wasteful.' Schwemmer wagged a finger archly at him, an amused frown on his chubby, sweating face. 'That's the whole point, John. Even an on-target shell only decimates those within a certain close proximity to it. Beyond that close proximity you get blast-effect, a lotta wounded, some repairable, others not, and that's cool because it means they won't be fighting for a while, either way. But beyond that again you still have guys who're raring to go, spraying rounds, still operational. The optimum is an army that is utterly fucked at a stroke, totally out for the count, and at a cost of only a very little effort expended.'

'A nuke'd do that,' said Esteban mordantly.

Schwemmer winced. He looked genuinely horrified.

'Please, Phil. Wash out your mouth. A nuke'd do a fuck of a lot of other things too, none of which bear thinking about. Y'see,' he became serious again, 'this is where it's at. Sure, there are guys who've got the hots for nukes, both sides of the Iron Curtain, but in a weird kinda way gas is cleaner.'

'*Cleaner*!' exploded Hardin.

'Okay, okay.' Schwemmer waved his hands. 'Loose use of words. But you gotta rationalize, John. Ya gotta cut the emotional response. Gas *is* cleaner than a fucking nuclear holocaust. That's a fact.'

'Now look . . . ' began Hardin angrily, sitting up suddenly.

'Hang-fire, John.' Esteban cut in fast, leaning across the desk and holding up a hand. 'We can argue this one out some other goddamn time. The philosophy of the thing is of no fucking importance right now. If they have what Harry thinks they have, we gotta shift into top, head for the fast lane. There are no priorities except stopping the bastards.'

Still simmering, Hardin sank back into his seat. He knew that Harry Schwemmer was half-jesting, the way one does when faced with the unbelievable, the unthinkable. At the same time he knew that Schwemmer, whatever his own private emotional response might be, was also curiously attracted to the prospect of a chemical or gas whose sheer frightfulness might be on a scale as yet unknown to humanity.

Esteban said urgently, 'For Christ's sake, Harry, just give us the facts.'

76

Schwemmer shook his head, gestured at the gas-mask lying on the desk.

'Trouble is, with that fucker there are no facts, no really concrete facts. 'S all conjecture. Well, most of it. We can, if ya like, extrapolate a certain amount from the way that face-mask is constructed, what's inside it, how it works, but what precisely – and I mean pree-cisely – it was manufactured to guard *against* is another crapping ball-game. It's like I said, it all gets down to speed. What our guys and their guys, the Russians, have been trying to discover is the fastest effect possible, the agent that kills the quickest. The Russians, as I said, chose the Kraut agent soman as the basis for their chemical research. We know they've synthesized the original formula into a kind of very oily thickened soman which doesn't evaporate. We don't know what they call this shit but we've coded it VR-55. Our own newest agent, VX, is, we think, similar to it in consistency and, more to the point, toxicity. It sticks to your skin so you can't wipe or rub it off, no matter how small a droplet hits you, and when I say droplet I mean one microscopic particle that's part of a mist-haze. One droplet of that on your skin and within minutes you don't function properly. After that it just gets worse. Death occurs within ten minutes. There's no reprieve. The filter in this,' he tapped the mask, 'is far more sophisticated than anything I've ever seen, and that means it's geared to stop something we don't know about getting through.' He shrugged. 'If you want it simple, that's it.'

The silence that lasted for some seconds was finally broken by Esteban.

'Antidotes?'

Schwemmer laughed harshly.

'How the fuck are we supposed to dream up antidotes to something we don't really have the key to in the first place? Sure we have antidotes. We gotta whole bag of blasted antidotes. But against whatever this is, none of ours may work. In any case, even if we knew what it was, a specialized antidote would take a hell of a time to brew up in sufficient quantities to be effective. We know the Chinese are backing Charlie, we suspect the Chinese have the capability to create fairly fucking fearsome nerve weapons – simply because we have intelligence to the effect that not all of their high-grade scientists were knocked off in the Cultural Revolution, although a hell of a lot were. Therefore, unless this is black propaganda at its most in-fuckin'-genious, we may infer that the Chinese have in fact come up with a real zippy little number in the chemical line, faster than anything we possess, and a damn sight nastier.'

Esteban leaned back in his chair, his eyes pensive.

'I doubt this is a fake. Sure, our three reports are vague, but it doesn't smell like some bunco artist in the Chinese Command structure has come up with the bright idea of putting the frighteners on us. This smells real.'

It smelt real to Hardin too. A gigantic confidence trick on the part of the Chinese did not seem at all likely, although it'd be as well to keep one's mind open on that score, given the tricky nature of Chinese political strategy.

He said, 'And that's the breakthrough?'

Schwemmer said, 'If I'm right, yeah. If this guy – this Chinese and whatever back-up team he has – has created what I think he's created, an agent that's far faster and far more potent than anything we've got or the Russians have got, then he's so far ahead of us he's outta sight.'

Hardin thought about that.

'Yeah, but if we're going on these reports of the fire from the sky, or whatever the hell it was, it wasn't that fast.' He looked at Esteban for confirmation. 'You said the hillman took a long time to die – or at least he was able to trek through the jungle, get to a safe ville, spill his information to our asset. That all took time.'

Schwemmer tapped his file again.

'I got all that in here. Don't forget, John, those reports go back six months or more. We figure those were trial runs by the Veets. In any case it's the sickness itself which alerted me, specifically all that internal bleeding. Our asset was positive about this. The guy he talked to was shitting blood and throwing up blood. He was a fucking mess, a walking fucking toilet. But there were other indications of something we hadn't encountered before in research into nerve agents. F'rinstance, the guy had blisters all over him, blisters that were erupting, then turning black. But a blister agent – like mustard gas, say, even a highly sophisticated version – doesn't make you shit blood. At least, not like *this* dude was shitting blood. The guy had headaches all the time, too. Blister agent doesn't give you headaches. The guy was having spasms. Blister agent doesn't give you the kicks. But then something that does give you the kicks doesn't give you all the other symptoms he had. From the descriptions of the guy, and what the guy said about what happened in his village – and allowing for exaggeration and sheer damn getting-it-wrong – it sounds to me like our Chinese friend has created a super-cocktail, a chemical stew, a ferocious brew-up of all the dirtiest agents you can think of, and a hell of a lot you can't even imagine.'

Hardin looked at Schwemmer. His whole tone had changed. Now he was serious. More to the point, now he was actually sounding worried.

'And if the Chinese do have a powerful new agent you can bet they'll be refining it and refining it. Lemme tell ya, a lot can happen in this game in six months. All ya need's the breakthrough, the way to work it. Once you've figured out what to do, the rest comes easy. All they need now is a factory facility.'

Hardin breathed out, stared at Esteban. 'Your maybe-maybe-not building programme beyond the DeeEmZee.'

Esteban said, in a voice that was stripped of emotion, 'Like I told you, John, there's no maybe about it . . .'

The tall man with the wizened face walked quickly down the corridor, his boots echoing on the tiled floor, a folder clutched in one hand. He paused for a moment half-way along and stood loosely to attention, as one of *them* came out of a door and stared at him before turning away with a faint look of contempt and marching briskly off in the opposite direction. The man with the wizened face curled his lip, muttered a coarse expletive and carried on up the corridor until he reached the penultimate door, where he knocked.

'Come!'

He entered, nodding at the dapper little man who was studying some documents at his desk.

'Seen this?'

He waved the folder with one hand and back-heeled the door shut with a bang.

'I've seen a thousand of them,' said the dapper little man irritably. 'Probably ten thousand of the buggers. Once you've seen one bloody file you've seen 'em all.'

The man with the wizened face smiled craftily as he opened the folder and took a single sheet of paper from it, sliding it across the desk towards his master, who scowled.

'No. Read it. I took a copy. Thought you might be interested.'

The dapper little man reluctantly ran his eyes over the opening paragraphs, then spat out an earthy curse.

'Another fuck-up! You'd think some of those idiots'd be more careful! You'd think . . . '

'No, not there. Further down.' The wizened-faced man jabbed a finger at the paper. 'There.'

The room was suddenly quiet as the dapper little man took in what his aide was pointing at. He stared at it for some seconds, then his eyes shifted back to the top of the paper and he read everything on it carefully, every word. He did this twice. Then he looked up.

'Ah.' His voice was colourless.

'Thought you'd be interested,' said the tall man with the wizened face. 'Bit of a coincidence, eh?'

'It does make things simpler,' agreed the dapper little man.

80

V

The girl was saying 'Ohh *yes*, ohh *yes*, ohh *yes*' but in time with her breathing, sucked in deep on the 'ohh', expelled harshly, urgently, almost despairingly on the '*yes*'. As she did this she reared up on him, ground herself down, reared up, ground down.

She'd been doing this at a steady rate for some time now but Hardin was aware that the strokes were gradually accelerating, the tone of her voice becoming if anything more frenzied, more tormented. With a detached part of his mind, while his hands played with her body, stroking her sweat-dewed skin, pinching and rubbing and roughly fumbling at her bouncing breasts, he watched her above him and knew that she was a thousand miles away, not on him at all, perhaps not on anyone in particular. She was simply surrendering to the blinding shafts of pure sensation exploding through every part of her system, across every naked nerve-end, every time she plunged down so frantically to the base of his penis.

He was aware that she was nearly there, heading for the precipice, was aware that he too was approaching climax. Suddenly she sank forward towards him, her hands clutching at the pillow beneath his head, her breasts inches from his face. He pulled greedily at her left breast and gnawed at the hard, flushed nipple, rasping it roughly between his teeth. In his nostrils was the heady smell of sweat and sweetness and the powerful musky stink of sex; in his ears were the girl's moans

81

of pleasure which, as she suddenly slowed her thrusts to a long, grinding, heaving rhythm, became animal grunts, frenzied choked gasps. Her face, damp and flushed with exertion and excitement, dropped down further, onto his shoulder, long silky strands of hair brushing at him as he bit harder into her nipple, rasping and chewing at it. He closed his eyes as a sharp gnawing sensation grew along his cock, a slow warm sucking itch that needed to be assuaged. It felt as though her cunt was ballooning around him, as though its soft, slippery walls were not even touching most of his length. Blindly he reached around her with his free left hand, the right still moulding her breast as his lips and teeth worried at the nipple, and stroked her smooth flesh, moving down over her buttocks until his questing fingers found the tight puckered hole.

Half of him felt as though he was floating in a warm cocoon someplace else. The blankets, the bed, the cheap hotel-room with only two flickering candles for light, were not really there at all. The other half was greedily relishing the physical flesh-contact, the frenzied surge and thrust, the passionate release of lust. He was beginning to lose control and so was she. He thrust roughly at the hole, sank a finger deep into her, and she screamed out loud and began tearing at his arms and shoulders, raking at his flesh with her nails as she climaxed, now grinding with all the force she could muster at the base of his shaft, milking his cock with an immense sucking power. It went on and on until he could hold back no longer. He let go, still with one finger in her arse, still with his mouth closed hungrily around her hard nipple, and yelled into her breast as he came too, shudderingly, with each spurt trying to drive deeper and deeper into her both with finger and cock.

The wind-down took a long time. She lay atop him and around him, exhausted, murmuring lazily and incomprehensibly into his ear. Hardin drifted, enclosed by her warmth. He had a vague feeling that he'd been used, even though she was clearly attracted to him, but that didn't matter. He'd got out of the past two hours as much as she'd got. It was the nature of the situation: the war, the country; simple animal need. Nothing wrong with that. Remembering a similar past attraction, he thought about Eileen Satkis, wondering if there was something about photojournalist femmes that sparked his libido. Possibly so. Or maybe it was girls in flak-jackets. Maybe he was kinky. This amused him. He knew what it was really. It was the new breed of decision-making, life-style-creating women; women who fought their own fights, didn't give a shit either way, were raunchy and romantic at the same time. That was it. That was what attracted him. They'd always line set in plantin for gunships to see if the density is near or women who'd cut loose and made their mark. But it was only in the past decade or so, with new social conditions, that more completely than ever before, and in greater numbers, women were cutting themselves free of the old paternalistic crap and finding out they could be as resourceful and individualistic as the next – well, *person*.

He shifted slightly to scratch at a sudden itch on his leg.

'This is a tacky hotel, Ms Berry.'

'I told you. Kate.'

'I don't feel I know you well enough. Any case, we were never properly introduced.'

'Oh?'

'Yeah. To be properly introduced you have to have someone else do the introducing. I read that somewhere. Old book of etiquette my grandmother had, I think.'

She said, 'It's the best hotel there is around here. So the lights go off at night. So what?'

'It's not the lights I'm worried about, it's the goddamn bed-bugs.'

'That's swell. So now you accuse me of keeping an unclean nest . . .'

He slid a hand down between them and lazily fingered the hairs at her crotch.

'Your nest is okay, don't let no one tell you different.'

She chuckled in his ear, a deep and melodious sound, full of knowledge.

'Tell me what you do.'

'No.'

'Why not?'

'What I do's got nothing to do with the here and now. When I fuck I'm not interested in what goes on outside.'

'I don't think I believe you, John Hardin.'

His eyes closed, Hardin thought about that. There was an element of truth here. More than an element, in fact. She was very perceptive. Even now there was a part of him pondering the future, what Halderling was going to be doing with him, VC booby-traps, keeping your piece clean in the jungle, whatever. The externals. He thought irritably: Fuck Lew Halderling. Why the hell should I worry about what he wants to do with me, how he wants to make use of me. I should be thinking about what *I* goddamn well want to do.

The trouble was, it came to the same thing. Or roughly so. Already he was automatically thinking about that no-go zone beyond the DeeEmZee, about the possibilities of actually, physically, getting there – have to go up through Laos, then across, east, penetrate the EnVee border that way. He'd done it before, although never that far south, never that close to the DeeEmZee, never . . .

Disgustedly he thrust all that out of his mind. There was an attractive and very sexy and active lady on top of him, so why in God's name was he letting his thoughts run along those lines? Often he didn't make sense to himself, and that was worrying him more and more.

She murmured, 'Listen, I'm a working girl. I have to have my beauty sleep . . . '

His hand was still cupped around her crotch, fingers lazily playing with the lips of her cunt. She moved against him restlessly and Hardin could feel her sudden wetness, could feel himself hardening again in response.

'Not yet,' he said.

Hardin nodded to the aged boy behind the desk, yawned, and walked across the darkened foyer towards the side door. The front windows that looked out on to the street were all blocked off with pierced-steel planking in case of bombs, shells or grenades. Inside the windows were bars, then strips of fine-mesh wire to stop the glass blowing inward in case of a direct hit. Hardin idly wondered why no one had thought to put up screens in front of the windows too, just in case the glass penetrated the fine-mesh. And then of course you'd have to fix tne screens to the floor to stop them falling over from the blast and then hang blankets over the screens and . . .

Jesus, he thought, as he stepped through the door into the street.

There was not much moon to speak of, and what little there was might just as well not have been there for all the light it gave. His eyes adjusted automatically, through long practice. There were one or two parked cars up the street, an abandoned cyclo-taxi. Outwardly Do Thon was a dead town at night, even this early, although there were bars and hotels in the hootch-ville area down near what the Do Thon citizenry quaintly referred to as the river – actually a stinking sewer. He glanced at his watch. Fifteen minutes short of eleven o'clock. His car was parked around the corner and he had plenty of time to get back to the SSG base outside town and phone Will Steeger in Saigon, who would almost certainly have not only a deal of hot gossip and scandalous rumour but the urge to impart it.

He thought about the girl. The phone call from her had come as a mild surprise. He'd imagined that she would've been well on her way back to Saigon, civilization, assignment completed, a story to hustle back in the World. Up here it was the boondocks. Why bother remaining?

She hadn't said. He found it hard to believe that she'd stayed simply to have a so-so meal with him in a so-so restaurant and then back to a so-so hotel for bed; although *that* was by no means so-so, it had to be said. On the other hand, why not? Harry Schwemmer had done weirder things in his Quest for the Perfect Screw – but then Schwemmer was Schwemmer; there weren't too many guys, or gals, like him.

A fat rat shot across his path, fled out into the road, disappeared in the shadows. A door opened somewhere off the street ahead of him and a burst of laughter cut the silence like a hacksaw. A bar. The door banged. Silence. Hardin walked on.

He wondered where his men were, that ragamuffin bunch of dopers, fraggers and murderers that now, oddly, seemed closer to him than many of the comrades-at-arms he'd known over the past four or five years.

He thought it was a strange thing, but . . .

And then he stopped thinking about them, cut them out of

his mind completely. Thrust them from him along with all thoughts of Steeger, Kate Berry, the night, the tacky bars and tacky hotels. In a microsecond his mind was clear and clean save for one burning image.

Men. Up ahead of him.

Waiting for him.

Not only ahead. Behind him as well, goddamnit.

Still maintaining his laid-back, ambling pace, Hardin let his eyes rove along and across the shadowy street in front of him. There was nothing he could actually see, no visible evidence of any kind of human activity. But his senses were now all on hair-trigger alert. He couldn't be wrong about this.

Or could he?

His mind bounced back to the temple in the jungle. He'd been wrong there, damn it. Or so it had seemed. He'd been convinced there was someone listening in, but there'd been no one. No one at all. Maybe, he thought with a chill curdling his bloodstream, I'm losing my touch, losing my grip. Maybe nearly fifteen years of danger and dancing with death in the hotspots of the world is catching up with me. Maybe I'm tipping over the edge into total paranoia.

He wanted very much to turn round and peer back over his shoulder, but couldn't. If he did that and he was right, it would tip off whoever it was following him. If he did it and he was wrong, he felt it would almost blow his mind. He felt that his training, his background, everything he'd learned in the war of shadows in which he'd been immersed for most of his adult life would be shattered utterly and completely.

He gazed ahead. He had, he gauged, roughly forty paces left before the corner around which was his car. In between him and that corner was the parked cyclo-taxi. He could see nothing remotely resembling a human form under it or beyond it. A guy hiding on the blind side would have to be the size of a goddamn monkey not to be seen. Christ, thought Hardin, maybe they're using kids for this one . . .

Part of his mind still refused to believe that he could, with all his considerable experience, be wrong. But the other part was putting up an insidious and debilitating fight. He walked on slowly, forcing himself to relax, to whistle softly and tunelessly through his teeth, his left hand in his fatigues pocket, his right hanging free.

He was suddenly aware of engine-noise, growing louder. Automatically he tensed, his right hand inching towards his belt. Headlights sheared into the darkness, growing brighter; a car came round the corner, its gears grinding at it slowed. The headlights caught him and Hardin knew that if there was someone in that car with any kind of a piece he had no fucking chance at all. The wall beside him was too high and even if he jumped he'd be cut down in milliseconds, the perfect target. His back felt as though a thousand needles were being slowly driven into his flesh; his shirt stuck to him tackily. The light grew brighter, dazzling him, blinding him. Then the car moved slowly past, gathered speed and rocketed off behind him.

Jesus Christ, he thought disgustedly, a car, a late-night car is all. Sure it slowed. There was a corner. The guy didn't know the roads. What the fuck is the matter with me?

He noted with tense amusement that he'd automatically identified the car by its engine sound and the shape of it, just caught out of the corner of his eye as it accelerated past. A Citroen, a four-door, old, maybe from the late 1940s.

He walked to the corner, turned it.

The relief that hit him as two figures sprang towards him from a shadowy doorway was enormous, much stronger than the surprise. He'd been *right*.

It was as though someone had pulled a switch. Instantly he shrugged off the clammy hand of paranoia; adrenalin surged into his system, and made him feel like he was on fire.

And yet, too, it was as though suddenly everything had slowed down, as though he was a character in a slow-motion film. There were still two Hardins, two quite separate and distinct personalities, but while one now acted, the other watched with a cool detachment the almost ballet-like sequence of violence that erupted.

Both men had knives. Hardin's right hand clenched around the haft of his own knife, double-edged with an eight-inch blade, and slid it smoothly up and out. His arm went back and round in a graceful curve and the weapon disappeared from his ungripped fingers, its haft appearing as an ugly, alien knob in the chest of the leading attacker, the man on his left. The man gagged, mouth sagging foolishly, his free hand clutching at the haft, tugging feebly. His own knife tinkled on the sidewalk as he lurched sideways.

Hardin jumped him, heaved at the stumbling shape, thrust him into the path of the second man.

The second man let out a hiss of breath from between gritted teeth and staggered. Hardin smashed the iron-hard heel of one hand into his nose, heard the crunch of bone, saw blood spray. The second man whimpered, became entangled with the dead weight of his companion, collapsed to the sidewalk.

Hardin scooped up the fallen knife and swung round like a well-oiled machine, dancing to one side as he turned. There was no need. The third Vietnamese, the one he'd known with a stone-cold certainty must be somewhere behind him, had lagged too far behind, been too slow to catch up. Now he was running toward Hardin cat-footed, making no sound at all, holding his blade thrust out like a sword, trying to make up for lost ground.

The two men circled round each other warily. Hardin's palms were dry; there was a feral smile on his lips. He was too close to jump, too close to throw. The Vietnamese jabbed at him but the blade plunged harmlessly into thin air. Hardin stabbed upwards but the knife felt wrong, the blade was too short. The Vietnamese twisted to one side, bobbing up, chopping at his wrist, tearing through cloth, slicing a long furrow down his arm. Fire shot up Hardin's arm as the flesh parted but he paid no attention. The Vietnamese was now stupidly close, fatally close. Hardin pulled back his knife, blade up, and sheared down into his attacker's wrist. There was a thin, almost soundless scream as the man's eyes widened, as the blade sank into flesh, tendon and muscle. Then Hardin lunged, flicking his knife up and driving it tearingly into the man's guts. It was a messy one. The blade was none too sharp. Hardin had to carve like a butcher's apprentice, using main force, left hand gripping right, to heave the knife upwards through the stomach wall and into his rib-cage, grinding against bone, opening him up.

88

Arteries parted, pumped red stuff all over him. His hands became slick and wet and sticky. The Vietnamese was making a snorting, squealing sound, like a hog whose throat has been cut by an amateur. Blood was coming up out of his gaping mouth and down over his chin in a thick, treacly gush. He sagged away from Hardin, taking the knife with him.

Hardin didn't bother about that. He spun round and saw that the second man was groggily trying to shove the first man off him. Hardin reached down and tugged his own knife out of the first man's chest. It came cleanly. He heaved the stiff off, kicking the second man between the legs. The man choked, then threw up noisily. Hardin, grimacing, grabbed at his shirt-front, yanked him up. He smacked his face hard with a vicious backhander and the Vietnamese's thick black hair sprayed up wildly with the force of the blow. Hardin rammed him back against the stonework of the wall.

He stared into the man's face, now slack with exhaustion and pain. He gauged him to be in his early-30s, a city-dweller and not a farm-boy turned guerilla. Still, he stank of VC, that was for sure, and in a way this was almost a relief. The thought that had been nagging at Hardin was that this was a hit-squad from some rogue element of the Company, the CIA. Those fuckers did not wish him well, he knew that, and it would be just like them to set him up, using a South Vietnamese spook or a bunch of Saigon gangland hard-men, and put the job down to a random VC killing. US forces walking alone in darkened streets were prime targets for those who ruled the night.

But this guy was the genuine article, there was no question about that. Hardin had seen too many, interrogated too many, to be mistaken. The difference between a Chinatown hood and a cadre-indoctrinated civilian was stark.

So this looked like a case of random attack.

Except for one thing. It wasn't random at all but deliberate.

The random attack was a grenade through a window, or a shot from down the street, the attacker almost invariably a lone man who didn't give a shit whether he was killed in return or not. Sometimes, maybe, you got two men.

You never got three, two up-front, one a backstop behind. That was sophisticated, professional. That was a directed attack.

He grasped the man's jaw with his left hand, shook it roughly. The guy groaned, opened his eyes.

Hardin said, 'Talk now. Quickly. Who put you up to this?' He spoke in fluent Vietnamese.

The Vietnamese stared back at him, blood still oozing from his crushed and broken nose. He was breathing quickly, harshly.

'Talk. Talk now and I'll make it easy for you. Don't talk and you'll be in a world of pain. No one could ever teach you about the pain I can give you.'

The man's lips twisted in a sour smile. He said, in mocking English, 'No talkee, American monkey.'

Hardin thrust his right knee forward, between the man's legs, and suddenly jammed him downwards viciously, using both hands. The Vietnamese gave an agonized gasp, his free hands flapping wildly then clutching at himself, his eyes rolling upwards.

Hardin muttered, 'When I've finished with you, buddy, you won't be donating any more goddamn children to Uncle Ho.'

Again that smile, stubborn and mocking.

'Uncle Ho dead. You know that, Colonel. No threat.'

Hardin tensed. There was no way the guy could identify his rank, no way at all.

He hissed, 'You're gonna talk, pal. Believe me if you believe nothing else. You're gonna spill it all.'

'No spill. I'm a dead man, Colonel. You get left with many questions, no damn answers.'

Hardin cuffed him across the face, spun him round. His car was fifty yards along the narrow street. He wrenched one arm round and back in a tight and agonizing lock, half-way up the man's back. The man grunted with pain.

'Move,' snapped Hardin.

Then he heard the car engine again. Not his, of course, but the car that had sped past him only minutes before, the late-night car. It couldn't be any other, the engine-note was too distinctive. Lights appeared at the far end of the street. There was a squeal of tyres, a roar of exhaust. The car was moving fast towards him, its lights blinding.

90

'Shit!'

He flung the Vietnamese from him and dived for the pavement where it met the stonework of the wall.

As he did so automatic fire ripped apart the night-silence hideously, a roaring, racketing burst of rounds that hammered into the wall above his head, spraying him with brick-shards and dust. There was a tortured scream from the Vietnamese, who'd already started to run. Now he was flung back towards Hardin, propelled by the hammer-blows of maybe half a mag on full auto. The rounds thudded into him, tore through him, ghoulishly transforming him into a dancing puppet on a string held by a puppet-master with *delirium tremens* before he collapsed on to Hardin.

Crouched there on the sidewalk, huddled into the wall-angle, Hardin still had a full view of the car as it hurtled past, muzzle-flashes stabbing at the darkness like crazed fireflies and weirdly lighting the scene. He had a glimpse of a face behind the automatic rifle, a glimpse that kicked something at the back of his memory, deep, and then the car, tyres shrieking once more, careered round the corner and out of sight, almost out of earshot, the sound quickly fading to a foggy murmur, then nothing.

He struggled free of the body, cursing savagely. This was getting out of hand.

The Vietnamese was dead, his white shirt-front turned into a torn and bloody patchwork quilt.

Hardin gazed around but, not surprisingly, no windows opened, no doors, in that silent street. He looked down at himself and saw that he was greasy with other men's blood. He stooped quickly, went through the man's pockets. Nothing. He went to the first man. The result of his search was exactly the same. He'd have been surprised if it weren't. The third man still lay where he'd fallen, surrounded by a horrifying pool of thickening blood. It was going to take a whole sackful of chloride of lime to dry that motherfucker up, Hardin thought grimly.

He bent over the body, once more went through empty pockets, his fingers now starting to glue together with all the blood.

Then, at a sudden faint sound behind him, the scuff of shoe-leather on grit, he whirled around, his own knife back in his right hand again as though by magic, his face twisted up into an ugly rictus of anger and menace.

Kate Berry stood there, at the corner, white-faced. She was holding a small .32 automatic in one hand. She looked like she knew how to use it.

They gazed into each other's eyes for what seemed like centuries and there was no recognition in either of what had taken place only a half hour before. Then she breathed out hard, through her mouth, her eyes flicking to the scene of slaughter behind him.

She said, 'What goes on?' Her voice was slightly frayed at the edges.

Hardin relaxed, slid his knife back into its rig.

'More to the goddamn point,' he said, his voice still taut, 'what the hell are you doing out?'

She shrugged, gave a nervous laugh.

'Even more to the point, why am I the only human being out on the street apart from you after what sounded from my room like a full-scale battle?' She gestured to the camera slung round her neck. 'I thought I had an exclusive.'

'You have.' Hardin was still angry: angry at the loss of the VC, angry at being shot at, angry at the menacing but unidentifiable shadows that seemed to be hovering over him like death-angels. 'But automatic fire means you keep your head down, lady, and blood on the sidewalk is penny-ante stuff out here. Gallons of the shit, tanker-fucking loads, have been spilled on the streets of South Vietnam. Take your snaps. It's old news.'

'The boy back at the hotel kept grabbing my arm, told me I was crazy.'

'He was right.'

He turned away from her, walked purposefully towards his car.

'But what about these?' She pointed at the corpses.

There was something in her voice he couldn't for the moment identify, some emotion that in any case he didn't feel like analyzing right then.

92

'Leave 'em. Let the civil authorities worry about 'em. I have too much on my goddamn plate already.'

He made it to the car, automatically checking petrol-cap, bonnet, the two doors for any signs of tampering. There were none. He unlocked the door and climbed in, switched on. He hunched wearily down in the seat, bleak-faced, backed the car, then swung out into the street. In his rear-view mirror the girl was a lonely figure standing on the corner, soon merging into the darkness and the night.

He drove fast, hands clenched around the wheel.

Paranoia was back, like a black dog biting deep into his psyche.

VI

'Heard the latest?' said Steeger. He sounded in fine form even through the mush and crackle of the line down to Saigon.

Hardin took a generous slug of the gin gimlet he'd just made for himself and stuck one booted foot up on the desk in front of him, leaning the chair back so he was perched somewhat precariously.

'Tell me.'

'CIA got this hot scheme to send Giap a bottle of poisoned apricot brandy. Seems the good general is partial to apricot brandy. Got the habit from us, when we were helping him and Uncle Ho back in '45.'

'Is that a joke?' said Hardin. 'Where's the punchline?'

'The punchline is, it ain't no joke.'

'Are you serious?'

'Swear to God. I had it from the guy whose boss thought up the idea. They're now discussing ways-and-means. Gonna set up a committee.'

'Buncha fucking clowns,' grunted Hardin.

His disgust with the CIA was so profound that he never gave a shit about trashing them verbally even on an open line. Although not with Will Steeger, a friend from his San Francisco days in the mid-fifties, when Steeger had been on a university newspaper and Hardin had been behind the counter of the once-notorious City Lights Book Store.

Steeger was now a highly regarded newspaperman and commentator who had strong links with the spooks who operated out of the Embassy on Thong Nhut Street. The spooks thought they controlled him, but the joke was that, while playing along with this and shit-eating when it was necessary, he blew most of the stuff he got from them to various radical rags and counter-culture acidhead papers back in the World. He also ran an asset on the Embassy staff who brought in cart-loads of dope in the Diplomatic Bag. Steeger liked the element of danger associated with his extra-curricular activities. He liked walking the tightrope, feasting with panthers.

Even so, Hardin would have been rather more circumspect had this been an open line, which it was not. All SSG lines were secure; tight as a gnat's ass, as Halderling – who liked his privacy – was fond of saying. And in any case Hardin saw to it that a friend of his moonlighted in Steeger's rented villa on plush Pasteur Street every month, sweeping for bugs, checking the wires.

'Buncha dimbo crapheads,' he muttered.

'Hey,' said Steeger, 'these guys are fighting the Red Peril, you know. Making the world safe for democracy.'

'Boy, have I got a tale to tell you,' said Hardin heavily. He extracted a cigarette one-handed from the pack on the desk and lit it.

'Is it a hot one?'

'Hot as hell. The Big H. The Company's been shifting it around.'

'Well, Jeeze!' said Steeger disgustedly. 'I know that. *Everybody* knows that! They've been doing it for goddamn years. Shit, John, Air America's been flying junk up to Laos on a regular contract since Christ was a teenager, more or less.'

'Uh-uh. This is different. This is ten keys worth, and that's just for starters.'

'Tell me more.'

'Too complex. You put me on to it in the first place anyway, kind of. So I owe you.'

'I'll hold you to that, buster.' Where news was concerned – or at least the real dirt – Steeger could be hard-nosed, but

Hardin didn't hold this against him. They went back too far together, although even Will Steeger had never managed to plumb Hardin's full depths. There were times when even Steeger felt it wise to call a halt to the digging.

'When you gonna be back down here?'

'Depends.' Hardin was unsure. Unsure about a lot of things. He was still angry over the attacks on him, although there seemed to be no connection as far as he could see between those and the business of the EnVee gas-masks. That there might be a link was not beyond consideration; it was just that he couldn't put it together for the moment. In any case he was tired already of Do Thon and the confinement of the SSG camp. Getting right down to it, Saigon was no different, just bigger.

He said, 'You remember Bill Pronzini? That temple out in bandit country?'

Steeger chuckled. 'Mezzrow, how could I ever forget it? Didn't the army have to retake it four times so the photogs could take their snaps?'

'Something like that. I jumped into another one couple of days back. Girl from *Pix Magazine*, Kate Berry, and a squad out in the wilderness. Same situation. The great American public sure loves an old temple.'

'Who'd you say?'

'Berry. Kate Berry.'

'Don't know her. *Pix* pay well, but they're kind of choosy.' Steeger sounded slightly sour and Hardin forbore to ask whether he'd been turned down by them at some time; there were some things you didn't question your friends about. 'She must be good.'

'She is.'

Steeger chuckled again.

'Oh yeah?' he leered down the line.

'Yeah.'

'Well, I ain't gonna embarrass you by trying to find out the sordid details. Won't tell on ya to Satkis either, my friend.'

'Bastard.'

'Hey, listen. I'm extending my power-base.'

'Oh?'

'Yeah, contact I have over in the World wants me to do a thing for one of them comix. You know – with an 'x'? Funnies these ain't, I'm tellin' ya! Wants me to do, like, a script and they've got an artist who'll draw it up. One of them dope-head acid-freak fuckers in San Francisco. It's called *Hot-Shit Comix*, and I'm gonna be spilling the beans on a certain far-famed government agency whose probity is by no means a proven fact. Really looking forward to this one. Even got me a new pseud. Gonna call myself "Rand McWilly". How d'ya like it?'

Hardin laughed.

'It's a winner, Will. A goddamn winner.'

After putting the phone down he wandered restlessly around his apartment. It was comfortable, as were all those in the SSG senior officers' complex. Lew Halderling had determined many years before that the men and women who worked for him in the SSG would get as near the best as was humanly possible.

The SSG was obscurely named and equally obscurely funded. SSG stood for Strategic Studies Group, although what strategies the group was supposed to be studying had never been made clear. More often than not its members worked on those tasks considered by other government agencies to be either impossible or just too damn complicated. Halderling's budget was scattered through the books of a score or more departments and bureaus, his agents listed on every roster but their own. Officially, it and they didn't exist. General Lew Halderling himself, tall, gaunt, craggy, a tough and downy old bird, sometimes appeared in public and gave yawn-inducing lectures on army pension schemes; these rarely had high attendance figures.

This was not to say that Halderling and his group were not known. There was no doubt at all that fat files on Halderling and many of his top agents, including Hardin himself, were held by a strange miscellany of intelligence networks, not only in archives in Moscow, Peking, Hanoi, Tirana, Prague, East Berlin and all the obvious places, but also in Bonn, Paris, London, Rome, Tehran, Johannesburgh, Tel-Aviv and even weirder and wilder locations closer to home. Like for instance the euphemistically named 'communications' centre owned by

Howard Hughes in the San Fernando Valley, or the curious conglomerate known as Resorts International which on the surface seemed merely to be the umbrella organization for a number of casinos in the Bahamas. Not to mention that vast and ugly complex of glass and concrete out at Langley, Virginia.

Hardin pondered once more the Vietnamese knifemen and the ancient Citroen with its murderous passenger. Could be the latter had been 'minding' the former; an automatic rifle had been allocated as backstop if the knifemen failed. But that seemed too stupidly complicated. He was fairly certain the two were not linked at all. And if it hadn't been for that Vietnamese calling him 'colonel', he would have put both attacks down to the whole craziness out here: some guys'd kill for nothing. But the Vietnamese had certainly known who he was and that inevitably meant that the knife-attack, at least, had been deliberate and premeditated. Maybe the car had been manned by a couple of crazies. But then why hadn't they shot at him first time round? There was an answer to that, maybe. The street outside the hotel was, despite being narrow and unwholesome, a main thoroughfare, whereas the street he'd turned into was more of a back-alley. Maybe they'd figured they could do the job easier there than on the first pass, which was perhaps too near the hotel. Sleazepit as that hotel was, it was the biggest in Do Thon. Maybe they were worried about who might come tumbling out if they'd iced him virtually on its steps.

It occurred to him that he could worry and gnaw at this one for weeks, months maybe, and still be no nearer to a plausible solution. Weird and starkly inexplicable events were two a penny out here as well. In any case, long ago he'd realized that when you worked for Lew Halderling you had to accept that you were a target for someone or other; some vicious bastard somewhere had your name at the top of his list. That two separate sets of vicious bastards might coincidentally hit you at the same moment should come as no shock.

He lay on his bed and smoked a joint, wondering idly where Olsen and the rest of his so-called squad were, what they were doing.

'I lick her cunt, she lick mine,' said the Vietnamese girl brightly. She had her arm round another girl, who was also smiling. Neither looked to be more than thirteen or fourteen, but that was only to the Occidental eye. On the other hand it could have been true. 'Then I lick her titties and she do same to me.'

To Leroy Vogt the whole thing sounded depressingly mechanical, especially when explained like this in words of no more than two syllables. It was not that he was against such a performance in principle. Theoretically the idea sounded fine; in practice, and under different circumstances, he had no doubt he'd enjoy it immensely. The actual idea of a threesome was great; terrific in fact. The *idea* – fuelled by images that were already swelling up in his mind – was in the process of giving him a hard-on.

The snag was, what was on offer was more like an eightsome. Vogt stared round the crowded, smoky, unbelievably filthy bar. Both Olsen and Fuller were staring at the two girls with interest. Doc Pepper was leaning back in his chair with a dumb grin on his face. Garrett and his buddy Griswold both had their tongues hanging out.

Vogt was, in a sense, a romantic, and this would be a far from romantic interlude. He was also, at heart, a realist and he knew damn well that all these girls were after was bucks, greenies, paper. Money. It was going to be a show, was all. Sure, they'd all get a chance at some slit, but Vogt positively yearned for something a little more than a fast two-minutesworth with five other guys lining up behind, their goddamn pants round their ankles.

Garrett said, 'Then we all get some fuck-fuck, right?'

The girl giggled.

'You fuck-fuck me, lick her cunt at same time.'

Garrett leaned forward, his face oozing sweat.

'Tell ya what, you sit on me, the other bitch can squeegee my face, okay? Ya get what I'm talkin' about, huh?'

The girl opened her eyes wide, gave him a lascivious smile.

'Sure thing, big boy. She sit on your face, make you real messy.'

'You got it, bitch. I like some hot sauce, I do.'

Doc Pepper chuckled.

'You'll regret it,' he sang, his voice a light mocking tenor. 'You're really a dumb prick, Garrett. And you've *got* a dumb prick. Jesus! You never heard of the dreaded South China Seas cock-rot?'

'I know all about that, shit-for-brains,' snapped Garrett.

'I'll tell you,' Doc Pepper leaned towards him confidentially, 'sometimes amputation is the only possible cure. Take it from a medical man.'

'My ass could medicate better 'n you, Pepper.'

The girl stooped slightly and reached out for Garrett, grabbed herself a generous portion of his crotch. Garrett reacted by pulling her on to his knees and mauling her breasts. She whispered in his ear.

'Jesus!' said Garrett. He looked stunned. 'I ain't never heard of that before.'

'You know,' said Doc Pepper to the others, 'and this is God's honest fuckin' truth, there are guys who caught a dose in '65 and they're *still here*!'

'Ah, shit, Pepper,' said Fuller.

Doc Pepper was keeping a very straight face.

'They've been *in quarantine* for *five fuckin' years*, man. Two guys I know, they woke up one morning, their dicks fell clean off. Now they both gotta squat to piss.'

'No way, José.' That was Garrett's buddy, Griswold. He had a deep cavernous voice. 'Fuckin' Command propaganda. When I was up in Tran Nam there was so much gook cunt up there the Colonel hadda get up an' tell us ta jack ourselves off instead. They was comin' out in the jungle on fuckin' scooters. In the middle of a fuckin' firefight! Off the scooters, up with their skirts. Grenades and mortars poppin' every-crappin'-where. Shit!' He spat at the floor, adding to the gunk already there. 'So the Colonel, he hadda do somethin'. Started these rumours, guys gettin' fungus growin' outta their crotch. You could farm fuckin' mushrooms off some-a these dudes, he said. Story was, these gooner cunts was impregnatin' theirselves with a real vicious strain of dick-rot, so we hadda beat our own meat. Crap!' He spat again. 'Fuckin' propaganda was all. Ain't nothin' wrong with dink pussy a jab can't solve.' But he still sounded uneasy.

Vogt stared at Garrett's buddy Griswold. He was a big man, bigger even than Garrett and that was saying something. Griswold had one eyebrow that stretched across his face in a thick bushy bar, like a second moustache. His real moustache was thick too, a luxuriant growth. The face itself looked like it had been carved out of wood that had been cured for a long time. He had bulging forearms and fists like a couple of rocks. Vogt decided that he would never do anything to incur Griswold's wrath.

But – Garrett's *buddy*? Vogt couldn't imagine such an animal; couldn't imagine Garrett having a friend, a buddy. It didn't seem at all right somehow. It didn't *fit*. And yet when Garrett had spotted him earlier, across the bar, he'd near thrown a fit, rushing across the crowded room, shoving guys aside, pounding the bigger man across the shoulders, even *embracing* him! Or at least throwing an arm around the guy's lumpy shoulders and hugging Griswold to him. And *smiling*, goddamnit! Generally Garrett's smile took about as long as the wink of an eye, but here he was, grinning and beaming as he propelled the guy back across the room, swiping a chair from a nearby table and jamming him down on it. And buying him a frigging drink!

Vogt thought: Whoever said it was damn right, there's good in every man, even the blackest-hearted, most evil sonofabitch there is. Not that Garrett was quite that, but the principle applied.

Of course, when they got to reminiscing, turned out they'd both been hitmen for the same mob at the same time. Vogt already knew that Garrett's pre-army days had been taken up with all kinds of gruesomeness. Well, you had to take the rough with the smooth, although with Garrett it was mostly rough. The talk had been mainly about powdered kneecaps, meat jobs, bodies dumped in wet concrete – 'Yeah,' Griswold had nodded thoughtfully at one stage, 'there's a lotta flesh mixed into some-a them new apartment blocks in Atlantic City.'

Vogt took some more beer down inside him and belched. He was beginning to feel dazed.

Garrett said, 'You could sure do with some pussy, Vogt. Be the makin' of ya.'

'Shit, Garrett. Quit putting me down. I can fuck as good as you.'

'You ain't never had what these cunts is offerin', kid,' Garrett leered.

The girl on his knee was whispering in his ear again and at the same time pulling her dress up. Vogt could just make out her bush, which was not exactly profuse, but then he'd noticed that Vietnamese girls, even older ones, were thin down there. Some shaved themselves so that the growth would thicken, under the impression that Americans preferred it that way. As it happened Vogt found a sparse growth of hair quite exciting. Thinking about Garrett and his buddy Griswold had, not unnaturally, caused a certain amount of detumescence. Now, staring up the girl's skirt, Vogt found he was getting horny again. Suddenly it didn't seem to matter that the whole business was essentially Sleaze City.

'Come on,' urged Garrett. He gazed round the table. 'They gotta place couple blocks away. Nice an' quiet. Real cathouse. We can take our pick.'

Olsen, across the table, nodded thoughtfully. He ground his cigarette out in the ashtray. He said, 'Speakin' for myself, I gotta say, I gotta wife an' two kids.'

'Suit ya fuckin' self,' snarled Garrett.

'On the other hand,' said Olsen slowly, as though he'd been pondering the question deeply for two or three hours, 'I ain't had nookey for a month or more, an' what the eye don't see the heart don't, an' this is a goddamn fact, grieve on.'

'I'm warning you,' chuckled Doc Pepper, but Vogt noticed that he got to his feet with the others.

'Hey,' said Griswold, 'gimme a minute. I'll go round up some-a the guys. They gotta right cathouse, we'll have a fuckin' party.'

The girl on Garret's knee shot a glance at her companion.

'No. No party,' she said. Then, pointing at Griswold, 'Not you. These all Numma One. You Numma Ten.' She groped Garrett again. 'You a real Numma One. I can tell.'

'Hey!' Griswold had a pained expression on his face.

102

'S'matter with me? You don't like my face, for Chrissake?' He guffawed noisily. 'You'll like my dick, sweets. You ain't never been screwed by me, you ain't never been screwed.'

'No!' The girl now sounded quite angry. She turned to Garrett again. 'Only you, big boy. You and your friends. No one else.'

'He is my friend,' protested Garrett. 'You're my friend, aincha, Griz?'

'Sure fuckin' am, Charlie.'

The other girl chimed in. 'Hurry-hurry.' She gestured round the table imperiously. 'Only you. Not him.'

'Fuck this,' said Griswold. Vogt could see he was getting angry too.

The argument went on for some minutes, back and forth, back and forth; at times heated. Vogt's horniness was decreasing again by the second. This was what appalled the romantic side to his nature: the element of hard bargaining that necessarily had to be a part of any commercial undertaking. He was gloomily thinking he might as well slip into the nearest can and give himself a hand-job, when the two girls, with bad grace, surrendered. Griswold could come.

'You bet,' agreed the big man, laughing oafishly, 'like a fuckin' fountain. You'll find out.'

They stumbled out into the darkness outside. The night was hot, sticky. Vogt's knees felt weak; he had to keep swallowing. It appeared from what the two girls had said that the place they were headed for was something special. They were all going to be getting preferential treatment, individual attention. Vogt didn't believe it, not for a moment. Of course not. No way. On the other hand, why not? These things happened. Sometimes you had to strike lucky. He'd noticed that both girls looked clean, didn't stink themselves up with a load of cheap perfume, were not – apart from the bout of bad temper over Griswold – as loud-mouthed and brash as most girls of their calling, especially those in Saigon. Pit-city, Saigon was, for the most part. Maybe this was the real McCoy?

They turned into a shadowed doorway, the two girls leading, chattering brightly. Inside was an ill-lit hallway with rugs on the floor. There was a faint smell of incense from somewhere.

103

Two doors led off to the right; another opened onto an enclosed staircase to which the girls, now giggling, pointed. Garrett stepped towards it but Griswold, booming with laughter, shoved him to one side, turned in through the open doorway, began to mount the carpeted stairs.

From above Vogt could hear a record-player, the mournful drone of the Grateful Dead. The sweet burned-straw smell of marijuana hit his nostrils, caught at the back of his throat. Griswold was near to the top with Garrett close on his heels, followed by Doc Pepper, then Fuller, then Olsen jostling with Vogt. Behind them were the girls, one of whom was now pushing a hand up between Vogt's legs from behind, rubbing and fondling his balls.

'Hurry-hurry!' she giggled.

Through the banister-rails to his right Vogt could see a door, slightly ajar, on the landing above him. A warm, red glow emanated from the room beyond. Another staircase led up to a higher storey and darkness. The smell of incense and Mary J was much stronger. He was suddenly aware that the girl had withdrawn her hand and that Olsen had stopped, half-way up the stairs. He glanced at the big man.

Olsen was frowning, his eyes, seen in the half-light, shifting about restlessly. Fuller, Doc Pepper and Garrett had reached the head of the stairs, but Griswold was well in front, heading for the door.

'Here I come!' said Griswold. He was rubbing at his crotch. 'Shit, I need this motherfucker, I'm tellin' ya!'

Vogt was all at once aware of a horrible tension that seemed to be powering off of Olsen in solid, tactile waves. The sarge was standing beside him like a guy turned to stone by Medusa's deadly gaze. Only his eyes moved. Then a hand came up and clamped itself like a vise on his shoulder, the fingers almost biting into his flesh.

'Hey, Sarge,' Vogt mumbled, wincing.

Olsen suddenly bellowed, '*Don't go through the fuckin' door!*'

Griswold guffawed. 'Waitcha turn, asshole!'

He pushed through the door.

And blew right out again, bits of him, in a terrible wash of eyeball-searing orange.

The roar of the blast beat against Vogt's ears, pounding at them. He found that Olsen had jammed him down by brute-force onto the stair-treads as bits of bannister rained down on them, bouncing off their heads, bowling down the stairs. Chunks of Griswold, too. Dazedly, Vogt heard yells of shock, then a terrible cry like someone had his stomach or legs blown away and, after the shock of instant trauma, had only just discovered that grisly fact. It sounded like Garrett. Other sounds now, too. The harsh punching clatter of Kalashnikovs. He heard Olsen gabble, 'Christ on a crutch, we been set up!'

Vogt clawed himself into the stair-treads, trying physically to dig himself into the woodwork. The lights on both stairs and landing had gone, but he could see muzzle-flashes stabbing the darkness at the top of the second flight of stairs and could hear rounds smashing into wood and plaster, ricocheting around like angry hornets. Someone was yelling 'Get the fuckers!' but Vogt didn't see how any of them were going to be climbing out of this one alive. The crash of shots erupted behind and below him and that meant that someone had been waiting on the ground-floor as well. He swore that he could feel the wind of bullets zipping up past him.

He half-turned as Olsen suddenly moved. The big sarge had launched himself into a wild suicidal leap down the stairs and Vogt heard a scream, the crash of bodies colliding and smashing into the floor. Several more voices could be heard now, adding to the din, although Olsen's outraged roars were the most prominent. He was cursing and screaming with a horrible profanity.

'*Vogt!*' he howled.

Vogt swallowed, scrambled round, thought resignedly, 'Oh, fuck it,' and simply leapt into space, his eyes closed. He hurtled through the air, crashed into someone. It wasn't Olsen. He flung his arms round the man and kicked and flailed and punched and bit him. They collapsed into the doorway, bounced off the jamb, flew out into the darkened hallway. Vogt had an impression of three, maybe four men fighting to one side and then had to concentrate on his own man, who was pulling at his hair, scrabbling for his eyes. Vogt's army crew afforded the guy no handhold at all but those digging, clawing fingers turned him mad. Freeing one arm, he smashed his fist into the guy's face, then kept on punching him again and again. He was suddenly aware that he was shrieking with fury.

'*Muthafuckin' shit-eatin' sonafabitch fuckin' crap-bastard shithead fucker!*'

They were rolling around on the floor and all at once Vogt knew he'd either beaten the guy's brains clean through his skull or turned him into a vegetable. At the same time his free hand scraped metal and he knew they'd rolled onto a fallen gun. He scrabbled for it, grabbed it, lurched to his feet and fired a wild burst up at the ceiling, spraying lead in a high crazy arc that brought down dust and plaster and bits of timber in a choking shower. He suddenly realized the fucking place was on fire.

Two figures leapt up out of nowhere and dived for the front door. Neither of them looked as bulky as Olsen so he let them have it, stitching rounds across and back and across again. His bullets flayed them, near-nailed them to the door.

'*Vogt, goddamnit!*'

Olsen's boot-camp bellow jolted his heart, because he could not see the big man anywhere. He stopped firing, suddenly noticing that Olsen was on his hands and knees below him, an angry, almost insane glare on his face as he stared upwards, his neck crooked back.

'How many fuckin' times do I have to tell you – *don't waste fuckin' ammo!*'

Sweat was streaming down Vogt's face. Wearily, he wiped his sleeve across his brow, still holding the AK-47 in his right hand, barrel pointed downwards. Olsen cursed ferociously and rammed the barrel to one side, away from him. He clambered to his feet.

'And don't, for Christ's crappin' sake, point that bastard thing at me.' Then he hissed air explosively out of his mouth. 'Shit! Don't worry, kid. You did all right. Fuckers were about ready to trash me, I gotta say, when you jumped in.'

Vogt said, 'The others?' hoarsely.

'Yeah, c'mon. Keep outta the line of the doorway or you'll frankly get a dose of rico-rupture.'

Olsen scrabbled round on the floor, gave a pleased grunt. He came up with another AK-47. In the flickering light that washed out from the staircase his nimble fingers checked it out, coolly, calmly. His face was grim. He stepped to the doorway, yelled upwards, though without putting his face round the jamb.

'Fuller!'

Sergeant Fuller's voice came back, faint.

'Yeah!'

''S tight down here.'

''S fuckin' loose up here!' Vogt could hear the freaked-out disgust in the man's voice.

Whoever was on the top floor opened up again, a short burst. Rounds racketed down the staircase, buzzed out in all directions. Olsen flattened himself against the wall, slamming a hand against Vogt to move him even further back out of the line of fire.

They could now hear the crackle and roar of flames quite clearly. The room in which the booby-trap had been set up was almost certainly an inferno by now, and it was not going to be very long before the stairs and landing went up. Looking up at the ceiling Vogt could just make out faint wisps of smoke curling down from above; he was uncomfortably aware that it was a hell of a sight hotter now than it had been only seconds before.

'How many?' bawled Olsen.

'All. They can't hit us. Back of the landing. Stairs and top-floor ceiling in the way. But we jump down the fuckin' stairs, we're gonna get lead poisoning in a big way.'

'They're gonna burn up there,' said Vogt forlornly. He could see no path of escape.

'No they ain't,' said Olsen irritably. 'Just fuckin' pray, Vogt. Are ya prayin'?'

'Uhh . . . yeah, Sarge, if you say so.'

'I do say so.'

Olsen was on the floor again. Vogt saw that there were two other Vietnamese, either dead or out cold, near the one he'd kicked, punched and bitten. He screwed up his face at the memory. Olsen was pawing at their clothes and suddenly gave a crow of triumph.

'Rely on the gooners to be weaponed-up,' he muttered. 'Yer prayers are frankly answered, son.'

He held an egg-shaped object in one hand and was grinning ferociously.

'Olsen!' That was Garrett's frenzied scream. 'Fire up the fuckin' stairs, you fucker. We're gonna fry up here, Goddamnit! Fry!' Vogt remembered that just about the only thing to twist Garrett up was the thought of being roasted alive.

Olsen stepped to the doorway holding the grenade with his left hand, fingering the pin with his right. He bulked tall against the furnace-glow from above, his face stretched into a demonic smile.

'Garrett!' he yelled. 'Now you learned a lesson tonight. Just remember, next time ya see a half-open door in an insecure situation, don't you go through.' He turned to Vogt, winked broadly. 'See, kid. OJT.'

'*Cunt*!' shrieked Garrett.

Vogt felt stuff coming down through the floorboards, ash or dust or something. The sound of the fire was now like the full-throated roar of a jet engine. Various crackings and snappings told him that the ceiling was going to be vomiting blazing death down on them any goddamn moment and no reprieve. But he stayed where he was. Olsen had that effect upon a guy, he thought gloomily.

'When I say now,' Olsen bawled back up the stairs, 'you come a-running. Straight down the middle and don't even fuckin' think about it.'

Fuller yelled 'Rodge!'

Olsen suddenly yanked the pin, counted, sprang through the doorway, his body twisting like a ballet-dancer's, his left arm powering back like he was throwing the discus. Then his arm shot round and up in a tremendous throw. He leapt back into the hallway again, at the same time bellowing '*Now*!'

There was a vicious cracking blast from above and almost in the same moment a rumbling, crashing sound and three figures came tumbling down the stairs and bucketing out of the doorway in a flailing, yelling heap.

'Move it, *move* it!' shouted Olsen.

Blazing timbers followed hard on the heels of the three men, collapsing walls, a dragon's-breath blast that seared the air. Above them the ceiling groaned, beams snapped. Vogt dragged at the dazed figure of Doc Pepper, saw Olsen shoving at Fuller and Garrett. They sprinted for the front door, hurled it open, for a second log-jamming themselves in the narrow opening, then boiled out into the street. As they rolled and tumbled away from the house an incandescent tide of flame roared out of the doorway as the building collapsed in on itself, a spray of fire shooting up into the night.

'I warned you,' said Doc Pepper. 'You guys wouldn't listen. Don't say I didn't fucking warn you dingbats.' His grimy, smoke-blackened face was set in a sardonic grin.

Sergeant Fuller wiped blood, sweat and snot off his face with the ragged sleeve of his fatigues. His eyes were dazed white circles in a Christy Minstrel's face.

'Me,' he muttered, 'I'll go for cock-rot every time ta bein' turned inta barbequed spare-ribs.'

They watched from the safe haven of a doorway way down the street. Firemen were trying with not much success to control the blaze, which was threatening to spread both ways along the street. A chattering crowd gawped at the sight and angry-looking Arvins were yelling at them and brandishing M-16s. Any moment now, on track-record, they were going to start shooting.

'So much for special treatment,' said Doc Pepper. 'Jesus, that was special all right. That what she was whispering to you, Garrett? Burn your dick off for a couple of bucks more?'

Garrett stared at him blindly. He looked stricken. Vogt couldn't believe what he was seeing.

'The fuckers,' whispered Garrett, his voice harsh, rasping. 'They got Griz. The bastards! *They got Griz!*'

Vogt couldn't believe what he was hearing either.

'Shit,' said Doc Pepper. 'Well, at least they didn't get me.' He breathed out gustily. 'Goddamnit, the Cong'll do any damn thing to waste a few of the good guys. We should've taken in reinforcements!'

'Didn't you hear that little bitch?' said Olsen. 'They didn't want any more.'

'Yeah,' said Doc Pepper, 'but we should've taken a whole goddamn regiment.' He chuckled wearily. 'Should've insisted, man. They wouldn't have jumped us then, no way.'

'Just us,' said Olsen flatly, as though Doc Pepper hadn't said a word.

'Yeah, but . . .'

'You ain't frankly got it yet, Pepper, have you?' said Olsen sourly. 'You don't *listen*, an' even when you do listen you don't frankly take it in.'

'Well, Christ, Sarge . . .'

'They didn't want anyone else. Not Griswold, not anybody. It wasn't a random hit. They just wanted us. Got it, dumbfuck. *Us!*'

VII

'Frankly, Colonel, and I gotta say I'm talkin' in all seriousness, it has to be that. It's the only answer. It's the only thing that frankly fits the fuckin' facts.'

Hardin sat back in his chair and stared at the five-man ragtag squad that seemed to fill his office.

He thought of all the men he'd been with on missions over the past decade, all the agents, male and female, who'd been his companions in times of hardship, vicious danger and grim survival. Sure, there'd been some fuck-ups, some treachery; there had been occasions when disaster had threatened through stupidity or crass overconfidence on the part of fellow-agents. But in over ten years you could count those occasions on the fingers of only a little over two hands, and that was a hell of a record in the dark and murky shadow-world that had almost become his natural habitat.

But these guys – how the hell did you classify them? Into what goddamn pigeon-hole could you place them? In many ways they were a fucking shambles, he thought. And yet . . . and yet . . .

The fact of the matter was, he felt close to them and he still couldn't figure out why. Maybe it was simply down to the fact that they'd saved his carcass in the Dempsey business, even if they'd been forced into it in the first place.

He zeroed in on Olsen again. Olsen was standing by the desk, staring at him, talking to him. He might have fragged his

Loot, but that was centuries ago, another time, another place. Fuller was beside him, nodding grimly at what Olsen was saying. To one side, Pepper was leaning against the wall, gazing sombrely up at the ceiling fan which whirred and clattered, dragging smoke from cigarettes upwards and scattering it to invisibility. Garrett was a hunched figure, oddly subdued for Garrett, on the other side of the room. Vogt gazed glumly at the desk, almost certainly wishing to hell he was back in Peoria, Knoxville, Spokane, or wherever the fuck he came from.

Hardin shook his head gently, mystified.

'You don't agree, sir?' said Olsen worriedly, catching the gesture.

'Uh-uh, Olsen. Keep going. I was, ah – thinking about the matter.'

Olsen said, 'I mean there ain't no other fuckin', beggin' your pardon, Colonel, explanation. We was frankly set up.'

'Olsen's right,' nodded Fuller. 'Hunnerd-one per cent.'

Hardin tapped fingers on his desk thoughtfully.

'You didn't report any of this to anyone?'

'Uh-uh, Colonel.' Olsen shook his head. 'Fuller an' me, we hadda talk-out on it, figured the wisest course of action was frankly to get the hell outta there, be as circumspect as possible. We just snuck away fast. It seemed like something else, you know, sir? Seemed like it might be connected, if ya get my meaning, with, well, you know, sir, like . . . us. I mean, the squad. I mean,' he looked confused, 'us guys, we're in a funny fuckin' position, with all respect to you, Colonel, statuswise.'

'Affirmative on that, Sergeant,' said Hardin dryly.

'I mean,' said Olsen unhappily, 'apart from Fuller here, sir, us guys really oughta frankly be in the goddamn slammer.' He thought for a moment. 'Oh yeah, an' the Loot, sir. I mean, he's like Joe here, if ya get my meaning.'

Hardin frowned.

'Where is Lieutenant Comeraro?'

He stared round and was greeted by a parade of blank faces. Joe Fuller shrugged.

'Last I saw, he was in the bar, officers' bar. I was walkin' past, saw him in there.'

Hardin nodded. Comeraro, like all these men, was now marked with what Hardin tended to think of as the Plague Spot, through association with him. He knew the guy felt bad about it, could not understand why he should be lumped in with scumbags like Garrett when originally he'd been dragged into Hardin's problems almost by the scruff of his neck, and certainly through no fault of his own. He'd have to talk to Comeraro, sometime.

Right now, however, there were other things to talk about and it was difficult to know exactly where to begin, how much to spill to these men. The 'need-to-know' philosophy had never appealed much to Hardin. It was often the case that you needed to know *everything* – every last jot and tittle – even when on the surface some aspects of a situation, and perhaps some of the background detail, seemed to have little relevance to whatever it was that you were embarked upon. But the guy who was only told what his control figured he needed to know, and no more, might well make an error of judgement – precipitating a shit-storm of the first magnitude – which he would not have made had the whole picture been revealed to him.

Hardin stared back at Olsen, then glanced at Vogt. He said, 'At that temple in the jungle, Lieutenant Comeraro found something and brought it back to me. Did you see what it was?'

Olsen said, in a neutral voice, 'Sure, sir. A gas-mask.'

Hardin nodded.

Makes it easier, he thought. He lit a cigarette. 'In a nutshell, we think the EnVees are manufacturing a highly sophisticated form of nerve gas. Almost certainly the Chinese are behind them. I say "we think" because we have no direct evidence, apart from that mask. We have stories picked up by our I-people, rumours, the theoretical possibility that the stuff is being boiled up not too far beyond the DeeEmZee. *If* it exists at all, because all of this may be a gigantic and brilliant piece of deception. Even the mask itself, although our labmen have checked it out, may be false. That is a serious possibility. On the other hand I don't believe that. I think the EnVees are making this shit, and I think they're seriously intending to use it. Our guess is that they're in the early rather than late stages

113

of manufacture, which is good news. But the bad news – its very existence in the first place – enormously outweighs that.'

He stared round at the faces of the men watching him, looking for reactions. Garrett, clearly, had something else on his mind; he registered nothing. The two sergeants were pros to their fingertips. They merely looked bleak; but then sergeants normally did. Vogt looked worried as all hell. Pepper, the medic, had ceased taking an idle interest in the ceiling and was now riveted to what Hardin was saying.

'You ain't kidding, sir,' he whispered hoarsely.

'No,' agreed Hardin grimly, 'I'm not. And there's something else. At that temple where the mask was found there's a strong possibility now that we missed at least one North Vietnamese in our sweep. That's the only explanation I can think of for these attacks.'

'Attacks, Colonel?' Fuller had noticed the use of the plural.

'That's affirmative, Fuller. Attacks. I nearly got nailed myself by an EnVee hit-squad. I now believe there was a guy hiding at that temple who either recognized us, or heard my name and put two and two together. Or reported back to his superiors, who put two and two together.' He gave a bleak and frostly smile. 'I strongly suspect that all of your names and descriptions are now on file with EnVee Intelligence. They've been known to screw up, but they can also be fucking smart when they want to be. We know damn well they have assets in Do Thon, they gotta have. They have assets in Saigon we still don't know about, although they must be there. And I'm not talking about farmers by day, guerillas by night. I'm talking about deep-cover assets, cadre-trained: interpreters, guys with the EssVee military secretariat, that weight of agent.'

Vogt gulped noisily. 'Jesus!'

'Don't worry. They won't know every goddamn thing there is to know about you. They won't know your date-of-birth, high school education, first time you went on a heavy-petting date. But they'll know enough by now about you to put a face to a name, or a name to a face. They hit me, they're gonna try and hit you too. It's as simple as that.'

Olsen frowned, mystified.

'Yeah, but with all respect, Colonel, *why?*'

'Why?'

'Well, yeah. I mean, I figure it has to do with this gas-mask, right? I figure that has to be important. They maybe didn't want Command to know about it, or something. But once you got that damn thing back here the fucker, beggin' your pardon, was blown for ever. Wasn't a secret any more. So why try an' ice us?'

Hardin stubbed out his cigarette.

'Simple. Like I said, the EnVees can be very cute at times, very very smart. We still tend to think of them as fucking peasants with the brains of a louse, which is by no means the case. But they can also screw up to nine on a scale of 10. They can panic. They can go fucking batshit. You can bet your life,' he smiled toothily, 'or what's left of it, that as soon as it was known that I, and therefore you guys as well, had something to do with the recovery of that gas-mask, the order went out: hit 'em! Sure, it was too late. Didn't matter. *Hit 'em!*'

'My God!' Leroy Vogt stared at Hardin, mouth sagging. 'That's creepy.'

'Penalty of fame, I'm afraid,' said Hardin. 'When you got pitched into the SSG, Vogt, even in the manner you were pitched in, you lost your grunt status. Forever. From now on, whatever you do,' his voice was chilly, 'you are a *name*.'

'But I don't wanna be,' gulped Vogt.

'I don't blame you. But that's the way of it. It's a case, I'm afraid, of tough shit.'

He felt sorry for Vogt, but it was better to be level with the kid than not.

'Okay,' he went on, 'so that is why the EnVees tried to blow you away, that's why you were picked on deliberately.'

Olsen suddenly looked up from frowning at the floor.

'They could win, sir.'

'I'm sorry?'

'The EnVees. Nerve gas. That's a powerful card to have in your hand. And a frankly dirty one, too. They could win this fucker. Do we have a retaliatory mode?'

Hardin said, 'You ought to know, Sergeant, that the President of the United States, on 25th November last, banned the use of all chemical and nerve agents.'

Olsen managed to look uncomfortable and sceptical at the same time. A not inconsiderable feat, thought Hardin.

He said, 'You don't look convinced, Olsen.'

Olsen gave a weak smile, glanced at Fuller.

'Scuttlebutt says we used it in Cambodia, sir. Not, uh . . . too long ago, frankly.'

'Scuttlebutt also says, sir,' chimed in Sergeant Fuller, 'Da Nang and Tuy Hoa got a stack of funny cans stored away, that no one seems to know what to do with. Not ta mention a stack of funny cans at Bien Hoa. I wouldn't know if that's true or not, just tellin' ya what the word is.'

Hardin smiled bleakly.

'Scuttlebutt is sometimes a good indication of what's really going on, Fuller. You might also be wondering about all that shit we're dumping and spraying over the local terrain, Agents Purple, Blue, Orange.'

'I thought that was pesticide,' muttered Vogt.

'What's pesticide to some guys, Vogt, is a whole different brew to others.' He rose to his feet. 'All this is to some extent beside the point. You guys just pray that we never have to use this crap, and just about the only way to stop that happening is to hit the EnVee supplies and source of manufacture.'

Olsen half-raised a hand.

'Do we take that as some indication that we frankly might be doing some hitting?'

Hardin shrugged.

'Frankly, I don't yet know. To hit a source of supply you have to know where it is, be able to zero in on it without any goddamn fuss. We believe there's a possibility that a plant has been set up somewhere beyond the DeeEmZee, but 'somewhere' covers a hell of a lot of ground. Until we know more precisely we might just as well not know anything at all.' He nodded briefly. 'That's it.'

There was a movement towards the door. Fuller and Olsen went first, muttering to themselves. Vogt and Pepper followed. Garrett didn't shift an inch.

He'd been in exactly the same position the whole time he'd been in the room, hunched against a side-table stacked with documents, staring blackly at the floor. Suddenly he lifted his head, glared at Hardin, pointed a stubby finger at him. Hardin wondered what the hell was coming.

'Those fuckin' sonsabitches. I'll cream the bastards, I'll blow the shits away,' Garrett hissed.

Hardin sat back, eyed him warily.

'Very admirable, Garrett.'

'I'll screw 'em, screw the cocksuckers to the fuckin' wall.'

'Your attitude is to be commended.'

'They won't know what massacree is, time I've finished with 'em. I'm gonna massacree 'em okay. I'm gonna waste the fuckers, *waste* 'em!'

Hardin leaned forward.

'I take it you are referring to the Cong?'

'You bet your sweet fuckin' ass I am. Those bastards better watch the fuck out. From now on, *no more Mr Nice Guy*!'

'Garrett, what's on your mind?'

Garrett's face was scarlet. He was breathing fast and heavy, stertorously, great gulping breaths in, gasped profanity out. Hardin recalled Garrett's murderous woe after he'd lost that ten million bucks worth of heroin, but this was something else again, something quite different. Suddenly he brought both his lumpy hands up from his side, clenching them and unclenching them.

He said, through his teeth, '*They got Griz!*'

From Garrett this was amazing, stunning. Hardin felt he was seeing the man in an entirely new light. Olsen had mentioned something about this Griswold character on the quiet before the meeting that had just finished. Some ex-Mob buddy of Garrett's in the same line of business: professional muscleman and hired killer. Olsen had said that Garrett had seemed put out at his death, but that was putting it mildly. Garrett was clearly as mad as hell. It was obvious that Griswold had been extremely close to him; maybe there was a blood-tie. Even so, Garrett really was not given to wearing his grief on his sleeve like this. There had to be more to it. Hardin wildly cast around for some reason for Garrett's rage and grief and came up with what seemed the most likely solution.

He said, 'Yeah, I'm sorry about that, Garrett. He, uh . . . save your life once, or something?'

That had to be it; it had to be the explanation. Astonishing as it might seem, Garrett clearly did have some finer feelings behind that brutish exterior. Probably in the bad old days Griswold had pulled Garrett out of some hair-raising situation, the details of which were almost certainly pretty bloody and nasty, not to be gone into too deeply. My God, thought Hardin, the older you get the more you fucking learn.

'Saved my life?' snarled Garrett, now seemingly more enraged than ever. 'What the fuck're you talkin' about?' His voice rose to a bellow of outrage. '*I* saved *his* fuckin' hide!'

Hardin kept his face neutral, as blank and expressionless as was humanly possible. The pieces of the jigsaw rearranged themselves in his head, fell back into place in an entirely new pattern.

Of course! *Garrett* had saved *Griswold's* life. Therefore – and the equation, instead of being alien in the extreme, was simplicity itself – Griswold was in hock to Garrett, was massively indebted to him. But now this indebtedness was a card that Garrett was never going to be able to play. This was so irrational, so illogical, so far fucking out – and so normal coming from Garrett – that Hardin accepted it instantly and utterly.

'That motherfucker owed me!' screamed Garrett. 'Them bastard fuckin' slant-eye shithead sonsabitches cancelled the fuckin' debt! Well, I'm tellin' ya,' he jabbed his fist out at Hardin, waved a grimy finger under his nose, 'I'm gonna cancel them, ya hear? Gonna cancel their fuckin' cheques an' nail the bastards to the fuckin' *cross*!'

He turned and stormed out. Hardin watched him go, wincing as the door was slammed violently into place with such force that he felt the floor shake.

Well, there was one good thing to come out of all this. It would probably be a while before Garrett began moaning and bitching about wanting to get back to the World. His rage would probably keep him fuelled for a good few weeks, if not months. Which, certainly in the short term, might prove extremely useful.

The phone rang, his one outside line. He picked it up and grunted, 'Yeah?'

'John.' It was Steeger.

'Hi, Will. What's the problem?'

'You tell me.' Steeger's voice was guarded.

'I got a thousand of 'em, Will. The main one right now is guys ringing me up and making damn-fool comments.'

'Maybe not so damn-fool as you think. That girl Kate Berry. When'd you see her last?'

'Couple nights ago. I told you. Why?'

'Funny thing. I mentioned her to Arch Shipley. He doesn't know her.'

'So?' Hardin was becoming irritated.

'So Arch strings for *Pix*.'

Holding the phone to his ear Hardin leaned back in his chair, stared at his blotting-pad. It was clean, virgin-white. Hardin never used it; it came with the furniture. Nevertheless it was changed every goddamn day while he was in Do Thon. And probably every goddamn day when he wasn't.

He said, 'So what, for Christ's sake? So *Pix* sent her out on a solitary, didn't bother to inform their man Shipley. Far as I know it wasn't a battle assignment anyhow. Like I said, a kind of *National Geographic* piece on this temple in the jungle.'

Steeger said, 'Bullshit, John. *Pix*'d tell their stringer. She'd have to come through Saigon anyhow. The Press Corps stick together like glue, except when someone's got a beat and then they wouldn't tell their own mother. *Somebody* down here would've known about her.'

'And you're saying . . . ?'

'I've done some checking. It started out as a joke, then it got serious. I know Arch, he's a jealous mother. Like I said, I mentioned her. I was ribbing the guy. Just threw her in over a glass or three at the Continental. He said, Fuck you Jack, I'm on exclusive. So I said he'd have to watch his ass, *Pix* were sending in this femme to steal his thunder. He went bananas, telexed them. He was really mad. *Pix* came back, disclaimed all knowledge of the dame.'

'So maybe she was bullshitting . . . ' Hardin said uneasily. He was beginning to get chilly about this one. 'Trying to nose in front of Shipley, grab herself some glory, present *Pix* with a *fait accompli*. You said they pay top dollar.'

'For a fucking temple story?' yelped Steeger. 'I'm tellin' ya! She'd still have to come through Saigon even if she was doing it on spec. And she had some muscle with her, you said. Where'd she get that from? Damn well not down here she didn't, I can tell ya. I got interested, started to nose around. Listen,' he said urgently, 'there's no such person as Kate Berry. *Pix* don't know her, press bureau don't know her, JUSPAO don't know her, MACVee Information Office don't know her. No one goddamn knows her. *She doesn't exist . . .*'

Hardin put the phone down, got to his feet, began to walk around the office. He lit a cigarette, puffed smoke up at the rattling ceiling fan.

As Steeger had signed off, he'd suddenly had a flash of memory. The car that had tried to nail him. The face behind that spitting automatic rifle. Blurred as the car shot past, but triggering off something in his mind – and now that something had broken, just as when sometimes a dream one can't quite remember one morning is suddenly broken, often days later.

One of the girl's cameramen, the guy with all the equipment strung across him – Harry something. Vronsky. Velikovsky. *Verblosky.* That was the guy. He was suddenly as sure of that as he was that the world was round, that night followed day, that the moon was not made out of cream cheese.

They'd had all the right IDs, all the correct papers. But it was no big deal to manufacture shit like that if you had the back-up, and there was really only one outfit that had that kind of clout. The goddamn Company. *The CIA.*

Christ, he thought, now what? What dark and murky waters am I sliding into here?

Those grunts. Captain Reisman. From the same source, you bet your life, he thought, extrapolating onwards. But why were they there in the first place?

Could be two possible answers to that. Answer One was that they were mounting some kind of operation up there which he'd unwittingly butted in on. He couldn't recall anything out of line, but maybe he'd missed something. They knew his name, so the word had gone out. Nail the bastard.

Two, however, was even darker, even more devious. The

gas-mask. They'd seen Comeraro hand him the mask, or at least the girl had. So was that what all this craziness was about? If the CIA were running an operation up there, was it *connected* in some way? Linked with the EnVee nerve-gas project? Did the Company have some kind of a hand in that?

Were they, in short, *backing the EnVees*?

'Christ Almighty,' he muttered aloud.

It was not at all an outrageous theory.

On the other hand, why try and knock him off back in Do Thon? The same illogicality existed there as for his theory that the EnVees had sent hit-squads out to nail him and his men *after* the mask had reached SSG HQ.

Really, none of this made any rational sense, but then much of what the CIA planned and carried out lacked logic. The apricot brandy scheme for decking Giap that Steeger had mentioned, for instance. Way out. Bizarre. *Ludicrous*! That Steeger was correct and that such a scheme had indeed been mooted Hardin had no doubt at all. It fitted in with all he knew and all that he'd experienced at the hands of those madmen who planned and plotted and tried to juggle the fate of nations out at Langley.

One of these days, he thought, I'm gonna have to declare outright war on those bastards, launch a full-scale assault, throw every dirty punch outside the book at them. Have my revenge on them just as Garrett is planning his on the EnVees.

He thought about the girl; an image of her naked body sprang into his mind, the sheen of sweat down the valley of her breasts, the glow of excitement in her eyes.

The gun in her hand as he straightened up over the dead Vietnamese in the Do Thon back alley.

Why hadn't she shot him then? It was perfectly clear now that she'd set him up in the first place; why not finish him off? He didn't know, couldn't imagine, what held her finger from tightening on the trigger right then and there. A romantic would have theorized that she'd fallen for him, but that only happened in books; hardly in real life.

It didn't matter. He dismissed her from his mind, rang Esteban, gave him a fast rundown on events and his interpretation of them.

He killed half a pack of cigarettes, chain-smoking them. Esteban rang back. There was no such guy as Captain Reisman. Hardin wondered why the hell Phil had even bothered checking. He killed the rest of the pack, started on another. He was also slowly sinking a bottle of Jack Daniel's. He thought, Why the hell am I doing this here? He thought, Why the hell didn't I try and find Marco, smoke a pipe or five with him? He was thinking this when the phone rang.

Comeraro said, 'Something weird, Colonel.'

'You ain't cotton-pickin' kidding, Lieutenant. The whole fucking world is weird. The whole fucking universe is weird.'

'Colonel.' Comeraro, now he came to think of it, sounded weird too.

'Yeah? What?'

'I have to speak with you.'

'So speak, Lieutenant.'

'This is something . . . ' His voice slid into silence. 'I've got to see you, Colonel. I'm in the town. It's about the mask.'

'What the hell is this?' Hardin was beginning to shuck off the effects of the bourbon.

'There's a bar. The Purple Pussy Cat.'

'Jesus Christ, Lieutenant. That truly is the goddamn pits!'

Comeraro slammed the phone down and Hardin glared at the handpiece he held. He didn't glare for very long.

He drove the jeep fast, one-handed. The night air cooled him off, revived him. He wondered what in God's name Comeraro was up to. The thought oozed into his mind that Comeraro was somehow behind all this, that he'd had the gas-mask all along, had sneaked it out into the jungle. Maybe he was a part of this gigantic conspiracy . . .

Hardin gripped the wheel tight, clenched his fingers round it until they were white, livid. This wasn't merely paranoia, for God's sake, he told himself. He was exhibiting all the signs and symptoms of someone whose mind was decaying beyond repair! Of course Comeraro wasn't behind this; he wasn't behind *anything*, goddamnit! He drove on, reached Do Thon itself, parked the jeep.

The purple Pussy Cat, he thought contemptuously. Sleaze

City, if any bar in town was worse than any other. Still maybe Comeraro had picked something up, some dangerous piece of scuttlebutt, some indication of treachery in high places. Maybe that was why he'd sounded so damned odd.

The gaudy neon sign was yellow and purple, a scrawny-looking cat in purple against a yellow flashing background. Every ten seconds the light died and when it came back on again the cat's tail was erect and wagging. Then off and on again, and the cat's tail drooped miserably. Hardin pushed through the door, noted Comeraro sitting by himself at a table at the far end. There were one or two drinkers, but on the whole more bar-girls than customers. The juke-box thumped deafeningly.

Hardin was half-way down the room when he realized two things. One, Comeraro was not looking at him but staring down at the table, one hand clutching a beer. Two – far more worrying – not one of the bar-girls had got off her high stool to greet him. A tingle of anticipation ran up his spine. No goddamn bar-girl in the whole of Vietnam would sit still when a fresh mark entered her grubby demesne.

His eyes flicked round. There was no one near Comeraro. The nearest drinker was four tables away, a little Vietnamese who was slumped across the table in a stupor, his face half in the ashtray, half in a pool of liquid that flowed from an over-turned glass. Drunk, or unconscious? Or dead? Or faking it? Hardin slid a hand to his belt, resting fingers lightly on the leather, millimetres away from the holster that housed his automatic.

He reached over and clutched at the slumped Vietnamese's hair, jerked his head up roughly. The guy's eyes remained closed; liquid dribbled out of his sagging mouth, dripped down from his drenched cheek. Hardin let go of the man's head and it thudded back down onto the table-top with a fearsome crack. The guy started snoring. Hardin moved on.

He stopped feet away from Comeraro, eyeing his surroundings. Behind the lieutenant was a curtain which probably hid a door to the rear regions.

He snapped, 'Comeraro!'

Comeraro looked up. He didn't look happy. He was saying

something but Hardin couldn't hear what it was. The music –
the scream of guitars, the thump-crash of drums – seemed to
have got louder. Then he realized that Comeraro wasn't
speaking out loud but mouthing the words. He lip-read them.
'Pis-tol,' Comeraro was mouthing, 'bee-hind.'

Hardin's fingers jerked at the flap of the holster then stopped
moving. He didn't even twitch a face muscle. Something cold
was digging into the back of his head and he knew exactly what
it was. You didn't mistake the barrel of a gun. Shit, he thought
disgustedly.

The barrel prodded at him and he walked slowly forward,
bleak-faced. Ahead of him the curtain suddenly swished back,
jerked from behind by a Vietnamese whose face was expressionless. An open doorway beckoned. Hardin slowly paced past a
mirror and noted out of the corner of his eye that the man
holding the gun to the back of his head was the same guy
who'd been slopped over the table. Not unnaturally, he was
grinning widely. Really fucking pleased with himself, thought
Hardin, and so he goddamn should be; I doubt even I could've
done that without even a twitch; goddamn head must be made
outta teak.

As he reached the doorway the Vietnamese standing there
shifted to one side and pointed. Hardin went through the
doorway, tense now, ready to jump – and walked into a booted
foot which smashed straight into the pit of his stomach.
Agonized, he jack-knifed, threw up, tried to get his breath.

Then his legs were kicked out from under him.

As he fell to the floor two pairs of hands grabbed at him,
relieved him of his weaponry, then pulled him fast along a
corridor, his feet dragging at the floor. He saw through blurred
eyes the street door, open, a car waiting. He was bundled into
the back, jammed down behind the front seats. The gun barrel
was rammed into the back of his neck again.

Dazedly he heard the slam of car doors, but another car, not
this one. For Comeraro, he thought. What the hell was he up
to? To what depths of treachery had he sunk? Not that it
mattered. This looked like the last car-ride of all for him. The
doors banged; the car jerked off.

A voice said from the front seat, 'Do not be stupid, please,

124

Colonel. It is not worth it. You will only be hurt.' The man spoke in English. Hardin didn't recognize the voice.

He kept quiet. There was no point in doing otherwise. He tried to relax, even though his humped position made this virtually impossible. Still, he let his muscles ease as far as he could and began to deep-breathe, trying not to make this obvious.

He visualized the lay-out of Do Thon in his mind. To the south the shanty-town area; south-west, the feeder-road to Highway 9; west, the town gave way to farmland and rice paddies; north, the old French quarter which opened out to treed terrain with a number of colonial mansions set in their own grounds, now owned by fat-cat entrepeneurs for the most part, and a few remaining Frenchmen. He hazarded a guess that the car would head in that direction.

He knew what he was going to do once they reached their destination. Attack. Explode into action. He knew exactly where the door handle to the near-side door was. If he could burst out when no one was expecting it, he had a chance. He groaned aloud, began to make gagging noises.

'He's going to be sick,' said another voice, in Vietnamese.

'Let him,' said the man in the front.

Hardin gagged some more, aware of the gun barrel, still squeezed into the back of his neck. He shifted himself lumpishly, groaning. His left hand was now in a good position, free of him. His right was still underneath his body but that he didn't mind. When the time came that would be extra leverage. He conserved his energy, fuelled his rage.

All at once the car slowed; he felt it turn sharply. This looked to be it. He gagged again, muttering incomprehensibly and thickly.

The voice of the gunman was sharp with irritation. 'I do not clean this mess up. Someone else has to do it.'

The man in the front said, 'If *he* says you do it, you do it.'

Hardin could feel the car slowing. He relaxed even more.

The man in the back seat said, 'Is he waiting?'

'Of course he is.'

Hardin powered up from the floor, arching his back, thrusting with his right hand and feet ferociously. He heard the man with the gun cry out and then his left hand found the door handle, was jamming it down, heaving the door wide. He shot out, hearing the bang of the gun and the 'zang' of metal as the round ploughed into the swinging door and ricocheted off. He hit grass and rolled, unable to stop himself somersaulting wildly. Already the car was yards further on, tyres screeching as the driver hit the brakes. There was a lot of shouting and then Hardin, still rolling, banged against something. Legs, damn it. A man loomed up out of the darkness, was grabbing at him. Hardin's right hand lashed out in a power-packed arc, its heel smashing into one leg just below the kneecap. There was a hoarse, animal-like bellow – and the guy he'd decked collapsed on him.

Cursing, Hardin struggled to free himself, but the guy was heavy, a dead weight atop him. Seconds later something stabbed down at his exposed fore-head. Gun-barrel again, this time a goddamn rifle.

He froze.

'I knew you'd try something, Colonel Hardin . . .'

A new voice, one he recognized instantly; light in tone, almost bantering. Hardin's mouth went dry. Torch beams bounced and jerked as men ran across the grass towards him.

'*You*!' he croaked.

VIII

'It was really the only way, Colonel. You have to believe that. You have to believe *me*.'

Hardin, seated in a cane-backed chair, watched the dapper little man with the jolly smile pacing across the room. He walked slowly, carefully; despite his beaming face, or perhaps because of it, he reminded Hardin of a panther padding deliberately toward his chosen prey. There was no chance that the prey would escape, no chance at all. Hardin, despite repeated assurances to the contrary, at the moment felt very much like that prey.

The room was large, comfortably furnished, perfectly positioned – 'ideally situated' as an enthusiastic estate agent might have put it. One wall, with two tall, wide picture windows in it, faced east; in the morning the room would be warmed by the rising sun, but would become deliciously cool once it had passed its noonday zenith. Now, at night, the windows were curtained. In between them was a desk with a shaded lamp on it which cast a warm glow across its polished surface. Two tall standard lamps were the only other source of illumination. Native rugs were scattered casually across the floor.

Near the desk Lieutenant Comeraro sat slumped in a chair, his head in his hands. Standing in the shadows to one side was a tall Vietnamese with an oddly wizened face. He was like a statue, arms folded across his chest. Hardin remembered him vaguely.

The dapper little man, however, he remembered all too well. How could he ever forget him?

His name was Hoang Van Tho.

Hardin knew that in many ways he was a civilized man with a civilized palate, a taste for fine wines, probably a love of good music and literature as well. Hardin wouldn't put anything past him. Though a Vietnamese, he seemed perfectly at ease in surroundings that were utterly Occidental.

All this, of course, was by no means unusual. The French influence was still all-pervasive even today, though Vietnam had become now a largely Americanized country, almost a colony, a state of the Union. It was not at all surprising that the educated, upper-class Vietnamese retained strong vestiges of their European-dominated past, a liking for things done in the French manner. Hardin acknowledged to himself that Hoang Van Tho looked the very epitome of a member of the cultured, cultivated South Vietnamese ruling caste in his immaculate off-white linen suit, laundered shirt, silk tie and highly polished shoes as he paced slowly and meditatively back and forth across the room, occasionally taking a delicate pull at the cheroot smouldering in his right hand.

Except that Hardin had never seen Hoang Van Tho in a suit before. Not a civilian suit. Hoang Van Tho normally wore uniform.

The uniform of a *thieu tuong*, the equivalent of a Major-General in the North Vietnamese Army.

'Seems like I'm fated to get bounced by you,' said Hardin.

Hoang chuckled, but Hardin noted a raggedness at the edges. In his experience, Hoang Van Tho was an arch-dissembler; this slight nervousness could be real – or it could be put on for his benefit.

'Yes, "bounced",' murmured the *thieu tuong*. 'I hope my men were not too hard on you, Colonel. As I said, it was the only way to bring you here.'

'They didn't kid around,' Hardin pointed out.

'Nor, it must be said, did you. Poor Ngoc. You nearly shattered his knee. He will be hobbling for some time to come.'

Hardin reached out a hand and took a tall wine glass from a small table at his side. He rolled some of the contents round his mouth, savouring it, and thought about the strangeness of the situation. Here he was relaxing over a bottle of wine with a big wheel of the opposition – Saigon would kill its collective grandmother to get hold of this dude – and the truly weird thing was, all his confrontations with Hoang Van Tho had started in much the same way.

The first time they'd met they had chatted in a Laotian headman's hootch over a bottle of 1962 Margaux, chateau bottled. Shortly thereafter Hoang's men had taken turns banging his head around with rifle butts. The second time Hardin had discovered himself surrounded by Hoang's men in Cambodia. The time the drinks had consisted of slugs of Evian water out of an ice-bucket. Sometime later Hoang had tried to destroy him as Hardin was escaping in a chopper, although Hardin himself had been under the distinct impression that it was he in fact who'd destroyed Hoang – six 2.75" rockets from two side-mounted pods should, after all, have blown his shit away in short order.*

Now here he was again, bouncing up like a Jack-in-the-Box. On a sliding scale the booze this time ought to have been supermarket coffee-bags, but Hoang had poured out a robust, fruity 1961 Lynch-Bages.

Hardin took another pull. He said, 'This is getting to be a habit.'

Hoang said, 'And a pleasant one, surely. Merely because we are on opposing sides is no good reason not to address ourselves sometimes to the finer things of life.' He glanced at the curtained windows. 'Incidentally, should you be tempted to break out through the windows I would advise caution.'

'Oh?'

'Yes. I have positioned three automatic rifles in the garden, trained on them.'

Hardin put the wine glass down.

'Look,' he said, 'what the fuck is this about?'

* See *The Killing Zone* and *Fire-Force* by J.H. Teed

Hoang continued pacing the floor. He seemed to be pondering the matter.

'Do you not wish to know how I escaped your vicious, murderous and totally unwarranted attack on me outside the caves in Cambodia?'

'Frankly, no. Who needs it. You got away. That's it. "Unwarranted" I'd argue with. As I recall you and your men were about ready to turn us into hamburger. We got in first.'

' "Hamburger" .' Hoang winced. 'This war coarsens us all. My escape,' he went on, struggling, 'was not so miraculous. You destroyed a good many of my men, but not me. That, as you say, is it. In the confusion I made a tactical retreat. It seemed best under the circumstances. A good general ought to know when to withdraw. Indeed,' he added thoughtfully, 'it is often a far more valuable lesson than when to attack.'

'Yeah,' said Hardin. 'I've read Clausewitz too.'

'Astonishing how even today Clausewitz says so much that is apt.'

'Strategy never changes,' said Hardin, 'only circumstances and weaponry.'

'Indeed.' Hoang took a thoughtful sip at his wine, first inhaling the bouquet. He frowned. 'A word of warning, my dear Colonel.'

'Another one?'

'Much more important. I am aware from a previous conversation that you are by way of being a slightly more than amateur drinker of wine.'

Hardin said, 'I try my best.'

Hoang nodded. 'Admirable, admirable. So many people do not. But my advice, should you need it and for what it's worth, is to avoid Bordeaux, even chateau bottled, from 1968 and 1969 – indeed, shun it as you would shun the Powers of Darkness.'

'I'll remember that.'

'Do. You will not regret it.'

Hardin caught sight of Lieutenant Comeraro following this exchange as though he were a spectator at a tennis match. There was an expression of baffled incredulity on his face. He suddenly realized Hardin was watching him and dropped his

130

eyes. Hardin knew Comeraro was feeling bad about this whole situation and sympathized. He now knew that Hoang's men had grabbed Comeraro off the streets of Do Thon and put him through the mill to get him to make that phone call. He said, 'Don't worry about it, Lieutenant.'

Comeraro now stared bleakly back at him.

Hardin said, 'It's what the major-general was saying. A smart man knows when to retreat.'

'Precisely,' agreed Hoang, toasting Comeraro with his glass. He said to Hardin, 'It took some time to persuade him. I'm afraid my men were perhaps a little hard on him. But it was . . . necessary.' He paused, looked up at Hardin with a particularly beaming smile. 'And do you know, Colonel, I do believe it was finally my own persuasive powers of oratory that did the trick. Your Lieutenant Comeraro did appear to believe at last that I was genuine in my desire to confer with you as an equal, not merely bring you here in order to destroy you.'

'Unlike the guys who jumped me the other night.'

Hoang's face lost its smile.

'Not my men,' he snapped. 'We'll get to that.'

'And unlike the guys waiting to shred me if I so much as take a peek through the curtains.'

'Merely a precaution.' Hoang's irritation was plain.

The man with the wizened face suddenly said, in Vietnamese, 'Why don't you get on with it. We don't have much bloody time.'

'I'm aware of that,' snarled Hoang exasperatedly in the same language. 'And don't forget Colonel Hardin speaks our tongue like a native.' He shot a hooded smile at Hardin, reverted to English. 'The servant problem. It is always with us.'

Hardin lit a cigarette, crossed his legs.

'The way I recall it, Marxist-Leninist theory doesn't have much goddamn time for the master-servant relationship.'

'True, true. But Tran is something special. Even my masters acknowledge that.'

Hardin wondered, not for the first time, who exactly Hoang Van Tho's 'masters' were. He had always had the strong suspicion that, not least in North Vietnam itself, Hoang was very close to the top of the pyramid. He seemed to be able to

131

come and go as he liked, indulge himself as he liked. He clearly had immense power. The very fact that he was here now, alive and kicking, after virtually screwing up on the Cambodia deal, was proof of that. Most guys who'd lost a prime slice of real estate to the enemy would have ended up either as Third Assistant to the Fourth Secretary to the Commissar in charge of the Rice Programme or with a bullet in the back of the skull.

'But Tran is correct,' Hoang went on, puffing at the cheroot, 'we do not have much time at all. This is a safe-house, although,' and he shot a darkly sardonic look at Hardin, 'naturally once you have left here it will have to be abandoned. I cannot take the risk that you might reveal it to your own masters, however agreeable you find my proposition.'

'I don't even know where the hell I am,' objected Hardin, straight-faced.

Hoang laughed.

'Come, come, Colonel. Don't take me for a fool. You would find out.' He took another sip of wine, his face losing its good humour. 'At the moment it is manned by my own men, those who are utterly loyal to . . .'

'What is this,' Hardin jumped in, 'a goddamn palace revolution? Is that what all this monkey business is about?'

Hoang Van Tho turned sharply, his eyes suddenly blazing, his face an angry mask. His voice cracked fiercely, like a whip.

'By no means, Colonel Hardin! Do not think that anything I have said or will say while you are here carries any evidence of disloyalty on my part!' His hand, the hand holding the cheroot, jerked out, stabbing at Hardin. 'Let me tell you, Colonel. You will lose this war. Whatever happens, you will lose it and we will triumph and you Yankees will run home with your tails between your legs. The tide of history is on *our* side. We have fought for our cause for 30 years, and this is *our* country. We have fought the French, the Japanese, the Americans. Where are the Japanese now? Where are the French? Soon it will be your turn. Soon you Americans will join those countries we have defeated. There will be no arbitrary and contemptible division of our land, no more accursed De-Militarized Zone. Our land will be one again, *one* country, *one* Vietnam! Nothing you can do can stop this! *Nothing*!'

He swung round again, marched stiffly to the desk. Hardin watched him. There was no fakery here, no play-acting. He knew this intuitively. But then Hardin had always known that whatever else he was, whatever else he did, Hoang Van Tho was a patriot, a true believer in the cause for which he fought.

From the shadows Tran said urgently, 'Tell him. Tell him now.'

Hoang breathed deeply, staring at the glowing tip of his cheroot. For a few seconds he seemed mesmerized by it.

'Yes,' he said, his voice still ragged. 'Yes, but it is difficult . . .'

Hardin suddenly turned his head to one side, listening. His ears caught the sound of a car, its engine-noise growing louder, then the hiss of braked wheels on gravel.

Hoang looked up sharply, his whole manner suddenly alert, like an animal that has caught the whiff of danger. He glanced at Tran. Hardin looked at the man with the wizened face, too, but it was difficult to see what was going on behind those lines and corrugations.

Tran said, almost apologetically, 'There should be no one . . .'

Hardin lit another cigarette, reached for his wine again. Adrenalin was beginning to pulse through his system. He still had no idea what was happening, but whatever it was, it was clear to him that Hoang hadn't expected a visitor. This too was no game. The North Vietnamese *thieu tuong* was genuinely disturbed. Hardin glanced at Comeraro, saw bewilderment writ large across his face. You and me both, Hardin thought.

There was the muffled sound of a car door banged shut, followed by other, less identifiable sounds. A short silence. Then shouting, growing louder, and determined footsteps jarring the passage floor outside.

'Tran!' Hoang rapped out, nodding briefly at the closed door.

The man with the wizened face was already moving smoothly across the room towards the door's blind side. Suddenly the shouting was very loud and the door burst open.

133

A Vietnamese strode in, his face angry. Hardin guessed him to be in his 40s.

For a moment the man did not appear to take in Hardin or Comeraro. He was shouting at Hoang, haranguing him, demanding to know what the hell he was doing this side of the border so near to an American Special Forces unit. Then his eyes widened. It was as though they'd just that second focussed. He stared at Hardin as though the American had suddenly metamorphosed into a creature from outer space. He pointed a quivering finger, an outraged expression on his face.

'What . . . what the hell . . . ' he spluttered. 'What's *he* doing here?'

'Kill him!' snapped Hoang.

Some instinct must have warned the Vietnamese. Already he'd begun to swivel to his right, one hand diving inside his jacket. But Tran was too fast. He slid behind the man, kneeing him in the small of the back, left hand grasping at his forehead and tugging. The Vietnamese bent backwards like a taut bow – and yelled. Tran's right hand whipped up, and the knife he now held sliced across the Vietnamese's jugular, shredding the scream into a terrible bloody gargle. Tran sliced once more and the blood welled up over his hand, over the knife-blade. Tran shoved the man contemptuously forward and he pitched onto the floor, a crumpled heap, blood gathering blackly around his motionless head.

Footsteps, running, now clattered outside. Another Vietnamese appeared, younger, an automatic in his hand. He gaped at the sight of the body on the floor, but that was all he had time for. Hoang, bleak-faced, leaned forward across his desk, pistol in hand, a suppressor extending its snout by six inches.

Hardin heard the *Fwip, fwip* of two shots almost as one, saw red blotches appear like magic on the younger Vietnamese's shirtfront. The man gagged, his arms flying up, the impact of the bullets sending him reeling backwards into the passage. Hardin watched as he slammed into the wall, slumping down it, his head sagging forward, a shock of hair fanning out like a veil with the sudden movement. Hardin eased his tensed right leg off his left knee.

Hoang rapped, 'Stay there!'

He gestured at Hardin angrily with the gun and suddenly the end of the silencer seemed like the mouth of a cannon.

Tran was wiping himself down with a handkerchief, cleaning the blade. The handkerchief had been white; now it was deep, dark scarlet. Tran's face showed nothing.

He said, 'I hope you know what you're doing,' in a neutral voice.

Hoang glared at him, then transferred his gaze to the doorway where more Vietnamese had appeared. Hardin noticed that one of them was the little guy who'd jumped him in the bar, the one whose head had clearly been fashioned out of teak.

Hoang said, 'Were there any more?'

The little guy shook his head.

'Just the two, sir.' He grinned at Hardin, turned back to Hoang. He spoke in Vietnamese. 'They said they'd come from Da Nang. Said there was a meeting here to be arranged. They seemed surprised to see us. I told them it was not convenient. That a comrade from . . .'

'Never mind all that. Get rid of them. If necessary cut them up, burn them in the boiler, bury what's left in the garden. Deep. And I mean deep. Whatever happens I want those two to disappear for ever. Get rid of the car too.'

'The river?'

'Well away from here. Someplace where the dry season won't expose the bloody thing.' Hoang thought for a moment. 'Better go through the car. Destroy anything identifiable.'

The Vietnamese disappeared, dragging the bodies off down the corridor. Hoang Van Tho breathed out harshly, putting the gun back in a drawer of the desk. He glanced at Hardin as he sat down again.

'You see? I don't need the gun, my friend. Not for you. You're safe.' A thin smile flickered across his face. 'Safe. Yes,' he said thoughtfully, 'I'll give you this safe-house on a plate. It must have been known by my people that those two were coming here, although I did not know. They were not of my faction. It will be thought that they were caught by the oh-so-clever Arvins, then vanished; perhaps to the tiger-cages, eh?

135

Or anywhere. Men often vanish in Vietnam under your country's administration. What a pity.' He tut-tutted, smiling like a tiger-shark. 'So loyal too.'

There was silence in the room. Tran, impassive, watchful, had rejoined the shadows. Lieutenant Comeraro looked as though all this was a dream from which he hoped to wake up in due course. Hardin got up slowly, walked to the desk. He leaned forward slightly, stared down at the dapper little man.

'Faction,' he said quietly. 'That was the word you used, Major-General. Faction. Now spill it.'

Hoang Van Tho nodded briefly. He took a deep breath.

'That gas-mask you found. That is what lies at the bottom of all this. We are manufacturing poison gas, an agent ten times,' he shrugged, gesturing vaguely, 'a hundred times more powerful than anything that has been known before. I want you to destroy the factory.'

'It's really very simple, Colonel Hardin,' Hoang went on, now back in control once more, an urbane, bantering expression on his face. 'There is a factory complex where this agent is being created. Tests have proved its effectiveness conclusively; now a process is being formulated whereby large quantities of the agent may be speedily and safely manufactured.'

'Just to the north of the DeeEmZee,' commented Hardin.

'Correct.' Hoang did not comment on this, merely accepted it. 'But I doubt that you know exactly where.'

'We know enough,' murmured Hardin. Even now it was difficult not to play the dissembler's game; shadowland move-and-counter-move, bluff-and-double-bluff, were deeply ingrained in him. 'We know it would be difficult to bomb. In any case, we can't bomb. The latest moratorium still holds good, and even a black flight wouldn't stay black very long.'

Hoang leaned forward tensely.

'Colonel Hardin,' he said urgently, 'it is important, extremely important, that at this stage in the proceedings we do not indulge ourselves in petty bourgeois scoring matches. And I say this with all due respect to your undoubted intelligence. It is clear that although your informants may have indicated a vague location, you have absolutely no idea exactly where our laboratory complex is situated. It would not only be difficult to bomb, it would be impossible. I will tell you why. The exact location is deep within a series of natural caves below the Annamese Cordillera.' He relaxed slightly, still grim-faced. 'There is only one way to destroy it. From the inside. Given a certain amount of aid, a small party of determined men could with comparative ease not merely disrupt the complex but bring the entire mountain down upon it. I am proposing to offer you that aid.'

'Why?' said Hardin.

Hoang smiled. 'I am under the impression that it is an axiom of the Occidental races never to look what I believe is called a gift-horse in the mouth.'

'Tell that to the Trojans.'

This time Hoang laughed out loud, a genuine belly-chuckle that shook his dapper frame. He reached for his glass and drank.

'Yes,' he said. 'Why. Why indeed? Let us be frank and open with each other. As I have said, what we have developed is an agent of terrible potency. I have seen it in operation. Its effects are truly appalling. We know very well that you too have chemical and nerve agents stored in this country, ready for use. What we do not know is how potent these wepaons are. We *think* that our agent is like no other that has ever been developed – but we do not *know*. We do not know what you have up your sleeves. Here is a simple fact: our airpower is not equal to yours. If we make use of our agent, even suddenly, without warning, in such centres of population as Saigon, Da Nang, Hue, and devastate those centres, we cannot be certain that within hours our own centres of population will not be turned into mass graveyards in a manner that would make the dropping of modern high-explosive bombs seem like the stone-throwing of primitive aborigines. Does that answer your question?'

'Of course it fucking doesn't,' said Hardin. He said this in a perfectly mild and reasonable tone of voice.

'No,' agreed Hoang, 'of course it doesn't.' He sighed heavily.

'Apart from anything else,' said Hardin, still in the same tone, 'this could all be a gigantic shell-game.'

'Shell-game?' Hoang looked puzzled.

'Swindle, sham, sting, fraud, deception,' said Hardin. 'Hocus-pocus. A confidence trick. The dropping of a bunch of specially manufactured gas-masks to lend credence to the imposture would be an obvious move. Sooner or later, over a period of time, someone was bound to find a few, put two and two together, make nine. The masks would be, on the face of it, an advanced type. This would blow the minds of our labmen, freak the fuckers out utterly, and cause a certain amount of discombobulation all round. A perfect example of how to create alarm and despondency in your enemy.'

'And the result?'

'Result would be that *we* wouldn't use those incredibly poweful nerve agents we have stored away, just in case of a retaliatory strike by something that is clearly even more awesome. The joke'd be,' he went on reflectively, 'if neither of us had very powerful nerve agents at all, and we were both conning each other.'

'Colonel,' said Hoang, his voice quiet, 'we have to strip these, as you call them, "hocus-pocus" layers off and we must do it quickly. We must tell each other the truth, the entire truth.'

'And nothing but, yeah,' nodded Hardin. 'Trouble is, Major-General, what if I tell you the truth and you tell me lies? I will then have put myself right up the fucking Swannee.'

'What if I were to give you twelve precise locations in Laos where this agent has been successfully tried out?'

'Prepped areas,' said Hardin. 'In a game like this you always seed the ground well in advance of the actual sting. It's one of the rules. You go into a thing like this half-assed, you get nowhere.'

'Colonel,' and there was just a hint of desperation in Hoang's voice, 'do you not want to know why I am in effect offering to betray to you the secrets of my country?'

'I can extrapolate any number of theories myself, from what I know and what I can guess. I don't need anything from you, buster.'

Hoang swore in vicious Vietnamese. 'You do not make this easy, Colonel.'

'Why should I?' asked Hardin reasonably. 'Why the hell should I, Major-General? You've screwed me in the past, even though, and let's face the fact, I've managed to win the final battle each time.'

'What do you want from me, damn it?'

'I want the entire truth, not a disconnected string of half-truths.' Hardin took a sudden chance, a leap in the dark. 'We actually know about some of your testing-grounds in Laos. We know that a major symptom of this agent is massive blood-loss. Why don't you take it from there?'

Hoang Van Tho stared at his desk-top, the cheroot forgotten between his fingers. He did not look up at Hardin but spoke fast, tonelessly.

'The agent is a mix of a number of different types of agent. Do not ask me for details; I am no scientist. But it mainly acts as an anti-coagulant, an anti-clotting agent. As I understand it there are two ways an anti-coagulant can work successfully. First, by simply blocking coagulation so that the blood does not clot and thus the victim bleeds to death like a haemophiliac. Second, by causing the blood-clotting factors to act all at once, using them up, so there would then be nothing left to halt the flow of blood and the victim bleeds to death just as swiftly. There has to be a burning agent included so that the body tissue is perforated, to let the blood pass through quickly. One of the agents in the mix sears the intestines, the lining of the stomach, as well as the outer skin layers.' He lifted his head, his expression sombre. 'As I said, I have seen the effects. At close hand. You must believe me when I say that, at maximum potency, it can destroy a man in less than sixty seconds. Not just kill him, you understand, but turn him into a mass of putrefaction.'

Hoang's hand went up to his face, slowly stroking his chin. To Hardin the gesture was oddly unnerving. Hoang Van Tho's eyes were glazed, as though he were staring into the far future. 'It is . . . a terrible weapon, Colonel Hardin. It ought never to have been created . . . ' His voice drifted into silence.

'But it could win you the war,' said Hardin quietly, reasonably.

'The price is too high.' Hoang's voice was now a whisper. 'Too high . . .'

Hardin watched him from under lowered lids. He was convinced that the North Vietnamese was on the level, was speaking the truth – though still not the whole truth. There would always be a fine-shading of deception. Hardin was also convinced that Hoang had other motives for betraying his country on this gigantic a scale, and perhaps those motives were much more important to him, perhaps more central to the problems of North Vietnan as a country, a separate and distinct entity. He had no doubt that Hoang hated the very thought of this chemical super-agent, but there was a strong probability that he hated something else far more.

He said, 'And using it, I guess, could put you in debt.'

Hoang's eyes flicked up, focussing on him. A bleak smile curved at the corners of his mouth.

'It could, indeed.'

'You wouldn't thank me if I used the phrase "in debt to your masters",' said Hardin.

'I would not.'

'Because you don't see it that way.'

'I do not.'

'The master-servant relationship, I mean. In this particular case.'

'I know precisely what you mean.'

'You, and those who think like you.'

'How perceptive, Colonel Hardin. I believe you are inching your way toward what may well be the very heart of the matter.'

'The Chinese,' said Hardin carefully, 'have given you a hell of a lot of aid over the past decade. Rather more than the Russians. Any guy who gives another guy a million bucks to play around with and helps him out of a spot naturally expects more than a slap on the back and a firm hand-clasp.'

'That is only to be expected.'

'And that price could be even higher than ten million decaying stiffs.'

Hoang Van Tho said nothing, merely stared at Hardin impressively. Hardin got to his feet and yawned, shoving his elbows hard back and cock-crowing his chest.

He said, 'You're using me, Major-General. To do your own dirty work. What do I get out of it? I and my country.'

'I would have thought that was obvious.'

'Tell me about the guys who attacked me.'

Hoang shrugged.

'Sheer stupidity. I would not have sanctioned it. One of our men put in a report about a skirmish in the jungle. He escaped, but recognized you.'

'Yeah,' muttered Hardin, 'that's what I thought. I missed the fucker. I knew he was there. I knew *something* was out of kilter. Didn't follow it up.' He grimaced. 'Must be getting old.'

'One of your men found a gas-mask, dropped by one who has since paid the penalty for his carelessness. It was thought best by some to deal with you, and the men with you. If I had known of this I would have stopped it. It was an unwise and incompetent response by certain people in our command structure, purely automatic. It ended in failure. A botched job. However, I noted your name in the original report.' Hoang smiled tightly. 'It brought back certain . . . memories.'

'I'll bet.'

'It occurred to me that here was an answer to my prayer! I had already thought of you, my dear Colonel, but was unsure how best to approach you. The coincidence of your name appearing on a report at the precise time I was pondering the greater problem convinced me that the workings of Fate are by no means to be derided.' He smiled thinly. 'Now here you are.'

'So,' said Hardin, 'it's war in Heaven, huh?'

Hoang stiffened.

'Any internal conflict our side may be engaged upon will not affect the course and outcome of the war, believe me,' he said coldly.

'Oh, I believe you, Major-General.'

'To your eternal credit, Colonel, I think you do.'

'Okay, so what you're proposing is that we knock out this place, for the greater good.'

141

'That is correct.'

Hoang Van Tho said this perfectly calmly, and Hardin had to laugh at the irony of it. In many ways, the sheer fucking effrontery.

'Because if you and your faction try and deal with the situation you might just fail, and that'd be you, screwed to the masthead. But if we try, and succeed, you'll have got yourself a painless solution to the problem. Even if we fail it won't matter. No one would ever make the right connection. Which was why you had to ice those two guys just now. Jesus, you've got a fucking nerve!'

Hoang jerked forward and thumped his fist on the desk, his face darkening. 'You are not treating this seriously, Colonel!'

'Sure I'm treating it seriously, but you have to admit there's a funny side to it.'

The North Vietnamese stared at him, his face suddenly as bleak as perma-frost. He said in a low voice, 'Colonel, let there be no mistake. Our side is not merely *contemplating* the use of this weapon. Production has started. At the moment the agent is being stored at the complex. Soon – indeed, within a month – there will be no more storage space and we will begin to transport batches to other locations. We already have a target-date.' He paused, winced. Hardin waited silently, knowing it was a major effort for Hoang to spill all this to him. 'On the third anniversary of the 1968 Tet Offensive, we intend to saturate the cities of the South.'

Four months. And in less than a month the stuff was going to be moving out from base. It was tight, thought Hardin, fucking tight.

'Is there an antidote to this crap?' he said.

Hoang nodded tightly. He reached down, pulled open a drawer, placed a leather satchel on the desk-top.

'It is . . . complicated.'

'Yeah,' said Hardin bleakly, 'that figures. It always is. We can go into that later.' He tapped the desk. 'Okay, let's have some detail . . . '

Hardin kept his eyes on the road. Like many roads this far north it was pot-holed and rutted. There was no money to repair it, nor any inclination by the authorities to find the money. It was a road that was never used by the Americans or the South Vietnamese: who cared what state it was in? The car jolted and creaked, the headlights slashing the darkness. Comeraro suddenly broke a lengthy silence.

'Do you believe all this, sir?'

'As it happens, yeah. In the main. There's a lot left out, but that's only to be expected.'

'But – in-fighting in the EnVee High Command?'

Hardin chuckled.

'Why not? You should see some of the goddamn conferences I get to. All the chairs round the table dragged right back to the walls, so no one can stick the daggers in!'

'But,' Comeraro's voice was incredulous, 'if this isn't a trick, he's just blown one of the biggest military secrets of the war!'

'Hoang's a pragmatist. We've known for some time that certain North Vietnamese are unhappy about the amount of aid China is giving them. The Chinese aren't altruists. They want something for something. The more money, men and matériel they give, the more North Vietnam's in hock, until maybe there just won't be anything left in the kitty to pay the Chinese back come reckoning day – except the country itself. This whole country, North and South, is a handy slice of territory. In its weakened state, with the Americans gone, it'll be ripe for takeover.'

Comeraro was silent for a moment.

'You figure we will evacuate? Finally?'

'In some way or other. For Christ's sake, Comeraro, we're getting the hell out already. Once we've gone, the South Vietnamese haven't a fucking hope. We'll have left nothing behind but a bad memory and a million illegitimate kids.'

Hardin's bleak analysis of the situation – one Comeraro had heard before from him in one form or another – never failed to disturb the lieutenant.

'I dunno, Colonel,' he sighed. 'Of all the weirdo deals . . .'

'You gotta learn, Lieutenant, life's like that. Nothing is ever simple. Uncle Ho kept his Command tight and together. He was a strong man, a man with a vision who could take his people along with him. Now he's dead and the rulers are split, some wanting one thing, others another. Remember your history – Alexander the Great. Once he was dead the in-fighting started. I'd guess Hoang wants two things: a whole country, and no Chinese intervention. To give the fucker his due, I believe he hates this nerve-gas thing. Apart from anything else, it's counter-productive. Saturating the South'll kill a lot of Americans. South Veets too. It'll also turn the country into a poison-land, unlivable-in. Hoang and his dissidents have a saner view. They know that sooner or later we'll be out and it won't take too much time, and a lot less destruction, to conquer the country after that. They've been waiting for thirty years. A year or two more ain't gonna hurt. These guys think in the long term. It's something we've never learned how to do.'

'If you believe all this, Colonel,' Comeraro said tentatively, 'why the hell are you still here?'

'It's very simple. I believe that the North Vietnamese, the Chinese, the Russians, if you like, have got it wrong. I believe we've got it wrong, too, but less wrong. As long as we're here I'll do my damnedest to fight – not for an Americanized Vietnam, not for the fat-cats, not for the money-men, but for the Vietnamese people and an ideal society, as I see it. I may be wrong but I don't think so. I'll do my damnedest to repel all boarders and screw the opposition. It's not enough, but it's all I can do.' He swung the wheel sharply to avoid a gaping hole in the road. 'That's it.'

Comeraro stared ahead at the road. There were more complex reasons than that, he felt sure; perhaps darker in form and in tone. But on the whole what Hardin had just said was a good enough, and honest enough, explanation of the man's philosophy.

He said, 'So we go in.'

'Looks like it. Halderling'll like it fine. It's wacko enough to appeal to him.'

'Just a small force.'

'Smaller the better. Hit 'em hard, hit 'em fast, beat it.'

'Garrett's not going to like it.'

Hardin chuckled.

'Oddly enough,' he said, 'Garrett'll be all for it.'

IX

The thunderous racketing roar of the Huey gunship's rotors was, to Hardin, no more than the faint rattle of hail pellets against a window in another room, as he pondered the sheer insanity of the mission they were now embarked upon.

And it *was* an insane mission, when you got right down to thinking about it coolly. Utterly dingbat. Seven men, and one of those a medic, out to destroy a top-secret scientific complex deep in bandit country.

Sure, Hoang Van Tho had given him precise details of where the place was, how to get there, lay-outs, plans, where to lay plenty of plas for maximum effort, even guard-duty rosters – and sure, the location wasn't as heavily manned as maybe it ought to have been, owing to the number of men the EnVees were currently throwing into the field in muscular and aggressive harassing drives. But it was still a crazy idea, and in any case there was still one half of one per cent of his brain telling him: It's a goddamn set-up!

But no. Even given the supposed wiliness of the Oriental mind, this could be no trap. That would be too absurd. A trap by Hoang simply to knock him and his squad off? Merely to gain revenge for past embarrassments? Far out! Too far out by a billion goddamn miles.

This was straight. Hoang wanted that nerve-gas complex destroyed, and he wanted it bad. Hardin could sense his line of thought. Hoang was a devious bastard who saw things essentially in the long term. The very long term. Not only did he not like the idea of Big Daddy China, but he could also foresee – and Hardin was convinced of this – a time when North Vietnam might reject its huge neighbour's aid entirely, go someplace else; go, wild as it might seem, to Russia. The Big Bear instead of Big Daddy. That was a distinct possibility, politically. Hardin knew that over a period of twenty years or so the idea of a reunited Vietnam, a dream of one single separate country, had become firmly embedded in the EnVee psyche. The thought that, once this was gained, Vietnam would then become a puppet to China – as the countries of Eastern Europe were all dangling on Russia's strings – would be anathema to Hoang and those of his particular faction. Better to take aid from Russia, therefore, a country separated from them by thousands of miles, than become a beggar to China. Destroying the Chinese-manned and Chinese-backed nerve-gas installation was simply one small but important move on the complex and bewildering chessboard of South East Asian politics.

And he and his men were pieces, dispensable pawns. As Lew Halderling had said, when he'd flown in from Da Nang just the day before, 'Sure he's using you. No fucking altruist he. He'll screw you first chance he gets. *Watch your back, John*!'

General Halderling had been in high good humour. The evidence of CIA involvement in a secondary and previously unknown heroin trade (everyone knew, of course, about their involvement in the Pepsi Cola bottling plant in Vientiane) with Mafia connections and EnVee links was a fat prize indeed. There was a good deal of digging to be done still and already he was briefing Phil Esteban to get a team onto that. The final result was bound to be dynamite – or, to make the metaphor more apt, unstable nitroglycerin. It was going to have to be handled very carefully; but used judiciously it would certainly blast the shit out of an awful lot of guys against whom Halderling held immense grudges. He was almost rubbing his bony hands with glee.

'Apart from anything else,' he said, 'if you're successful the guy's in our power and he knows it. Jesus, he must've spent

146

months fighting his goddamn conscience on this one. He gave you an optimum day so you can be damn sure his men'll be waiting for you. They'll let you finish the job and then they'll hit you. Beautiful! We couldn't save the plant, what a goddamn shame, but look! We got the monkeys who did it! Hoang Van Tho will come out of this smelling of fucking frangipani!'

'That's why we're gonna hit 'em early,' Hardin pointed out.

'I wish I could send a more muscular force,' Halderling brooded.

'Too unwieldly, too much hassle.'

'Yeah.' Halderling suddenly grinned. 'One thing to come out of this, John. Proves my point that Charlie can be as much of a stupid goddamn tightwad as us.'

'You mean the gas-masks?'

'Sure I mean the gas-masks. My God! Look at it! They make this crap first and then think, Hey! Wait a minute! What about some protection! So they make a few fucking gas-masks just in case some of their guys hit some pockets out in the jungle where this crap has lingered after their trial-runs – but only hand 'em out to their upper echelons, field-leaders, battle honchos. Forget about the grunts! Fucking gas-fodder. Mean and stupid, and an extra dimension of stupidity is that gas-masks were all they got. No other protective clothing, as far as we can tell. Situation normal: all fucked up. Just like us.'

Hardin had to nod in agreement as he recalled Frank Marco's oft-repeated bitch about the availability – or, more precisely, non-availability – of body-armour for gunship pilots even as recently as eighteen months ago. One piece per chopper; so before every flight, each pilot and co-pilot had to toss a dime to see who'd get lucky. And as a pilot normally outranked his co, even the spin of a coin did not necessarily govern the outcome of who actually got to wear the damn thing.

Thinking about Frank Marco brought him back to the present – to the stink of oil, the bellow of the rotors above, the blast of air smacking against him as he stared out at the Big Green below. And as though psychically prompted, Marco's voice cut in on his thoughts in his hooked-up earpiece.

'Clearing ahead, Colonel Hardin, *sah*!'

Hardin grinned.

''S what I like to hear, Marco. The acknowledgement of my authority and superior rank.'

Marco angled his mouthpiece away, leaned across and bawled 'Fuck that, bwah!' in Hardin's ear. He reset his mouthpiece and said in a normal voice, 'Should make this mother fine. This so random, probably ain' no Pathet Lao in fifty keys.'

Hardin checked out the clearing as Marco swung the bird round it in a wide, low turn. There was a lot of elephant grass down there, and small bushes. Surrounding it on all sides was jungle-wall, thick and tangled, matted and elemental; untouched by human hands.

On the other hand, this was ten miles west of the North Vietnamese border and it was hardly to be supposed that Communist Pathet Lao guerillas were not in evidence somewhere. Not to mention VC resting up in friendly terrain. This was an area where the population was constantly shifting; nowhere was safe for such a group as Hardin and his men.

He glanced behind him, saw that his men were weaponed-up, rucked-up; ready to go. He took off the intercom and reached for his AK-47, the weapon he preferred to the M-16. The latter was a far more sensitive piece, requiring much tender loving care, and thus liable to fuck up badly when you least wanted it to. That could not be said of the Kalashnikov.

Marco was taking her down, his eyes constantly shifting behind his aviator's spex. He snapped into his intercom, 'Massacre some bushes!'

Instantly both side-MGs opened up; Hardin watched his side as rounds flayed the jungle cover in short sweeps, chewing up vegetation, seeking out hidden watchers, almost begging for a retaliatory sparkle of muzzle-flashes. But there were none to be seen.

The chopper hovered briefly, then sank to the ground, flattening the tall elephant grass and whipping leaves and forest-floor detritus up into the air.

Hardin leapt down, waved briefly to Marco, sprinted for the treeline, cradling his AK. He dived into the cool shadows of the jungle, stopping by a big-boled tree to watch as his men scrambled past the forest curtain toward him. He heard the roar of Marco's chopper become a full-throated bellow as it lifted off, the sound beginning to recede.

'Olsen, point. Garrett, tail-end. Okay, let's move it.'

Olsen was already heading into the deeper jungle when the rockets exploded.

'*Shit*!'

That was Garrett. Hardin hit the ground as the big man dived for a bush inches from him. The others disassembled in equally swift manner. Hardin stared around, his eyes now accustomed to the forest gloom. He could hear MG-fire, tracers, but there was something wrong . . .

It took him a few seconds to figure out what it was. Then he jumped to his feet.

'They've bounced Marco!'

That was now perfectly clear. The high-pitched staccato yammering of MGs was coming from above, from the skies. Hardin leapt towards the jungle-edge, peered upwards from cover. Nothing. Marco and whoever was attacking him were out of sight, beyond the top-growth horizon on the other side of the clearing. Hardin swung round, stared, picked out an accessible tree.

'Vogt! Get up there fast. Find out what the hell is going on.'

Leroy Vogt, hoisted up by Sarge Fuller, grasped branches and heaved himself into the tree. Soon the ground was lost to sight and he was surrounded by foliage and the humid, sticky half-darkness of the upper forest. He wondered what he was going to see, but his main concern was how good a target he was going to be when the topgrowth began to thin out. He clambered on, twigs tearing at his face and hands, leaves brushing him. A fat spider plopped out of nowhere onto his right hand and he yelped and shook it off, hauling himself upwards with desperate haste. He thought: Don't you get yellowjackets hanging in bunches or nests or some damn thing at the tops of trees? Maybe Vietnamese yellowjackets were more ferocious than anyplace else. Most things in Vietnam seemed more vicious than they were elsewhere; why not fucking yellowjackets? He could still hear the angry stabbing clatter of MG-fire although it was becoming more distant by the second. As was the goddamn ground. And the tree-bole was getting slimmer, the branches more slender, more inclined to bend alarmingly under his weight. And it was getting brighter all the time.

Vogt broke out into the sunlight, clinging to the swaying treetop and gasping for breath. Oddly, although it was so close, he couldn't see the clearing in which they'd landed only minutes before; all he could see was a choppy sea of green extending away as far as the eye could take in.

And a chopper sliding down into it maybe a mile away, tail-boom smoking.

It disappeared from view. Vogt couldn't hear the crash because the clatter of a second helicopter drowned any noise it might have made. Nor could he see any signs of an explosion: no roar of fire, no thick oily smoke. There was smoke, sure, but it looked almost as though there was a hidden giant over there, lying below the treetops, idly smoking a cigarette.

He shifted his concentration to the second chopper, but that one was high-tailing it south and he could not now identify it at all. It could have been Captain Marco's Huey; on the other hand, the downed chopper could have been, too.

Why, wondered Vogt, not for the first time, did everything out here in Nam have to be so fucking *difficult*? He started to scramble back down.

'Fuck it,' said Hardin angrily, as though it was all Vogt's fault. 'A goddamn mile is a good two hours' hike through this shit, off-trail. Or more. And we don't even have five fucking minutes.' He turned on Vogt. 'You couldn't identify *either* of them?'

'Jeeze, sir,' Vogt protested, 'chopper-one was actually hitting the trees when I poked my head out of the topgrowth, chopper-two was starting to head off south bare-ass.'

'Okay, okay.'

Hardin stared at him, not seeing him, his mind a-whirl. Did he but know it, his own thoughts at this point were echoing Vogt's almost precisely. Why the hell did everything have to be so fucking complicated?

Was Marco dead or alive? Who jumped him? Could it have been a Pathet Lao chopper? – No reason why not, come to think of it; they were deep in the heart of bandit territory out here, and if it had been a PL patrol they might have taken strong objection to the presence of a US chopper in their bailiwick. Or – and his mind made a jump – was this something to do with the girl Kate Berry, the girl no one had heard of, the girl who didn't exist? Esteban had sent men out to the Do Thon hotel as soon as it was realized there was something more than a little screwy about her, but it had been too late. She and her companions, along with Captain Reisman and his grunts, had disappeared off the face of the earth. It was as though they'd never existed in the first place. Hell of a thing so near to the SSG camp!

Hardin thought about the girl briefly. He'd been thinking about her, off and on, for some days, tossing the CIA option around in his head, other options too. He was gradually coming to a quite different conclusion about Ms Berry than the initial and instant conclusion he'd originally reached. Quite different; eminently logical, when you got to thinking about it; chilling in its ramifications.

'What should we do, sir?'

That was Comeraro. Hardin stared at him, still pondering alternatives. If Marco had been the winner in that chopper duel, surely he'd've been back to tell them about it, warn them? Unless in the exchange of fire, he'd been hit – damaged fuel lines, maybe a couple of WIA, whatever. In which case he would indeed head for base bare-ass. A downer in the Big Green this far into enemy territory was no warranty of an old-age pension.

'Sir?'

Hardin glared at Vogt, then thought: Shit, it's not the kid's fault. He turned to Comeraro.

'Move on. Whoever it is, they'll have to hack it themselves.'

They moved on, faster, much faster than seemed possible. The terrain was bad but they were on a side-trail, a minor tributary of the main Ho Chi Minh Trail, that spectacular answer to the EnVees' logistics problems that snaked sinuously yet obscurely through the jungles of Laos and across the northernmost tip of Cambodia to strike deep into the heart of South Vietnam, carrying every month whole regiments of men, vast quantities of matériel: the Communists' main artery. Cut it, Saigon said, and the war was won. But how did you sever something that was rarely where it was reported to be? For the Ho Chi Minh Trail, though certain sections were fixed, was a moveable feast, its position influenced by external factors. Sometimes it ran through dry river-beds; but in the rainy season, when watercourses were transformed in a few moments into raging torrents, the Trail shifted to more accessible terrain. It was a phantom highway; you could bomb the shit out of it and clap yourself on the back and talk about how you'd slashed that main artery and the blood was spraying every whichway – and within days, sometimes hours, either the breach would be patched up by those busy little yellow men in their absurd sunhats and black pyjamas, or the goddamn trail had been shifted elsewhere and the stuff was still getting through. The Ho Chi Minh Trail was a constant source of depression in Saigon.

But to Hardin and his men, right now, it was a Godsend, a life-saver, for even side tributaries off the main trail were kept in trim by gangs of Cong who, every so often, went out slashing down bamboo and elephant grass and vine, clearing and cleaning, blocking the insidious encroachment of the jungle tending the pathway like a garden.

Hardin's party made good time in the steam-bath heat of the jungle, their pointman, usually one of the two sarges, always alert for local tribesmen or small guerilla bands or, a possibility even out here, a much larger and more muscular EnVee contingent heading south. But they met nothing, and with a man flung out on each side, Hardin was certain that no one was tracking them on a parallel course either. It definitely felt to him that, at least at this stage, everything was secure.

Sometime on the second day out they crossed from Laos into North Vietnam itself. No one, not even Hardin with his maps, was sure exactly where or when: the EnVees hadn't bothered to erect a chain of customs posts out here or put up signs with little men in funny hats saying 'Welcome'. But Hardin felt it, like a resonance in the air only half-heard. It was nothing that

152

was tangible, but certainly something you could feel in your mind. He knew they were near, relatively speaking, to their target.

The trail, no longer straight, was descending now. These were foothills they were penetrating, although it would need someone to shin up into the forest canopy to distinguish exact features. They skirted a deep ravine which fell sharply away from the trail, a place where there were weird accoustics, so that men brushing against branches and heavy palm fronds heard the rustling sounds repeated hollowly and strangely, microseconds later. This made some of them jumpy, unnerved, especially Vogt and Doc Pepper.

Hardin decided to move off-trail, merge into the jungle, go out at a deep angle maybe even by a couple of miles. They were getting to the point where they might well start bumping into serious enemy activity.

Now they had to cut and hack and slash their way through the soggy, slimy undergrowth, constantly alert for leeches, constantly using the foul-smelling insect repellent that didn't seem all that damn effective anyhow. To Vogt, slackman to Sarge Fuller's point, it was a miserable business. If he ever re-upped (hardly likely, under the circumstances) he wanted to make it conditional that they put him on choppers. They could shove him anywhere, he didn't mind; they could tie him to the tail-boom with an M-60 for all he cared, as a new kind of rear-gunner; anywhere. Even bucketing down out of the sky in a flamer was better than trying to wade through this shit, he thought. The only compensation was that on this mission there was no radio, and that, for Vogt, was a supreme bonus. Humping that fucker was a real pain in the butt and no mistake.

He was suddenly aware of a commotion behind him. Something was going on, though not an attack. He pulled up, turned. Lieutenant Comeraro had come up from the rear where Garrett was tail-ender. He was holding Garrett's MG and looking black.

'Garrett's gone.'

Hardin stared at him. 'He's *what*?'

'Gone. Beat it. Left the MG against a tree. I looked round and the fucker suddenly wasn't there. Went back. Found the

MG.' He said defensively, 'You didn't say to keep a special eye eye on the prick. I got the impression he wasn't bitching about this mission, that everything was tight.'

Hardin shook his head, frowning. If Garrett had suddenly taken it into his head to cut out at such an insane moment – right in North Vietnam itself – he must have done *dinky dau*. It happened. He thought: The hell with him. They were better off without him. In his present weird mood he could have gone bananas just when they needed him most, endangered everybody. The only problem was, if he was picked up by an EnVee patrol before the main squad had reached the Chinese installation, it would blow the entire enterprise.

'You think he's wigged out?' said Comeraro worriedly.

'Christ knows. But one thing's for sure, we don't have any time to look for the fucker. Maybe a tiger'll get him, save us all a deal of grief. I mean, the guy hasn't just taken time out to tap a kidney?'

But even as he said it Hardin knew that couldn't be the case. If Garrett had gone to relieve himself, front or rear, he'd have taken the MG with him; standard procedure. In any case, Garrett was not exactly Mr Coy. If he wanted to piss he usually did it when and where the urge struck him. No, he'd left the MG because it was an encumbrance. He had an M-16 anyway, so he wasn't weaponless – *the bastard*!

Hardin stared ferociously at the MG, then gestured to Fuller.

'Fuller, you're gonna have to hump the mother.'

Fuller said, 'Yeah, 's what I figured.'

'Okay, let's move.'

Vogt was now on point. It was not a position he enjoyed for the obvious reason that point usually got it in the neck first in an ambush situation, although he never failed to get a boost out of a story Garrett had once told him about how he, Garrett, had once been point on patrol in the Iron Triangle, down south, and had stepped over an unseen booby-trap which his slackman had then proceeded to trip. The wire had led to four mines which had all blown in sequence, pop-pop-pop-pop, decimating most of the rest of the patrol and leaving Garrett as the only man totally unscathed. The kicker was, all the mines had been Claymores, not looted by Charlie, but placed there

154

by Special Forces in the hope of killing a few Cong. Garrett revelled in stories like that, especially if they were true.

With his M-16 held out at the ready, on full auto, Vogt proceeded along the narrow path with the utmost care and delicacy. His eyes switched from the leaf-mulch of the path, to the bush-screen on each side, up to the network of intertwining branches above. His mouth was dry, but he was dying for a smoke. Also a beer. Miller's 'High Life' preferably, ice-cold, with beads of frozen perspiration on the can. He moved slowly, checking out the trail, stepping carefully, until suddenly, with a sound that made his heart seem literally to jump in his chest, a bird shot out of the bushes almost in front of his face and soared upwards with a raucous screech. Automatically he followed it with his eyes, stepping forward – and then froze, a feeling of horror flooding through his system and loosening his bowels, as his right foot snagged at something which gave almost imperceptibly. He looked down, trying to make as little movement as possible.

The toe of his boot was pushing at a tautened wire which, until he'd hit it, had been lying under a carpet of dead and sodden leaves.

He didn't know what the hell to do. There wasn't much give down there, but taking his boot away might just finish the job. Release of tension, now, might be all that was required to trigger off whatever the fuck it was that was lying either on the trail itself, or to one side, left or right.

He pushed the barrel of his rifle down and gently worked at the loose leaves, exposing some more of the wire. But that was worse than useless; it gave him absolutely no idea of how this particular booby-trap had been placed. If he flung himself forward the mine, if it was a mine, might actually be in front and in seconds he'd be hamburger. If he threw himself backwards, the goddamn thing might well be behind him: same result. Although he'd been standing there for only a few seconds, it felt like hours; already his leg was starting to ache from muscle-tension.

Lieutenant Comeraro was behind him, about ten paces back. Vogt knew that Comeraro would have stopped as soon as he stopped. He didn't want to make any kind of violent gesture in case the wire, so finely balanced on the toe of his boot, became dislodged, slack. He said 'Booby-trap' – but he could hardly hear himself, his throat was so dry. He began to turn his head round to the left, to make a face at Comeraro, but in doing so began to overbalance. He was falling and he couldn't stop himself. The wire twanged from his boot and he heard a terrible crashing sound high above him. He squawked '*Boobychrist!*' hoarsely and threw himself sideways, into the bushes on his left, and as he hit the leafy screen he saw out of the corner of his eye a huge ball, looking bigger than a wrecking ball and with long, vicious-looking spikes sticking out all over, hurtling down from the tree-canopy.

Next moment he was sprawling in stinking, soggy undergrowth and an LYF – Little Yellow Fucker – was diving at him with an AK-47, bayonet extended.

For an instant Vogt couldn't believe his eyes: the guy looked so young, almost like a kid. But that was surely the desperation of the moment triggering off strange and unreal sights, and in any case a kid, if he was a kid, could kill as easy as a grown man. Vogt brought his M-16 round and rolled, firing. He triggered a long burst, which he knew was wrong and was more than likely to bring the wrath of Sergeant Olsen down on him, but which saved his neck in spades. Rounds unstitched the Vietnamese with the bayonet, plus two more behind him, one of whom had his face burst apart in an explosion of blood and brains. Vogt scrambled to his feet, still firing, short bursts now, all points of the fucking compass. He dived back to the trail, saw more Cong appearing out of the bushes up the path, let them have it. He fired off his mag, rammed another one up. Firing had broken out all over now, and for the moment Vogt couldn't see anyone. Then he spotted Hardin, back down the trail, firing from beside a tree-bole, his bullets coming uncomfortably close.

I have two choices, Vogt thought, and both of them suck. Either stay here and get killed, or head back down the trail, through the bushes, and risk getting iced by my own guys.

He wondered where the hell that huge ball was, then realized it was only feet away from him, hanging from ropes in the trees, swaying and juddering as stray rounds thumped into it. The spikes looked like goddamn spears. M-16s were stuttering and Kalashnikovs hammering, although one of the AKs, Vogt knew, belonged to Hardin.

He began scrambling through the bushes, heaving branches and heavy creeper away from him, yelling, 'It's me! Vogt!'

Next thing he knew something was gripping his ankle and he was crashing to the ground, and Fuller's scowl was close to his ear: 'Don't make so much fuckin' noise, Vogt, you'll frighten the natives.'

Rounds were buzzing and whining overhead like a squadron of angry yellowjackets, flailing at vegetation, chewing tree-bark. Fuller snapped, 'C'mon kid, across the trail. Do it fast an ya won't get hit.' He gave a chilling chuckle. 'If yer lucky.'

Vogt didn't give himself time to think, just bolted after Fuller's disappearing form, bursting through the foliage and triggering half a mag off to his left as he flew across the trail-space and plunged into the greenery on the other side. A moment later Hardin dived through, nearly falling over him. Vogt gazed round; everyone was there, crouched and grim-faced, cradling their pieces.

Hardin said, 'That's a muscular bunch. You know what we hit?'

'Ambush? They were expecting us?' hazarded Lieutenant Comeraro.

'Nah! Check out some of those guys. They're kids. This is training territory and we've jumped straight into Lesson Five: "How To Damage The Yankees Using The Nearest Crud To Hand". Sheer bad luck for us, but I'll bet their instructors can't believe their good goddamn fortune. Main thing is, we have to kill them all, every one, without exception. Either that or wave goodbye to any hope of a successful mission and getting back to friendly territory alive.'

A grenade barked, though not near. There were a couple of shrill screams.

'Someone dropped an egg, you bet,' remarked Fuller cheerfully. 'Reckon you hit it, Colonel. But what if they send for help?'

'Doubt it. Only if things get really shitty for them. They'll

157

want to prove themselves, and this is too good an opportunity. By now they'll have some idea of our numbers and the fact is, I'd guess they outman us, maybe three or even four to one. Stupid as this may sound, this is one we could lose.'

They spread out, in three groups of two, diving into the dark, wet maw of the jungle. Hardin was trying to find a defensible position, but was soon confronted by the ugly fact that three or four to one was possibly an underestimate. The young EnVees seemed to be everywhere; behind, on their flanks, to the front. Bursts of firing from half a dozen different directions proved that these were real beginners because some were almost certainly shooting across at their own men, but it didn't make movement by the Americans any easier. Rapidly it became clear to Hardin, as he clawed his way through a tangled mat of vines and creepers, that they were surrounded. All it needed now was a grenade or two . . .

As if on cue there was another cracking blast, this time nearer, to his right. He fired a three-round burst in the direction of the sound, heard a Vietnamese voice yelling orders, trying to curb over-enthusiasm. He thought, with a flicker of grim humour: Deep-sixed by a bunch of kids; that's not just ironic, it's embarrassing.

A Vietnamese came bursting through the undergrowth, yelling madly, and Hardin nailed him with a single shot then rolled frantically away and dived under some bushes as he caught sight of a grenade sailing high through the air. The blast rocked him and hurled earth all over him, but he was mostly shielded from the frags by the dense foliage.

Then four more Vietnamese came storming into view – and Hardin's eyes widened as their triumphant yells suddenly turned into shrieks of agony. He watched, stunned, as blood blew outwards from their chests as tremendous kicking rounds hammered into them from behind. He knew the sound, the harsh pumping of an M-60 MG, but couldn't imagine where it was coming from, who was firing it. It couldn't be the Vietnamese or they'd have heard it before now, and in any case what he'd just witnessed had been deliberate, not a mistake by a trigger-happy kid spraying off rounds in the exhilaration of his first real combat situation.

More grenades blasted, but further away this time. Then there was a tremendous burst of firing, the high-pitched rattle of M-16s, but not coming from his own men at all. Hardin kept low, waited to see how things would develop. He suddenly remembered the downed chopper that, according to Vogt, had not exploded on impact, and light began to dawn. But he knew this wasn't Frank Marco.

Suddenly there was silence. It lasted for maybe half a minute then was broken by a high-pitched keening wail. Someone in pain, someone who couldn't keep quiet for a second longer, someone who had not yet learnt to button it and bear it – and now would never learn that all-important lesson, for the cry was cut off abruptly by a short burst of automatic fire. The silence extended, extended. Then ...

'Colonel Hardin!'

Hardin nodded briefly to himself, almost fatalistically. It was a voice he'd been expecting for the past few minutes. Everything was now fitting into place, neatly and precisely, without any fuss. The theory that had been growing stronger and stronger in his mind for some days was now a concrete fact. The loose ends were all tied up.

He spotted Comeraro in some bushes to his right, looking bewildered. Comeraro hissed. 'It's gotta be a trap.'

Hardin got slowly to his feet. 'Don't worry, Lieutenant. It's no trap. These people need us. Fact is, they need us more than we need them – although they're gonna come in right handy as back-up.' He called out, 'Yeah, I'm here.'

Kate Berry came slowly through the bushes towards him, no longer encumbered by cameras but holding an M-16. She eyed him warily.

Hardin said, in faultless Russian, 'Good shooting, comrade. Looks like we're all square now. Tell me, how are things in Dzerzhinsky Square these days?'

X

The man who called himself Captain Reisman said, 'I don't think they should be armed.'

He spoke in Russian and so did the girl. 'Don't be a fool,' she said.

Reisman retorted angrily, 'Don't forget my status, comrade. We have enough men to guard them, even after the helicopter losses. I think we should get the information out of them, then kill them.'

The girl laughed. 'Your status is worthless out here, comrade. You are political. Which means, frankly, you're just a bloody nuisance.'

'This will go down in my report, Major.'

'Don't forget, comrade, I have the ear of Director Andropov himself. Doubtless when he's read your report he'll use it in the appropriate manner.' She smiled frostily. 'To wipe his arse.'

Hardin, leaning against a tree and calmly smoking a cigarette, chuckled. He said, in Russian, 'That's good. That's very good. I like that.'

Major Katarina Berisovna of the KGB turned on him and snapped, 'Shut up!'

Hardin blew out smoke coolly and glanced to his left. His squad were outwardly relaxed, sitting around on the grass, close together, weapons to hand; Fuller was even playing solitaire. Hardin had noticed before that in a tight situation

Sergeant Joe Fuller tended to take things as they came; he was clearly a fatalist, although it was doubtful that he would recognize the word or agree with the philosophy if it was explained to him. Reisman's men were standing about twenty yards away, outwardly at ease too, but watchful. No one was pointing guns at anyone else, but there was a distinct tension in the air, and the big problem, as far as Hardin was concerned, was that the Russians outnumbered the Americans. There was no getting away from that.

Hardin now knew, from what the girl had told him, that they had tracked him in a chopper and had then foolishly tried to shoot Marco down, but Marco had been too damn quick for them. He'd smashed their rotors but had probably sustained a hit in his fuel lines. Which was why he'd beat it, leaving the Russians to plunge into the forest canopy. Luckily for them they'd been low to start with and had simply drifted into the trees. There'd been no explosion, but five men including pilot, co-pilot and the two 'photographers' had been hurled out, ending up with broken necks on the forest floor. That still left the girl, Reisman, and a dozen men – and those dozen men were well weaponed-up with American arms and the knowledge, almost certainly, of how to use them to maximum effect. They'd force-marched their way after Hardin and his squad, and had arrived just in time to pull their nuts out of the fire and mop up the EnVee training cadre. For which Hardin was duly grateful, although he knew full well there was a price to be paid. A hell of a price, if the Russians had their way.

'Look,' he said now, 'while you guys are chewing the fat, time's a-wasting. We could be on the move.' He spoke in English now. 'You got me out of a spot, but that doesn't mean you call the shots.'

'Are you blind?' demanded Reisman. 'We outnumber you. At a sign from me your men would be decimated.'

'Don't be fucking stupid,' said Hardin. He spoke without heat. 'I guarantee that at a loss of two of my men, tops, my squad could nail every mother's son of yours. In any case, you need us, buddy.'

Reisman glared at him. He held an M-16 and was gripping it so tightly his knuckles were white.

Hardin said to the girl, 'Let's talk.'

Reisman snapped, 'I forbid this!'

Hardin said, 'And without this yoyo, either.'

Reisman took a step forward, the rifle pointing at Hardin's stomach. Hardin noted that both his men and Reisman's were now staring silently at them, all holding their pieces. He said to the girl, 'Be sensible. We have a lot to discuss.' He started to move away.

From behind he heard Reisman say, 'One more step, Colonel, and you're dead.' Then he heard the girl hiss ferociously, 'Drop it, comrade, or I'll drop you. And I mean it. I'm in charge of this mission and you do what *I* say.'

Hardin kept on walking, his back prickling with tension. He reached the edge of the small clearing, passed through some bushes, leaned against a creeper-draped tree. He discovered he was sweating profusely. A moment later the girl appeared. She was looking furious and Hardin knew that she was angry with him as well as with Reisman. But that suited him. He shot her a dark grin but she didn't respond.

'That was close,' he said. 'I really thought he'd do it.'

'You owe me, Colonel.' Her voice was brittle.

'For that, yeah. I guess. Otherwise, like I said, we're square. Incidentally, who commands the grunts? You or him?'

'You heard me. I have charge of this operation.'

'And you really have the ear of Yuri?'

She hesitated. 'As it happens, yes.'

'I mean, that's not Yuri Grebochenko, deputy head floor-walker at GUM, or Yuri Tarkovsky who shovels garbage out in Smolensk? I take it the guy you're referring to is Yuri Andropov, head honcho at the KGB?'

'Yes,' she snapped. 'Through my mother's sister, if you must know.'

'Nepotism, huh? It's the same the whole world over. As American as apple-pie, my ass!'

'I was brought up in America,' she said tightly. 'For the first eighteen years of my life.'

'Uh-huh,' said Hardin laconically, 'then you went back to Russia for a three-year course at Moskva University, followed by the two-year intensive course at the State Institute for

Foreign Languages at Lomonosovsky, followed by the one-year even more intensive course at the far-famed but curiously named State Institute for Cultural Activities out at Sheremet'yevo, the one with the extensive and interestingly equipped dacha where culture has nothing to do with it. I'll bet that was the way of it.'

'We are not here to discuss my education, Colonel.'

'Am I right?'

'I repeat . . . '

Hardin grinned at her. 'C'mon, admit. I'm right.'

'Damn you, yes.'

'You'd be surprised how much we know about KGB recruitment and training. Or maybe you wouldn't be.' He was deliberately goading her, eager for any useful tidbit which might drop his way.

'And you would be surprised at how thick your file is, Colonel Hardin . . . ' She snapped the words out, glaring at him.

'At Central Files in No. 2 Dzerzhinsky Square? I wouldn't be at all surprised, actually. It'd be nice to think I was totally anonymous, but I have too much respect for you guys to believe that.' He spoke dryly, knowing that he was speaking nothing but the truth. 'In our line of business even no-account pieces of information add up. Even some of your people don't know it all, and neither do mine. Thank Christ.' He offered her a cigarette which, after some hesitation, she took. He lit it for her with his Zippo, admiring the fine bone structure of her face, the intense blue of her slightly almond-shaped eyes, still wary but not quite so much as before. He lit one for himself, then packed the Zippo away in a breast pocket of his fatigues. 'Look, let's cut the crap and get down to business, or that guy Reisman, or whatever the hell his name is, is gonna come in here blasting. Incidentally, what is his real name?'

'Reisman will do for now.'

'Sure.' He shrugged. It didn't matter. Reisman, or whatever the hell his name was, was going to die before this mission was through; so were the rest of his men. About the girl he was undecided. She was the opposition – or one of them; one of the many – and she was a cool customer. One of these bright days she was going to be very dangerous indeed, if not to him then to some other guy. Better to nip her in the bud right now than leave her to flower into the kind of highly-trained agent the Russians seemed best able to create: an *istrebitel*, or 'terminator' – almost invariably a beautiful, cultivated and sexually active young female. Which reminded him . . .

'Tell me, why didn't you ice me back in Do Thon? Finish off the job your guys botched?'

She sucked at her cigarette, stared at him with a look that was unfathomable, then finally said, 'I might have been compromised.'

Hardin didn't know whether to accept this or not. It was a reasonable explanation, given the fact that he'd been so near to the hotel, but didn't quite fit . . .

He said, almost pleadingly, 'Look, we really don't have too much leeway on this one. You wouldn't be crazy enough to follow me simply to finish the job, so there's only one reason you and your men are out here. The Chinese poison gas. It has to be that, doesn't it? But you don't know exactly where it is, and you figure I do. There might be a case for pooling our resources. It's as simple as that.'

The girl took another pull at her cigarette, then dropped it at her feet, stepping on it with her boot.

'Your I-people got wind of it, right?' Hardin went on. 'Sent you out on a recce mission with full US army rig and a chopper. I'd guess you were getting stories about weirdo deaths in the jungle, people frothing at the mouth, that kind of pitch.' He spoke quickly, quietly, his brain sorting it all out like a computer picking options. It was, after all, very simple really. 'You got jumped by Luke the Gook and that's where I blew in, and by chance you lucked in on one of my men finding a gas-mask and handing it to me right before your very goddamn eyes. You relayed this information back to your people, told them my name . . . ' He lifted an eyebrow, watching her.

She nodded suddenly, as though she had come to a decision.

'Your name is not unknown,' she said evenly. 'You have caused us much trouble in the past. We were ordered to dispatch you. That failed, but instead of being reprimanded our orders were then changed, and we were told to keep a watch on you. I imagine the signficance of the gas-mask outweighed any desire on the part of my superiors for . . . how shall I put it – revenge?' A brief smile flickered across her features. 'It was thought that, on your past record, you would become involved in this business, find out where the gas was being manufactured.'

'Taking a chance, weren't they?' murmured Hardin. 'Your people?'

'Oh, come now, Colonel,' her tone was lightly teasing, 'you have a certain reputation for getting things done.'

Hardin thought that, bizarre as it might sound, what she had just been telling him was almost certainly true. He knew the way the KGB worked, how they thought. He'd had enough experience of the bastards, after all – in one way or another, over the past ten years or more. Yeah, he thought, this was probably the way of it: Keep on Hardin's tracks because he might well lead you to the crock of gold at the end of the Chinese rainbow. He's the type of sucker that *shevnitch* Halderling would sent out on a mission like this. Keep tight up his ass and he'll lead you to the goods. Hardin grinned. He had no doubt that the Russians were spooked about this chemical agent complex and would be desperate to find out all they could about any Chinese involvement in nerve or chemical warfare; he remembered what Harry Schwemmer had said about the Russian agent, which the US had coded VR-55. It seemed the Chinese agent was far more deadly than that and the Russians would be wanting to get themselves a piece of this gruesomeness.

So here they were. It was chilling that the girl's KGB masters had charted his own movements and involvement so correctly but also, in a weird kind of way, flattering. When you got right down to it, he thought, we're all one great big band of brothers: KGB, SSG, CIA, British SIS, French SDECE, and all the goddamn rest. We each know roughly what the other guys are up to, and we each try to throw spanners into everyone else's works. Like a bunch of brawling kids. After a while, you realized that that was what it was: a goddamn game. And half the fun of the thing was outwitting the other guys, for no particular reason except the pleasure of beating them.

'Well, you've found me,' said Hardin. 'What now?'

This took her off-balance. He realized she hadn't really thought out too many moves beyond the here-and-now.

He said, 'You think I can lead you to this place where they're boiling up the potion, huh?'

'You wouldn't be here now unless you knew where it was. At least roughly.'

'Could be, could be.' There was one thing she didn't know about, and that was the rogue EnVee involvement. He was sure of that. He was also damn sure he wasn't going to let her in on it, either. 'And Reisman's idea is that you should screw the location out of me, set fire to my fingernails or something, then go in yourselves and blow it to shit.' He glanced at her slyly. 'And maybe grab as much documentation as you can, and maybe a scientist or two, before you actually finish the job.'

'And what are your orders?' she sneered. 'Exactly the same!'

Hardin thought about what Lew Halderling had said to him, only a few days before. 'Bring us back a live one,' he'd said. 'Forget about the paperwork, forget about specimens of this shit – you won't have time to find the right stuff. But a scientist, that's different. Grab us an egghead, force-march the fucker. We need to know.'

But Hardin had his own views about the need to know in a situation such as this. As far as he was concerned, no one needed to know about such a monstrous weapon – no one in the whole Goddamn world. The ingenuity of man on this planet was frightful enough. Every one of those Chinese suckers and their EnVee counterparts and technicians was going to die and their secrets were going to the grave with them. He'd made up his mind about that; there was no argument on earth that could change it.

'This is a kill-mission, lady,' he said. 'We can argue over the spoils when the job's done, and not before. And if we work together we can get the job done quicker and neater, and get out with our hides more or less intact.' He stared at her.

She said slowly, 'How do you know even roughly where this place is?'

'Our Intelligence,' he lied. 'Plus we made a useful capture,

166

worked the guy over. So I have a pretty good picture of the complex itself.' He went on, 'The only tricky spot is their communications. We have to kill that first and fast. It's a pretty primitive set-up; seems all the money's been spent on the refining rooms, the laboratories themselves. Plus, too, the EnVee didn't want to man up the place too solid in case aerial reconnaissance fingered the location. That's to our advantage, but there's still a barracks about twenty miles away to the east, and a heavy complement of men who can reach the lab complex fast if need be.'

Hardin lit another cigarette, spoke quickly and urgently. 'There's also a smaller, less muscular guard-force actually barring our way to the camp area itself, which is built around and into the cave-complex. Way I see it is this: Their communications have got to be blown first; after that it doesn't matter how much bang-bang we make. A handful of men could break through their guard-line in the jungle, then take out their radio-room. Once that's done, the rest of the force can come in shooting. I don't care how much noise we make, how much destruction we cause, as long as the heat's taken off the handful who sneaked in first, because they're the guys who then go in and blow the caves. As a plan it has its faults, but' – and here he played his trump card – 'our I-people discovered there's a time-factor involved. Within days, maybe hours, the stuff is going to be dispersed all over North Vietnam. Once that happens you can kiss any chance of cleaning these fuckers up goodbye. We have to hit them while they're all together, so we have to hit them right soon. Now.' He caught her eyes, held them. 'Otherwise, forget it.'

She dropped her eyes, stared at the ground. Hardin knew she was weighing up the possibilities he'd presented to her, plus any others she could think of herself. She'd probably believed him about the urgency of the mission because he hadn't made a big deal of it. If he had she'd almost certainly have suspected him of trying to bulldoze her for reasons of his own. That would have made her even more uncooperative.

'All right, Colonel,' she said at last. 'I agree it might be wiser if we joined forces. Mikhail won't like it, but the men will do as I say.'

'Mikhail being Reisman.'

'Correct.'

'Well, in the words of the good Lord, fuck him.'

She shot him an old-fashioned look. Suddenly she was a different person, although Hardin could not tell if this was cultivated just for his benefit, to get something out of him, or real. Maybe, he thought, some of both.

'You never did tell me,' she said.

'Oh? What didn't I tell you?'

'Whether I do fuck like a crazed weasel.'

At that he laughed, a huge belly-laugh that erupted out of his gut and came out loud and rich.

It was cut off abruptly by the sound of a shot. Small-arms – automatic pistol, his ears registered. He whirled, unslung his piece, dived for the brush-screen as more firing broke out, this time automatic, M-16, and muffled shouting. Hardin jumped through the foliage, the girl after him. He took in the scene, his face dark with fury.

Leroy Vogt was lying on the grass, wincing and groaning, holding his left upper left. Doc Pepper was stooping over him, a wild expression on his thin face. Comeraro, Fuller and Olsen were each holding their pieces levelled at a white-faced and sullen Reisman, whose hands were in the air. Two of Reisman's grunts were on the grass too, but they weren't groaning. They weren't doing anything; both were clearly dead, ripped across the chest by lashing M-16 rounds. The rest of Reisman's men were semi-fanned behind Reisman, but helpless, knowing that if they made another hostile move Reisman would get nailed good.

'What the hell is this?' Hardin snapped. He used his AK to cover Reisman's grunts from the side. He noted that Doc Pepper was scrabbling at Vogt's fatigues, and that blood was coming out of the kid's side, staining the heavy material darkly. Pepper was working fast and professionally.

Comeraro stepped a couple of paces towards him, gestured at Reisman with his rifle.

'This fuck,' he snarled. He looked to be on the verge of shooting Reisman's head off.

'Cool it,' said Hardin. 'How did it happen?' He was aware of the girl at his side, was aware too that her gun was up, and pointing at Reisman.

'Vogt went over, offering cigarettes. This shit grabbed him. Vogt struggled, the pig-fucker pulled his pistol and shot him. Those two,' he stabbed his rifle at the prone figures, 'made to fire. Almost looked like it had all been figured out beforehand, but we nailed the suckers. I'd like to shoot the shit outta the rest of 'em, nail their fucking hides to the goddamn trees.'

Hardin controlled himself. He took deep breaths, exhaled slowly. He looked at the girl, whose expression was one of anger and disgust, and said, 'Was it?' harshly. 'Was it part of some fucking scheme?'

'Of course not!' she snapped back. She was, he could see, murderously angry. She took two steps over to Reisman and slammed the barrel of her M-16 against the side of his face, screaming at him in Russian, 'You stupid pig! What would've been the point? I warned you!'

Reisman yelled, blood springing from his torn cheek and brow, and keeled over. He hit the grass in a tumbled heap, clutching at his face and moaning. The force of the blow must at least have loosened some of his teeth, if not dislodged one or two. The girl turned on the rest of her men and began to shout at them in Russian. She had a good command of lacerating invective.

Hardin turned to Vogt. Pepper now had his top and shirt off, his pants half down to his knees, and Hardin saw that it was a flesh-wound; the bullet had slammed into his left side. There was a lot of blood, but none of it arterial; Pepper was wiping it off, preparing bandages. It would hurt Vogt but not too much. But it would also slow them all down because Vogt was going to be limping.

Comeraro said angrily, 'I want to kill that sonofabitch.'

'So do I, Lieutenant, but it won't help any.' Hardin stared cold-eyed at Reisman, who was rubbing the side of his face and wincing his eyes shut with pain. With half an ear Hardin was listening to what the girl was throwing at the Russians.

Comeraro said, 'What's she yelling?'

Hardin grinned bleakly.

'Smart move. She's pulling rank, and then some. She's

saying that she knows the head of the KGB and they better watch their ass.'

'And does she?'

'So she said. I have no reason to disbelieve her. She's saying that Reisman – or Major Resnovich – is basically a no-account bum and the head honchos at KGB are going to be extremely pissed off if for some reason Reisman makes it back and she doesn't. She's also giving them a lot of propaganda crap about the Chinese, Chairman Mao, and the Ussuri River incidents last year; China must be defeated, the Imperialist Yankees are of secondary importance in this great task; in war you sometimes have to jump into bed with a stranger; stuff like that.'

'Ussiri River?'

'Yeah, about a year ago, eighteen months. Soviet Army units had a punch-out with the Chinese on an island in the Ussuri. It's part of the border between Manchuria and Siberia. The Reds are paranoid about the Chinese, some atavistic memory which probably goes right back to Genghis Khan and the Mongol goddamn hordes. That's why they're here now, Lieutenant. If the little yellow men have something which puts them ahead, Russia wants a slice. They'd do anything to screw the Chinese. It's our ace in the hole.'

'So why does this Reisman or Resnovich prick want to make waves and do us?'

'Because, I'd guess, he's the Red equivalent of a Puritan, doesn't like strange bedfellows. Thinks he can do it all himself without any help.' Hardin shrugged. 'Typical party-pooper.'

The girl had now gone across to Reisman and was hissing venomously at him in a low voice, her expression furious. Hardin wondered what she was saying. He trusted her, but only up to a certain point – after that point their aims were by no means mutual; diverged, in fact, alarmingly. Once they were inside the cave-complex, he and his men would be on their own. It might even now be a wise move to deep-six all of the Russians right here; on the other hand their additional firepower was not to be sneered at. He pulled a face, shrugged. It was six of one, half a dozen of the other; a decision either way could go blazingly wrong.

The girl came back.

170

'The men will do what I tell them. If we can agree on strategy, there should be no problem.'

'Yeah, but what about Reisman?'

'He will receive his punishment back in Russia,' she said confidently.

'That doesn't answer my question. I just don't want him to get the Order of Lenin too, for shooting me in the back.'

She shot him a sardonic look.

'Do you think your despatch is worth the Order of Lenin. How arrogant of you, Colonel.'

Hardin leaned towards her, his face suddenly grim.

'I'll be watching that bastard and so will my men. One wrong move, he gets it.'

As he turned away from her, he thought sourly that this was not really the best way to go into what could be one of the most dangerous missions he'd ever undertaken.

XI

Hardin could see the North Vietnamese guard quite clearly, even though he was not touched by the watery radiance of the moonlight that filtered through scudding clouds. He was a darker shape to one side of a massive bank of shrubbery; Hardin could even see the black outline of the man's Kalashnikov, held one-handed, loosely.

He eased himself silently forward on his elbows into the grass. He'd found an animal track, a narrow canyon through the tall elephant grass which ensured stealth of approach. There would be no sudden warning ripple of the fronds as he made his way towards the man; the first thing the guy would know of Hardin's close proximity would be the sudden intense agony of an eight-inch steel blade slicing into his heart. After that, nothing.

On one level the forest was utterly still; there seemed to be no sound at all to disturb the quietness. But in fact the jungle was alive with sounds: the creaking of boughs disturbed by a sudden breeze, the rustle of leaves, the muffled crash of some rotten branch, overloaded with creeper and vine, suddenly giving way and hurtling to the undergrowth-choked floor. Hardin thought that the EnVee would have to be a very sharp monkey indeed to distinguish any noise he might make, as he crawled through the grass, from the normal nocturnal creakings and crackings of the Big Green.

Not that Hardin made a sound anyhow; he slid silently

through the grass, smoothly inching his way nearer and nearer to the motionless figure, the knife clasped between his teeth.

He knew how much time they had. As Hoang had said, sometime during that strange briefing confrontation in the old Colonial house outside of Do Thon, the guard was arranged in a two-hour shift. Hardin had watched the change forty-five minutes earlier, and forty-five minutes was enough time for the new guard to become bored with his duty; restless. Careless. Once he was dead, Hardin then had one hour and fifteen minutes to do what had to be done, blow the communications cabin which was situated, unless Hoang had lied (unlikely) very near to where Hardin himself was now sneaking through the grass. A half-mile at most, down into the small valley beyond, and underneath the nearest coppice of trees in the natural clearing that led to the caves.

One hour fifteen, thought Hardin. Skate! Unless something went hideously wrong, they ought to be *out* in one hour fifteen.

Hardin had already planned his route. He would take his men straight south and then make a dog's leg south west, cutting back over the border into Laos again. There, in a small ville that he'd used before, where the headman was more trustworthy than most – due to the VC having made the stupid mistake of killing his only son three or four years back, a disaster the headman had never forgotten and would never forgive – was an arms and clothes cache which included a radio. From there, Hardin and his party would be helilifted out within an hour of making contact.

He was still undecided about the Russian contingent; that asshole Reisman, or Resnovich, was going to throw all kinds of goddamn monkey wrenches into the works if he could. Hardin was still faintly troubled that he'd had to leave Reisman behind. He was the kind of guy that needed watching like a hawk. He ought to have killed the fucker there and then, back in the clearing, but it would have caused a problem; and that was the last thing he needed now, problems of any kind.

In the end, his small advance party consisted of the girl, Sarge Fuller, and two of the Russians, all of whom were in back of him, waiting for the kill before they moved forward. That left Reisman and eight lower echelon Russian military, plus Comeraro and Olsen, and Doc Pepper and the wounded kid. He'd had to take the girl's word that the Reds would play ball; there was nothing else he could do on that score. Comeraro and Olsen were tight, however; they wouldn't let Reisman out on too loose a rein. He hoped.

He slunk onwards, smelling the rotting jungle stench all around him. It was almost like a miasma; a powerful and heady stink of rot that seemed to penetrate everywhere.

He slowed; stopped. The EnVee guard had made a sudden move. Hardin froze where he was, confident that neither his face or hands, liberally smeared with cam cream and darkly striped, nor his tigers, could be seen even at close range for what they were, but still uneasy about that sudden movement. Then he heard the Vietnamese curse vitriolically and slap at his face. Hardin relaxed. Bug attack.

He took his knife out of his mouth, and a sudden flare of anger erupted as he thought that the ideal man for the job here was that fucker Garrett, king of the garotte. Garrett had shown his skill on more than one occasion in the past. Hardin wondered where the bastard was now; hoped he'd been eaten by the local fauna. He hoped he'd died in considerable agony.

The EnVee guard was now slapping and grabbing at himself like a man demented. Hardin watched, a wolfish grin splitting his camouflaged features, as the man moved towards him stumblingly, dropped his gun, turned his back. He was now only feet away, ten at most.

Hardin rose up, crossed the space between them in two long strides, and sheathed his knife in the guard's back, at the same time flinging his left hand round his face and clutching at his mouth, gripping it closed. The EnVee spasmed, his arms flailing wildly. Hardin tugged the blade out, swung the man round and struck savagely into his heart. He saw the whites of his eyes briefly, then let him sink to the ground slowly and noiselessly.

Hardin glared round, stock-still. No movement anywhere; no sound. No human sound. Then a faint rustle of grass where he'd been only seconds before, and the girl's face appeared. He beckoned, watched as she came towards him in a crouch, followed by Fuller and the two Russians.

Quickly Fuller grabbed the EnVee's shoulders, nodding urgently at one of the Russians, who heaved at the prone figure's legs. They took the body into the deeper undergrowth.

Hardin muttered, 'Okay, we're through here. We keep moving down now, toward the valley. There's nothing between us and the radio shack.'

Olsen said, 'With all respect, Lieutenant, I don't frankly see how we're gonna stop this fucker from talkin' to his own men. It's, and I have to say this, sir, gonna be difficult.'

'Yeah.'

'I mean, when ya get down to it, it's frankly just me and you, sir. That's it. Just me and you.'

'Yeah.'

'I mean, frankly, the kid's a liability, as of when he got it in the fuckin' leg. With all respect, Lieutenant.'

Olsen lit a cigarette and stared glumly across the clearing to where the Russians were sitting, weapons to hand, muttering amongst themselves. Reisman was leaning against a tree, smoking, his eyes hooded. To one side, not quite out of sight but half-hidden by tree foliage, a light tarp had been roughly rigged into a makeshift tent where Leroy Vogt was lying. Doc Pepper emerged from the bushes.

'He'll survive. It's nothing, just a flesher. But he's gonna slow us to a crawl, man.'

Comeraro thought: Jesus, what else?

He said, 'I'll go see him.' Then he glanced at his watch. 'We move in twenty.'

He walked past the sullen Reisman, threaded his way through the bushes, dipped down to poke his head under the lightweight tarp. He wiped the back of his neck, noting sourly that the tarp, borrowed from the Russians, had been cleverly designed to let water through in several strategic places. Vogt stared up at him miserably.

'Pepper says you'll do.'

'Yeah, sir. Jeeze, what a crapper. You don't think it'll have to come off, do you? I asked Doc that, but I don't trust his answers. He wasn't taking it seriously, the prick.'

Comeraro grinned.

'It was only a flesh-wound, Vogt. Went in, came out. Nice and clean.'

'Yeah,' Vogt said gloomily, 'but you hear stories, sir. Jeeze, I couldn't stand having my leg off. *Jeeze!*'

'Don't panic. You're okay. We're gonna be moving in twenty, and I'll get Olsen to whittle up a crutch. I was thinking of getting one of the Russkis to do it, but I guess they'd probably sabotage it. Just keep your piece handy, that's all.'

Vogt clutched his M-16, lying beside him.

'You don't have to tell me, sir,' he said with feeling.

Vogt watched Comeraro duck out, then lay back on the soggy tarp. His ruck supported his head. He reached for his pack of cigarettes and hoped that he was going to make out. He had feelings of doom about this mission, although that was nothing new. Every mission with Colonel John Hardin seemed to Vogt to be fraught with danger and disaster. There were times when he yearned to be just another fucking grunt out in the Delta, prime target for every VC nasty who drove an ox-plough by day and hurled grenades over the perimeters by night. And then he thought: The hell with it, Hardin gets us into tight spots, but we've always got out of them. So far.

His leg ached but didn't throb. The weird thing was, he felt sleepy. He thought: If I go to goddamn sleep the goddamn Reds'll sneak in here and kill me. He dozed.

Then jerked up with a grunted imprecation as the moon-light was blocked out by a bulky figure leaning over him. Wildly Vogt clutched at his M-16, tried to drag it over to him.

'Take it easy, kid.' It was Olsen. 'Kill me and that'll frankly only leave the Loot between you and the Russkis.'

'Sorry, Sarge, I dropped off.'

'Y'know, Vogt,' said Olsen kindly, 'sometimes I frankly think you got about as much brain as a whoopee cushion. Here.' He jammed a couple of lengths of wood down towards him and Vogt took them. 'They're thick and the crosspieces'll take your weight under the arms. Get used to 'em, because frankly you're gonna have to run with the fuckers at some stage, unless from here on this mission has no more foul-ups. And that, I haveta tell ya, I can't believe.'

He backed off, ducking down under the extended tarp and

disappearing back into the bushes. Vogt watched him go. He'd dropped the M-16 and now held the crutches only. For a quick cut-and-slash, Olsen had done a good job: the sticks weren't too heavy but were solid and the two arm-rests seemed smooth. Vogt wondered if he was going to have to use his M-16 at some point, whilst supported by the crutches. He tried to imagine this, but the whole operation seemed too cock-eyed to him.

He was suddenly aware that the mutterings of the Russians, up till now only faintly discernible, had become louder. One of the Russians was clearly arguing hotly with another, although Vogt couldn't tell what the hell they were arguing about. He heard the Loot call out, low but sharp, then the voice of one of the Russians rose high and there was the sound of a blow. Then another. Jesus, thought Vogt, in panic, the fucking Reds are beating up on each other! I don't fucking believe it!

At that moment a shadow from outside fell across him. He started. He'd been too absorbed in the noises of the fighting to keep his ears tuned for anything else. He stared up into the grinning features of a Russian. The man had his M-16 thrust out, the bayonet attached. Vogt was suddenly only too aware of the fact that his own M-16 was not in his hands and there wasn't going to be any time at all to grab it, let alone fire the fucker.

The Russian laughed suddenly – and lunged.

Sergeant Fuller muttered, 'Fuck this moon! Willya look at it! For the past hour it's been in an' out, in an' out. Now the fucker's like a crappin' searchlight!'

Hardin whispered, 'Easy, Sergeant. Couple minutes, that's all. Then we have a nice big fat cloud and you can take the guy.'

They were staring, from bushes, down a short grassed slope. At the bottom of the slope stood a small verandaed cabin, radio aerials sprouting from the rear, half-hidden in trees. Above them, all around them, hills climbed away to the night-sky; here, thickly wooded; further up mere rocky crags. This was a tiny natural bowl beside the foothills of the Annamese Cordillera that marched ruggedly deep into the Asian heartland. To the right Hardin could just see a road under the trees, almost certainly hidden from watching eyes high above in spy-planes; a typical EnVee workmanlike track, created in haste, yet solid enough to take a convoy of deuce and a halfs carrying heavy equipment and matériel. The EnVees were past masters at making do with what little there was to hand; turning it to good use.

Beyond what could be seen of the cabin was a wide open space that, again, would not attract any attention from above. Bushes had been left to grow in the centre, the grass had not been cut down to boot-height; yet the ever-encroaching jungle had been so cunningly cut back and confined around the edges that, from the air, it would seem to be a purely natural clearing. Rocky outcroppings hung over the cabin and above the trees, and Hardin knew that beyond the hut and round on the left, to the west of the clearing itself, there would be cave-mouths, inside which would be located the laboratories and office-complex of the Chinese contingent and their EnVee subordinates.

On the other side of the clearing Hardin could just make out a building, hidden in the trees. That, according to Hoang Van Tho's detailed sketch-map, was the barracks where probably twenty to thirty grunts were housed.

Hardin switched his gaze back to the slope immediately in front of him – and to the man leaning against a tree, half in shadow, only feet away from the end of the veranda that was their possible means of entry to the radio shack.

He turned to the two Russians.

'Stay put and cover our rear, but don't shoot unless you have to, unless it's absolutely necessary. Then follow in five, with Sergeant Fuller.' He said to the girl, 'We're gonna slide round the back of the shack, could be an entry-point there. Whatever happens, Fuller's gonna have to ice that guy down there or we'll all be in shit.'

Fuller watched as Hardin and the girl threaded their way through the undergrowth and out of sight. He turned to the Russians, knowing that they, like all the other men under the girl's command, spoke English like Americans; it was why they were on the job in the first place, why they'd been chosen by the KGB.

'You cover my ass,' he muttered. 'No fuck-ups, right?'

One of the men said, 'Okay, okay. We wanna get out of this in one piece too, buddy.'

'Buddy,' muttered Fuller dispiritedly.

Above, clouds drifted towards the moon, slid across it, plunging the world into a thick hot darkness. Fuller grunted, reached for the knife at his belt, and emerged from the bushes silently, cat-running downhill over the springy turf.

There was no other goddamn way but this, and in any case Fuller was a man who knew how to run soundlessly, on the balls of his feet, his breath held in as he sprinted down the slope. His mind held a picture of his target, starkly and sharply defined, and he knew that before he did anything he had to grab the guy's face, close off any kind of noise that might erupt with the shock of his attack: The knife was held tightly in his right hand; his left hand was thrust out, ready to grab that head like a catcher mitting a fast ball.

As he reached the man, who had not even stirred, the moon came out briefly. Too fucking late, Fuller thought gleefully, as his hand slapped round the man's face, clamping into it.

But he didn't smack home the knife into the guy's back.

Instead he did what he'd never in his life done before.

He yelled. With shock and horror.

The head had come rolling off the trunk, like a coconut on a carny stall, and hit his face, and all he could see was a mess of still feebly pumping gore.

The musette bag over Hardin's back was lightweight, but it was still a goddamn nuisance. Hardin liked to be free of encumbrances in a situation where the slightest addition to his own natural weight made a vast and sometimes terrifying difference to speed, balance, agility. But it had to be carried, for in that bag was not only plastic explosives, fuses, timers, spare mags, but possibly his own salvation. Maybe his *only* salvation. It was a frightening thought.

He peeled back foliage, slunk through vegetation, the girl tight on his tail. He wondered how she'd make out if things tipped over the edge, and then thought probably okay or she wouldn't be ramrodding a muscular KGB troop in the first place. Even so, this was not your ordinary, average, everyday mission by a long chalk; it could very easily get very hairy out there. He mentally shrugged. They were in the lap of the gods.

Pushing gently through some bushes he found himself at the rear of the shack. He stopped, listened; could hear nothing. No sound of muffled conversation, no scuff of movement, no crackle of radio static. That was a pity. You could hit someone easier, jump them without too much fuss, if they were concentrating on something else. He turned to the girl, his voice an almost soundless whisper.

'Round to the side.'

He catfooted alongside the wooden wall, peered warily round the angle. A vague impression in the blackness of more trees and bushes, thickly clustered, some actually encroaching on the building itself. Then he grinned as he made out the open window, chest-high, along the wall. He moved shadowlike up to it, sniffing for cigarette smoke but smelling nothing, his eyes endeavouring to pierce the gloom. He peered in, seeing nothing in the darkness, but sensing the room was empty. Probably a store.

'I'll boost you in,' he whispered to the girl.

She put her hands on the sill and Hardin gripped her legs, for a second feeling a weird spark of desire at her closeness as he heaved her silently upwards. That was crazy, he thought. There was a brief scuffle of sound, then she was gone.

He waited, counting seconds in thousands, every sense alert for danger, any sudden unnatural disturbance. Then the girl's head was leaning out of the window.

She said, not particularly quietly and in a tone that hinged on the bleak, 'You'd better come up.'

Hardin thought, Jesus, now what?, and hoisted himself over the sill. He unslung his AK—47, held it by his side. Adrenalin was beginning to pump into his bloodstream, firing him up; an invariable occurrence when he sensed that things were sliding out of kilter, and the girl's tone of voice and a sudden awareness that the small shack was totally void of man and machine warned him of that.

There was a door ahead, opening on to a larger room. He peered through the doorway and as he did so the moon broke

180

through the clouds outside, its wan light shafting through two windows and revealing bare boards, a few wires hanging from the walls, discarded valves on the floor, a tipped-over chair. And nothing else. Not a goddamn thing.

'So much for your detailed plans,' said the girl dourly.

And as she said that Hardin heard a human cry, a yell of terror-tinged shock, echoing outside.

Then, fainter but still clear enough for anyone within a half-mile to hear, the sharp thudding rattle of automatic fire.

XII

Fuller too heard the firing break out in back of him, high above in the trees. It was what steadied him now. He cursed savagely. Joe Fuller was normally a hard case, rarely responding to such outside stimuli as the horror and savagery and frenzied destruction of war. He was a man without fear, who could deal out bloody death and not give a passing thought to it after it was done. He had few feelings at all, apart from a sour disgust at the conduct of the war, the looseness of discipline, the quality of the draft, the sackashit nature of most of the brass he'd ever had the misfortune to meet.

Told to clean up a slaughter-house he'd have done it without a qualm, despite the reek of death in his nostrils and blood up to his armpits. Once loose head more or less didn't mean beans to him; blood, any amount of it, he could wade through. It was the heart-stopping shock of the totally unexpected that had caused that yell. So when he cursed, as he did now, he cursed at his own stupidity.

But he didn't curse long. Not at all. He took about three seconds of fucking and shitting, then clamped his teeth together and worked fast, with the speed of a desperate man. There was a screw-up behind him somewhere; never mind what it was, how it had happened. *He'd* screwed up too – that shout, he knew, had echoed and reverberated hollowly all around the valley. He could do nothing about the firing, but

Christ on a crutch he could sure as hell make an effort to nullify the effects of that one dumb yell.

Without thinking much at all but working on semi-automatic pilot, he tossed the bloody head into the bushes. The cut, he'd mentally noted in the brief glow of moonlight, was a cleanish slice. His nose told him now that at the moment of death the man, an EnVee guard, had emptied his bowels. The trunk still leaned against the tree and Fuller suddenly realized that the headless body was tied there. There were two lengths of cord. Fuller sliced through both, heaved the body after the head and kept the cord, stuffing both lengths into a pocket of his tigers as he heard running footsteps. He crouched down and saw, using the horizon gap between the trees, a lighter darkness than the jungle itself, that it was the two Russians, sprinting down the slope.

He stage-hissed the word 'Mask!', which was Hardin's designated verbal pass for this particular mission, and saw the two men, both with slung M-79 grenade launchers and holding M-16s, veer towards him. He rose up, joined them. 'Radio shack!' he snapped, suddenly thinking: Shit, these two jokers could turn ugly if those shots mean their buddies up there are trying to knock our guys off.

But the two Russians followed him, doubling down the slope and into the trees that crouched around most of the shack. Fuller wondered where Hardin was, if he'd iced the EnVee radio operators. He now gave a thought to that fusillade of shots that had shattered the night silence only a minute or so ago, but he was suddenly distracted by other sounds, the sounds of running feet. Only one thing that could be.

The three men lay low in the undergrowth as the moon again broke free of clouds, revealing an eight-man pack of EnVees running up the slope towards the jungle. They disappeared into the deep shadow of the trees.

'Eight less ta worry about,' muttered Fuller.

One of the Russians said, 'What the hell was that shooting about?'

'Reckon our guys must've tripped over some more of the gooks,' said Fuller, hoping to hell that was indeed the case.

183

He pushed around the silent shack, found the open window, whispered 'Masks' again.

'Climb in, Fuller.' Hardin's voice, bleak-toned, came from the darkened interior. The three men scrambled through the window-space, stared around at what was revealed in the shafts of watery moonlight.

'Shit,' said Fuller, 'we been set up?'

'No.' Hardin was definite. 'This was a radio shack, not a doubt of it, but they moved the equipment. Recently too. There's no dust to speak of, and the aerials are still up. Could've been done yesterday. I'm pretty sure my source knew nothing about it. Maybe Charlie didn't think there was enough protection here, shifted everything to a safer location. Whatever, the mission's starting to fucking unwind.'

'Say that again,' grunted Fuller.

One of the Russians said, 'That shooting . . . '

'Yeah.' Hardin's response was instant, smooth, natural; firm. 'Looks like there were more EnVees up in the woods than we thought. Too bad. They're just gonna have to look after themselves up there.'

The girl was standing back from one of the windows that looked out over the central open zone of the small bowl-like valley. She suddenly said, 'More men, but only half a dozen. They don't look very excited. They're moving east, away from us, into the trees.'

'Good,' Hardin turned to Fuller. 'What the hell happened to you?'

Fuller winced. 'Never done that before. It was piss-stupid.'

'So?'

'The guy's head had been sliced off at the fuckin' neck. He was secured to the tree with ropes.'

'Jesus!' Hardin was alarmed. What in God's own sweet name was going on? Maybe they *had* been set up? But no, he thought, I don't believe it; it's not how Hoang would have handled it. 'What did you do with the stiff?'

'Threw him away. Maybe they'll think he's takin' a leak or something. It was the only thing I could think of at the time. If I'd've left the fucker, sir, even with his head back on, someone'd've been bound to think it was kind of funny, you know?

So I figured, better if he just went missing.' Fuller shrugged. 'I mean, hell, whatever he was supposed to be doin' in the first place, he could be up in the trees by now, checkin' out whatever's caused all the fuss up there. That's the way I figured Charlie'd think it out.'

'Yeah.' Hardin dismissed the headless guard. Right now it was the least of his problems, almost an irrelevance. 'Okay, we've got to take it that by now Charlie's maybe sent out a low-key message about the disturbance. The main garrison, like I said, is maybe twenty miles away, and there could be a chopper presence there. I doubt that there are choppers any nearer.' He gestured to the cleared space in front of the deserted shack. 'I'd be happier if we could somehow mine that area, but we don't have a hope in hell of doing that. So you two,' pointing at the two Russians, 'are gonna have to hole up near the entrance to the caves with your grenade launchers. Any choppers arrive, hit 'em. Let 'em come down low, and just before they land blow 'em away. Meanwhile, we'll hit the caves, start fixing the plas as far into the complex as we can. My source says the caves reach back deep so it's gonna take time, but at least I know roughly where things are from the ground-plan.'

'What about the radio-shack?' said Fuller, 'wherever the hell it is now . . . '

'Forget it. We could take an hour looking for it and now we don't have a half-hour. We don't have five goddamn minutes.' He said, 'Pistols.'

He pulled out his own automatic and twirled a suppressor into its barrel, Fuller and the girl doing likewise. Hardin had frags on him and in his bag; he had his AK and spare mags. His knife was at his belt but he didn't think he'd be using it much; he wanted any enemy nailed hard before it got to close-quarter work. Both Fuller and the girl had back-slung bags too, with more plas and detonators, and the two Russians were well weaponed-up, at least for a short siege situation. Hardin hoped it wouldn't come to that.

'Let's move,' he said.

Out of the empty shack, they scrambled over rocks, crawled

beneath bushes, wriggled through dense shrubs, until they were over the brow of the foliaged rock-arm that reached out from the sheer cliffs and began to drop down over the other side. In the cloud-breaks, when the moon cast its fitful light, Hardin could see that the high entrance to the caves had been covered over, probably with a wood structure over which a wide awning had been draped, netting, camouflaged with earth clods and vegetation which was renewed every so often to stop it looking dead. From what Hoang had said, the place had been built in a hurry, and that was all to the good. It meant it could be destroyed in a hurry too. In places, the *thieu tuong* had mentioned, the roof of the cave complex sagged low, was weak; here pillars had been erected to hold the rock up. That too was good. Take the pillars away and the rock ceiling would not fall. *Blow* them away and the shock would literally bring the roof down. Plastic explosive, placed at strategic points, ought to bury the entire lab complex which, Hardin now knew, mainly consisted of hastily erected shacks and Quonsett-style huts. The laboratories were deep in the heart of the caves; built into the rock, almost a part of it in places, Hoang had said. Perfect, thought Hardin, goddamn perfect. Here there were testing rooms, decontam chambers, storage areas where the 'sky-fire' was quiescent in stacked drums and cylinders.

They climbed down towards the forward area, the entrance to the caves. From afar, or so it seemed to Hardin, voices could be heard, the excited chatter of men who were loudly trying to figure out what was going on up in the forest; it was something Hardin would have liked to know too. Since the initial burst of firing there had been no more shots and Hardin wondered what was happening up there right now. Had the Russians attempted to kill Comeraro and Co? Or had the whole party hit a snag, bumped into a patrol? Idle to speculate, he thought; the only reality is down here. All the time he moved, his ears were not only attuned to what was going on around him but also alert for the far-off clatter of approaching choppers. Thus far, there was nothing.

He crouched in a bush, the girl behind him, almost breathing in his ear. To his right were boulders and a track that led past to the front. To his left the track, wide enough to take a deuce and a half and then some, turned under the sagging camouflaged awning and down a shallow slope into the caves. Low-wattage bulbs had been hung farther down; their light would not be seen from the sky, even on the darkest night. The track itself was rock with a light sand covering. Hardin could see a man, a guard, walking hurriedly towards them, up the slope. He carried a Kalashnikov. Behind him, another guard. The first man passed Hardin's hide, only a few feet from him, then disappeared in the direction of the valley bowl which lay on the other side of a low ridge in the ground. From here, Hardin noted with satisfaction, a hidden man could command the immediate approach to the caves; could certainly fire off grenades at anything that might drop out of the night-sky.

The second man hurried along up the slope, slowed, stopped – five feet from Hardin's bush.

He was perfectly silhouetted against the dim light from down the cave tunnel, but was standing sideways to Hardin. Hardin cursed silently, knowing that a hurled knife at this angle might miss, even at that range. He didn't want to shoot the guy either, even with his silenced automatic. He was saving any firing until he was within the caves themselves, when it wouldn't matter much. He could feel the girl gripping his arm, tensely. There was really only one damn thing to be done, and that was a hugely risky undertaking. But it had to be done, and done fast. Now.

He listened, could hear no one approaching from the valley. Beyond the guard it was clear for thirty yards or more down the tunnel to a bend. He gently shook the girl's hand free from his arm, inched forwards and sideways, to get as close as possible without alarming his target. Then, knife in hand, he suddenly rose up out of the bushes, leapt towards the guard.

The EnVee jerked round, eyes wide, mouth beginning to drop open, AK swinging up. Hardin jumped at him, the knife-blade slicing through air in a tight thrusting arc. His judgement was perfect. The point of the knife hacked into the guy's throat, the jugular, cutting off any sound that was starting to vocalize, taking most of his throat out in a gush of blood.

Hardin fell into the man, clasped at him, blood spurting over his face, down the front of his tigers. He heaved him back the five feet or so into the bushes, dumping him onto the ground. He thought: If that took ten seconds, that was all. No damn more. He wasn't breathing too quickly. The tunnel was still clear; nothing, either, from his right. One of the Russians, behind him, said ungrudgingly, 'Nice work.'

Hardin muttered, 'Leave him here. One of you guys stay here, the other across the track and into the bushes on the other side. Let through single men, twos and threes. We can deal with them once they get into the cave system. Anything muscular, let 'em past then take 'em out. Use your M-16s, fuck the noise.' He said to the girl and Fuller, 'Check your rifles are tightly slung. From now on, it's small arms unless things get really tough. Okay, with me.'

He emerged from the bushes again, running down the slope and into the caves.

It was like a small town below ground. It might have been done in a hurry and it might have been done on the cheap, but, Hardin acknowledged, as he sprinted into the narrow, dimly lit network of passageways that spiderwebbed around huts and shacks, it had been constructed with all of the typical Chinese dexterity, care and attention to detail.

They were, he knew, fanatical tunnel-builders and tunnel-users. They'd taught the EnVees the tricks of living below ground in enemy territory – down in the Delta the US forces were continually excavating miniature cities that had been dug out of the earth, where whole families sometimes lived for months at a time without surfacing – but they were even more hot for the subterranean theory at home, in China itself; they practised what they preached. Hardin knew from Intelligence reports he'd seen that Chairman Mao had put the word out to 'heighten vigilance, store grain everywhere, mobilize the masses to dig tunnels deep'. And from Peking to Dairen to Mukden to Shanghai that's exactly what they were doing, toiling away like goddamn beavers – or, maybe more accurately, moles – constructing shelters, subways, tunnels, entire labyrinthine cities-beneath-cities, little worlds below ground; Microcosms.

These caves were natural, not man-made, tunnels, but even here the Chinese had adapted, transformed, engineered; had eagerly grasped what nature had offered, and turned it into a reasonably clean, reasonably comfortable system of underground burrows, where men could dwell – and where unknown horrors could be created.

It was of course one of life's little ironies that, maybe a couple of seconds after the thought hit Hardin, running silently, on his toes, that as yet he had seen no evidence of a Chinese presence at all, an eight-man squad holding rifles and dressed in Red Guard fatigues came marching around a bend up the corridor.

As he dived for the floor Hardin's eyes took in the scene with all the dispassionate detachment of a machine. What happened then took maybe six or seven seconds, although it seemed like five minutes in that weird timeline that exists in the brain when adrenalin is pouring into the system and every nerve-end is afire.

The Chinese marched like robots; carried on marching even after the initial shock of seeing three Occidentals in a place where no Occidentals should be. It was purely automatic, a reflex action. Probably they thought, for about two seconds, that they were dreaming. Then the disciplined ranks began to fall apart, topple, in a way, like a finger-flicked house of cards. Rifles came off shoulders, men started to jump to left and right, shock searing their faces.

Hardin was on the floor, his automatic held two-handed. Behind him KGB Major Katarina Berisovna crouched against the right-hand wall, US Army Sergeant Joe Fuller opposite her on the left. The *fwip-fwip-fwip* of silenced shots sounded like fast cars passing each other on a four-lane black-top. The Red Guards were punched back by the high velocity rounds; hollownose slugs exploded their organs, erupted out of their flesh in bloody sprays.

Six seconds. Maybe seven. Maybe even eight for the echoing clatter of dropped rifles on to the concrete floor to die out. Then silence. There had been no shouting, no cries.

Hardin jumped to his feet, sped up the passage followed by the other two. All eight men were dead.

'Take the mags, leave the pieces,' Hardin ordered.

They catfooted to the bend, Hardin point, Katarina drag, Fuller in between. Katarina moved sideways, one eye always to the rear, checking for unpleasant surprises. Hardin peered round the corner. Another corridor, short, dimly-lit by naked, low-wattage bulbs; at its end an opaque, frosted-glass door.

'Hold this bend. I'll check out the door.'

He ran to the door, inched it open. He could now see how this part of the underground complex had been constructed: a series of office-blocks, each with its own internal corridors, and separated from each other by outside paths and duckboarded walkways. Here the cave roof was low. Cables were draped everywhere, looped from jagged rock outcroppings, some carrying light bulbs. You couldn't see much as the light was bad; but then, Hardin thought, you didn't need to know what was outside if you were working in the 'bungalow'-style offices.

He beckoned urgently to Katarina and Fuller.

'Start fixing the plas. Forty-minute timers.'

They worked fast, moulding the pliant *plastique* cored with detonators, wiring it up. No one appeared. Hardin moved along one of the walkways, his eyes alert for movement, a door suddenly opening, a flicker of motion at the corner of the building.

Nothing.

He rounded a bend. And froze.

Ahead, in the shadows, at the end of the open passage, a man-shape. The shape didn't move. Hardin couldn't make out whether the man was facing him or turned away, and then suddenly realized that the guy must be leaning against a corner-angle of the passage. Peering intently he could now make out half a head, half a body. Fuller was suddenly behind him.

'Looks like a guard,' Hardin whispered. 'But it's too far to run at him without alerting the fucker, and it'd take too long to sneak down there as quietly as it ought to be goddamn done.' He raised the pistol, two-handed, went into a crouch. He breathed out, squeezed the trigger twice. The automatic spat two bullets silently – and the half-hidden man's head jumped clear from his shoulders, sailed away into the gloom.

The rest of the body stayed where it was.

'Jesus!' Fuller's voice was awed. 'What kinda fuckin' rounds ya got, Colonel? Ain't never seen the fuckin' like!'

Hardin stared. Nor had he. Still the man's headless body stayed lounged against the rock corner-angle. Hardin suddenly thought about the first set of timers, now ticking the seconds away; they didn't have any leeway for pondering miracles. He sprinted down the corridor, reached the still figure.

The head lay grinning up at him ghoulishly in the half-light, some yards away. Now blood could be seen, drenching the guard's uniform blackly from the severed neck-stump down.

Fuller muttered, 'Sorry, sir, you ain't such a hot-shot after all. That was how the guy outside was. A head-slice. Whoever did it, popped the head back on. See, he's tied to the wall – 's why he didn't keel over.'

Hardin thought, the image racing through his mind, Hoang's got to be behind this; it's the only Goddamn explanation. For some reason he's trying to sabotage the mission. But – why? Hardin couldn't understand it; any logical reason was, for the moment, beyond him. Apart from anything else, he'd been convinced that the *thieu tuong* had been on the level, had been desperate to destroy the nerve-agent and everything to do with it, chew the Chinese up and spit 'em out. So why the change of mind? Possibly some new twist in the political situation had caused it. South East Asian politics were in a state of constant flux: enemies could be friends at the snap of a finger out here; friends, enemies. But why was Hoang doing it in this utterly bizarre manner?

He had no time for further thought. A man in a white lab coat suddenly emerged from a doorway along the passage, light spilling out after him. He gaped at what he saw and Hardin shot him, banging the guy over onto the floor with one round then sprinting for the door as though a score of fiends from hell were breathing on his heels.

He swung through the open doorway and took in the scene. Four men staring at him as though he were a ghost, one already reaching for a telephone. Hardin hit him first, one round, then double-actioned the trigger of the automatic at another, slamming him against a whitewashed wall. Rounds zipped over his stooped shoulder from behind as Katarina finished the other two. Again, no cries; the raiding party had been too fast.

Hardin glanced briefly at the wall where, in sliding down to the floor, the third man he'd shot had left a scarlet smear, then he said, 'Might as well start here.'

They fixed more plas, retired to the corridor, set more explosive dough. Hardin slipped another mag up into his automatic, checked it. Using a suppressor was fine but you had to watch sometimes for barrel-burn when you were in a high-rate-of-fire situation.

The trio moved swiftly through the labyrinth, placing *plastique* strategically, in places where it would do the maximum amount of damage to buildings, cave-roof, and the structure of the rock itself. They worked smoothly and silently, unhurried yet fast. Thus far, Hardin considered, they were well within their time-limit at no cost at all. Judging by the silence no one had as yet found the bodies of the men they'd killed, but this did not surprise him. It was, after all, the dead of night; there was clearly a night-shift, but most of the personnel were sleeping in their quarters.

'Colonel!'

That was Fuller's urgent whisper. The stocky Sergeant was standing at a T-junction, pointing to his left. Hardin looked beyond him, saw that here at last was the storage area. What looked to be scores of long metal cylinders lay on racks along both sides of the passage. The racks went back deep. Not scores, thought Hardin grimly, drastically revising his estimate, but hundreds. No, damn it – there must be well over a thousand cylinders here!

'Plas it up,' he snapped. 'I want this crap blown and buried.'

Fuller and the girl started work. Hardin checked his watch and began to set the timers to thirty minutes. He wanted a maximum blow-out, everything going up together, or just about. As his fingers buried detonators into the doughy substance, nimbly connecting the timers, his brain was working at express speed. They were very near the main labs, where the actual agent was boiled up. And also very near the offices of Professor Xin Ming Lu, the man Hoang had said was responsible for the horrors piled up so innocently here in the heavy steel containers.

In those offices was a raft of priceless information: papers, documentation, test-reports, records, formulae. Hardin had no use for it; nor did he have any use for Professor Xin, despite Halderling's order to 'bring back a live one'. The papers were going to burn and so was the Professor. But he had an idea that Major Katarina Berisovna would not be seeing things his way. Out of the corner of his eye he watched her and Fuller finishing their wiring, then he glanced to his right. The other arm of the T ran down to another door, a steel door painted red and with an emblem stencilled on it which was familiar the world over – the skull-and-crossbones. Beyond that, unless Hoang was really pissing him about for some arcane reason, lay the testing-chambers, lecture-room, decontam unit, Professor Xin's office, and the main labs.

That was where the danger lay, Hoang had said. There had been one or two accidents, leaks which had been hastily and effectively controlled, but which had left a horrifying trail of death in their wake. Also, at the flick of a switch, if danger threatened from outside, Professor Xin could close off the entire area and flood it with the nerve agent.

That was where Hardin now had to penetrate. And that was where he did not want the girl to go.

He snapped, 'Sergeant, hold her!'

Fuller, trained to instant obedience whatever the command and whatever the circumstances, grabbed the girl. Her face reddened.

'What is this? You double-crossing bastard, Hardin!' Her voice was harsh, thick with anger.

Hardin said, 'I'm sorry. Ideologically we part company here. Fuller, take her back towards the entrance to this maze. I'll catch you in five.'

The girl began to struggle.

'Damn you, Hardin! I should never have trusted you! Mikhail was right! You want all this for yourself, you swine!'

Hardin shook his head, grinning faintly.

'Sorry, Major, but it's you I don't trust. Believe me, all this is going up. No one is gonna use this stuff. Not the Chinese, the EnVees, the Americans, *or* the Russians. *No One!*'

'I don't believe you, you bastard! You imperialist swine are all the same!' Her voice was growing louder, but was cut off abruptly as Fuller, locking both her arms with one hand, clamped the other over her mouth.

Then pulled it away quickly as she bit him.

'*Shit!*'

'Keep your voice down, Major,' Hardin advised. 'I don't think you'd want to be caught by the Chinese, under the circumstances. They have funny habits.'

He turned, amused despite the tenseness of the situation, and made for the door.

Once through the red door Hardin could feel a difference in the air. It was warmer, the atmosphere clammier. He was in a short corridor with doors leading off, all closed; he selected the nearest, opened it fast, went straight in with his automatic thrust out.

Darkness. He reached for a switch, tripped it. Lights flickered on. He was in a small lecture-room that contained maybe twenty chairs and desks, and a small podium at the far end with a table on it. Hardin closed the door and checked that the foot was tight to the floor. It was; no revealing light would escape into the corridor. This, he thought, will do.

What he had to do now was merely a precautionary measure, a just-in-case that would guard him against some monstrous, disastrous piece of bad luck. But it didn't make him feel any better.

He went to the table, unslung his bag. Inside was a small flat case, not much bigger than a cigar-box. He clicked the catch, opened it, stared impassively at the two plastic syringes nestling in cotton wool. He pulled out another box, bigger, squarer, and opened that too. He peeled back more cotton wool to reveal an assortment of medical supplies: two small bottles of colourless fluid, thick surgical tape, a rubber tourniquet band, raw alcohol, a jaw of cream, green-hued.

He pulled back his left sleeve to the elbow, began to apply the cream to his arm, thickly, though not massaging it into the skin. Then he smeared more of the gunk over his face and down to his neck. He pulled out an off-white silk scarf and tied it round his throat, buttoning his fatigues up tight. He daubed the cream liberally over his hair, his ears, the back of his neck.

He fixed needles to the syringes, thrust one into the neck of one of the bottles and sucked up the contents, gently tapping out the air bubbles. He fixed up the second syringe from the other bottle and laid it back on the cotton wool, closing the case. That was back-up; he hoped he wasn't going to have to use it. He tore some of the surgical tape into long strips, tamping the ends of each on to the table-edge for easy access, then tourniqueted his bare arm, tugging the rubber strap tight using his teeth and free right hand. He loosened the cap on the bottle of alcohol but didn't take it off. With the flat of his hand he banged up the veins on his left arm until they stood out like cables. He stared at the result for some seconds.

This was the sixty-four-thousand dollar question: to what extent had Hoang Van Tho lied to him?

The removal of the radio equipment could have been – almost certainly was – sheer bad luck. The headless guards, however, meant that something was seriously out of kilter somewhere. And if Hoang was screwing him somehow, for whatever reason, with regard to that – could he trust the *thieu tuong* on this?

The fluid in the bottle was, so Hoang had said, the antidote to the nerve agent, which the Chinese had stumbled across whilst creating the agent itself. It, like the agent, was a brew of a number of chemicals: primarily atropine to stimulate the heart, methyldexalene, parlodoxamine, and others, mainly to counteract the nerve agent's fearsome searing and blistering effects. Together they treated both the peripheral nervous system and the central nervous system. The main problem was, if you simply shot up before you needed to, it'd kill you: it was only effective during a nerve-gas attack, as a direct counter-measure, so it had to be administered only seconds before the stuff hit you. *Great*, thought Hardin sourly. The cream was a grease which did not absorb quickly into the pores of the skin, and was thus a second line of defence if the gas, droplet-based, got loose. There was nothing he could do about his clothes, but the serum was the main defence, and as long as he had it in his system he was okay.

So Hoang had said.

And maybe it was true.

On the other hand maybe Hoang had spiked the juice so that Hardin could function properly and destroy the complex, then die in terrible agony as a result of a delayed action toxin. Or maybe Hoang had had no time to fix something like that up and the stuff worked and he was going to be fine.

Shrugging suddenly, he said aloud, his voice echoing faintly and errily in the empty room, 'No choice.'

He unscrewed the cap of the alcohol bottle, placed a small wad of cotton wool over the neck, upended it. He swabbed at a vein near the elbow-joint, feeling the coldness of the fluid, then screwed the cap back on, placing the bottle in the box. He took the full syringe and inserted the needle into the vein, his arm lying on the table-top, then dexterously taped the syringe to his flesh, wrapping the strips round his arm. The syringe had a tiny bayonet clip which locked into place, so that the plunger was not forced out by the pressure of blood from the vein; but just to make sure, Hardin taped a second strip over the plunger, holding it in place. There were all kinds of appalling disasters that could happen – when taking the separate tape off to push the plunger home, for instance, he might jerk the whole kit-and-kaboodle off, losing his defences at the flick of a finger – but it was the best that could be done in the time.

He pulled on a pair of skintight surgical gloves and began packing the equipment away, keeping the box with the second syringe at the top of his bag. That was for emergencies. If he started to feel realy weird, Hoang had said, jab another needleful in and hope for the best.

Jesus, thought Hardin sardonically, the things I do to keep Western civilization alive and kicking.

He let his unbuttoned sleeve hang loosely around his wrists and slung the bag across his back. He walked quickly to the door, feeling strange; his fingers were fizzing very slightly, but that could be imagination.

He laid some more *plastique*, then flicked the light off and cautiously opened the door – and came face to face with Katarina.

She was angry; more to the point she had the drop on him, her silenced automatic pointing unwaveringly at his chest.

'Put your gun in its holster,' she said, her voice thin and harsh.

A feeling of wild panic starting to surge up inside him, Hardin said, 'You stupid bitch! You could die in here!'

'Sure. Now put the gun away.'

He did as he was told, breathing hard. 'Where's Fuller?'

'I knocked him out. In the KGB, training is far more creative than in your army. It was relatively simple to escape from his armlock.'

'Look,' said Hardin desperately, 'for God's sake get out of here. You don't know what you're doing. I swear to you I'm not taking souvenirs. We can all do without this shit.'

'I don't believe you, Colonel,' she said. 'And I don't trust you.'

Hardin's attention was suddenly caught by a movement up the corridor, beyond her. His eyes flickered uneasily. She sneered, 'Oh, don't be so ridiculous . . . .'

'Do not move! Either of you!'

The girl's face changed colour, became white and drawn. Her mouth opened. There was something comic about this sudden transformation, but Hardin felt no amusement at all.

At the end of the corridor were two men, both Chinese. One, very tall, unusually so for one of his race, had on a white lab-coat; the other, stockier, grim of face, held an automatic rifle. The tall man, Hardin knew from Hoang's description, was Professor Xin Ming Lu, the short one his assistant Dr Hua.

'Take off your weapons. Throw them down.'

That was Hua. He jerked the automatic rifle menacingly. Katarina dropped her pistol, unslung her M-16. Her eyes were tense, frightened. Hardin couldn't blame her for her fear; he wasn't feeling exactly fearless himself. He took off his Kalashnikov, threw it down.

'And the pistol.'

He pulled the pistol out and threw it to the floor. He was hoping that with all the cam cream on his face they wouldn't be noticing the greenish tinge to his skin, his hair. He also prayed that they might, for the moment, be too concerned about the weaponry to bother about his and the girl's bags.

'And the grenades.'

One by one the girl and Hardin divested themselves of their grenades. No use trying to throw one; they'd both be dead long before the damn thing blew.

Keeping his distance Xin stared at them as though they were beetles on a slide. Then suddenly he smiled, deathshead-like.

'If there are two, my dear Hua, there will be more. I will take these to the test-chamber. All is prepared. You will sound the alarm, find Colonel Su, capture the rest. Tell Colonel Su that there will be much unpleasantness for him over this.' He kept smiling toothily, talking as though all this was an everyday occurrence. He took Hua's rifle and gestured with it. 'Walk,' he said. 'Towards me, then backwards through this door. I want to see your faces.'

This suited Hardin. Hua waited until the couple had reached him then scurried past, crablike, grinning angrily. Xin jabbed the rifle at a door.

'Through here. Keep facing me.' He was talking all the time now: 'How did you get here. How did you get into the complex.' These were not questions; it was almost as though he was thinking aloud. 'Most curious. And Americans, too. Well, we shall soon know all, although not from you. It so happens you have arrived at an opportune moment. For me, however, not for you.' He chuckled ghoulishly. 'No. Certainly not for you. As you are here, you must know what we are doing. Soon you will experience the results of our experiments at first hand. Do you know,' he laughed, his eyes almost seeming to sparkle with delight, 'I find, with each experiment, I have a strong desire to see more. The results of our labours are quite impressive. Death in a score of seconds. Necrosis in less. *Actual necrosis!*' He laughed out loud. 'Extraordinary, is it not? You will have no need of worms to eat you up!'

It occurred to Hardin, as he stumbled backwards, hands in the air, that this guy had seen too much death, too many horrors. He was beginning to wig.

'Stop there!'

Hardin's eyes drifted. They had passed a large steel door, like the entrance to a bank vault. Xin began playing with a dial, then twisted a heavy handle. The door swung open, ponderously.

'Inside!'

Hardin was nearest. He edged in, keeping his face towards the Chinese, still holding his hands up. He backed into the room, the girl following.

'Gonna kill us now?' said Hardin.

Professor Xin wagged an admonitory finger.

'Wait,' he said softly, 'wait.'

The door swung closed.

As soon as it thudded home Hardin snarled at the girl, 'You goddamn stupid fucking *bitch*!' and began struggling with his bag. The room was bare, white-walled. A clock was set into one wall, high; opposite was an oblong mirror, wide and long.

'Get in the corner by the door,' he snapped. 'Get some plas out, two detonators. No good trying to blow the door, we'd blow ourselves out too. Two thin strips. We'll take out the mirror. It's gotta be a window. We can climb through.'

The girl didn't argue or hesitate. She crouched in the corner, working the *plastique*. Hardin joined her, began taking out the medical supplies. He was sweating profusely, and it felt extremely weird with all the grease on his face. His gloves were skintight but his fingers still felt like sausages. Breathing harshly he mumbled 'Shit-shit-shit! More haste less fucking speed!' He'd been in tight situations before, but never like this; never threatened with a death that made your guts erupt and blood fountain from every orifice and rot set in within seconds, no reprieve, and with only a maybe chance of survival in the form of an antidote that could just be tap-water, a vicious practical joke by Hoang Van Tho.

He didn't bother glancing at the clock as he tore up surgical tape, uncapped the alcohol. He thought: Xin'll want to gloat; surely he'll want to gloat; *please God let the bastard want to gloat*!'

'Done,' said the girl.

'Ninety second timer,' said Hardin.

He noticed her hands were trembling, then realized his were too.

'Left sleeve. Roll it up. Put some of that green gunk over your face, hair, hands, arms. As much as there is. *Quickly*!'

He took the plas, scrambled to the window, ducking low. He fixed the dough in long strips to the glass, tight to the frame, then ducked back to the girl. He said, 'Christ-Christ-Christ!'

He tourniqueted her arm with the rubber strap, glancing at her face as he tugged at it. She was trembling slightly, breathing quickly, but her eyes revealed no terror. They were wide liquid pools, strangely calm.

She said, 'Don't worry, we'll be all right.'

He said, 'For Christ's sake, *I* should be saying that!'

He swabbed her arm, banged up the veins, inserted the prepped syringe, taped it. He said, 'Hold the plunger, but don't for God's sake push it. Not till I say. And only a little.' Then he said, 'Look, okay, you're not a goddamn stupid fucking bitch, I'm sorry.' Then he said, jerking his head up to stare again in her eyes, 'You *could* have killed me in Do Thon. *And* gotten away with it.'

A smile trembled at her lips. She said, 'Yes. I couldn't pull the trigger. I still can't rationalize it. And only you will ever know.'

His face was close to hers and he could smell her, what seemed the very essence of her at that moment: a curiously heady compound of sweat and fear and her own unique woman's scent. He kissed her, passionately at first then gently easing back, tenderly nibbling at her lower lip. He did not close his eyes and nor did she, and her kiss was as passionate, as urgent as his; not yielding at all.

'How foolish.'

Hardin swung round, his heart jolting with shock at his first sight-flash of the grotesque thing that peered at him, snout pressed to the glass, now transformed into a two-way window, along the wall. It took him two or three seconds to realize that it was Xin dressed in a protective suit. Even the voice was grotesque, a travesty, transmitted through the facemask's voicemitter and out of hidden speakers in the room itself.

Harsh and buzzing and crackly, as though Xin were speaking from the moon.

Hardin stayed where he was. There was no point in getting up. He suddenly realized that ninety seconds had long gone and the plas hadn't blown the window out and an image of Katarina's trembling fingers as she set the timers slid into his mind. *Oh shit . . .*

'And how pathetic,' Xin went on. 'You intend to stay there, crouching like frightened animals? No matter. You will dance soon, all over the room. Just as your compatriots will dance very soon, in the crowded cities and bases. A dance of death.' He laughed, the sound macabre, unearthly in the chamber. 'I will set you dancing . . . '

Hardin muttered '*Now*' hoarsely. He tore at the tape, pressed the syringe's plunger gently, releasing some of the serum into his veins, at the same time hearing a faint hiss of sound, like a sigh. He caught sight of a faint mist appearing at a grille high in the wall, a scarlet fog.

Sky-fire.

'A medium dose,' Xin went on.

Hardin cut him off, concentrating on what he was doing. His mouth was suddenly very dry, his face felt cold. Then all at once his nose began to run. He began to feel panicky, pressed the plunger more, holding his left arm tight to his chest. He gasped to the girl, 'Put some more in.'

His voice sounded high-pitched and his ears were buzzing. He got to his feet, sniffing, swaying. He felt light-headed, as though he was high on marijuana; he wanted to laugh.

Xin shouted, 'What are you doing? What have you got there?'

Salvation, you insane fucker, thought Hardin. He swayed on his feet, laughing uproariously. His nose had stopped running.

Xin turned from the window, began to lumber across the room. And as he did so there was a brief flaring flash, a fire-cracker report, and the reinforced glass starred, shivered, blew out of the death-chamber. Xin swung round, staring owlishly at the sight, seemingly transfixed.

Hardin shot some more of the serum into his arm, feverishly taped up the plunger again. He staggered to the window-space, began to clamber through. Professor Xin gave a weird, wild cry, turned again, tried to run. Useless in such cumbrous garments.

'God damn you to hell,' snarled Hardin, spears of near-insane rage lancing through him. He reached Xin, grabbing at the voluminous folds of nerve-gas resistant material that swathed the lumbering figure, tried to pull him over. Xin wrenched himself free, turned, glared at Hardin's left arm.

'*How?*' he screamed.

He tried to grab Hardin's arm, tried to tear at the taped syringe, crush it. Hardin didn't give him a chance. He kicked at the man's legs savagely, homicidally. Xin let out a shriek of agony, toppled, still yelling, and Hardin knew he'd cracked a bone at least. He shoved at the man, sent him crashing to the floor face up. He knelt on Xin's chest, holding his left arm out of reach, and began to tear at Xin's mask, ripping at the material as Xin screamed, pleaded, struggled.

Soon he'd wrenched off the mask, or chunks of it, by main force and Xin's face was exposed to the air, the thin mouth gulping like a landed fish's. Blood suddenly came out in a thin stream that became a gush, thicker, darker. His eyes watered redly, weeping tears of blood. Blood flowed from his nostrils. Hardin sprang away from him, aghast, as the man began to spasm violently, throwing up blood and vomit over himself, his cries turning to inarticulate meaningless, bloody gurgles.

Hardin turned away, icy-browed, sickened. The girl was by his side. He took her shoulder, hugged her to him, and then went staggering to the door. Outside the room he mumbled quickly, 'Shoot some more, but only a little.' Then his voice pitched high. 'Christ, this place is gonna go up any fucking second!'

They ran shamblingly down the corridor, burst through the red door, plunged into the maze of duckboarded passageways. Hardin was holding his left arm to his chest, the syringe plunger now taped into place, his right arm flung round the girl. He suddenly realized she was having to hold her syringe to stop the blood-flow pushing the plunger back.

'How the hell. You climb through. Window.'

'Great. Difficulty.'

He started to laugh.

And stopped, staggering to a halt.

As Dr Hua, holding another rifle, came around a corner up ahead. He loomed demented.

'How did you . . . ?' He shook his head, dismissing the question. It wasn't relevant. He screamed at them, 'It is a madhouse out there! A full-scale assault! But we will defeat you filthy imperialist scum! And you will pay now!'

Even as he shouted Hardin was aware of the faint sound of grenade explosions and bursts of automatic fire. Hua's finger tightened on the trigger.

At that moment a man appeared behind him, hands held high. Something looped over Hua's head, tightened round his throat. The man jumped close, jerked his hands high. Hua stiffened, his body bowing outwards, and the rifle chattered viciously, Hardin and the girl dodging to one side as rounds hammered up into the roof. The next thing he knew, Hardin was staring at Hua's head tumbling to the floor, bouncing soggily like a fallen grapefruit. The body followed.

'Hey,' said Garrett, 'I been havin' myself a fuckin' ball!'

XIII

'You *prick*!' Hardin spat out at the man.

'I just saved your fuckin' bacon,' Garrett pointed out, his tone defensive. He stuffed the triple-strand piano-wire and toggles of the garotte into his shirt pocket, then stared at Hardin. 'Hey, you shootin' up, Colonel? Funny fuckin' place ta do it.'

Hardin said, 'Goddamnit, this complex is gonna blow to hell in . . . ' He glanced hurriedly at his watch, saw there was still some leeway: ' . . . seven minutes.' He picked up Hua's dropped rifle, said, 'We may have trouble getting out of here. Oh, and one thing . . . '

'Yeah?'

'Don't touch me. Or Major Berisovna.'

Garrett looked blankly at the girl. He didn't recognize her at all.

They began to run again, Garrett saying, 'Fuck, I've hadda time of it! Best thing I ever did was slip away from you guys. It was shit-easy gettin' in here, ya know? These slanty-eyed little fuckers, they won't mess Charlie Garrett around no more. Jesus, I lost counta the number of heads I musta taken off. I'm tellin' ya . . . '

'I don't want to hear about it,' snarled Hardin. Still holding his left arm to his chest he jammed the butt of the rifle into his side as he ran, so that the gun jutted out like an extra limb.

204

As they rounded a bend a figure came groggily out of the shadows, holding the back of his head.

'Fuller!'

The stocky Sergeant glared at the girl but Hardin snapped, 'Forget it. Run!'

He was aware that the sound of grenades exploding was getting louder, crisper; aware too that they were running out of time. But they were also nearing the cave entrance. They swung round a bend and ahead was the grassy slope up to the trees.

But now the entire area was lit up hellishly by flames. The sound of a firefight crashed in Hardin's ears. He saw a man-shape silhouetted up the slope, firing out from bushes; another silhouette on the other side. The two Russians. Hardin sprinted up the slope, avoiding bodies which littered the ground.

'With me!' he yelled.

He reached the top of the slope and saw that there were at least four choppers burning in the cleared area. The two Russians had done a swell job. He also saw figures dashing about in the flickering, garish light of the flames. A grenade erupted to his left, red-cored; then another. Tracer, streams of it, arced over the clearing from all sides.

Then he spotted Comeraro, an unmistakable figure in the bushes.

'Lieutenant!'

Comeraro turned, came crashing down through the under-growth.

'Colonel! Jesus, am I . . .'

'Where's the rest?'

Comeraro scowled. 'We nearly got blown all ways. That bastard Reisman! They started a fight. Deliberate. They tried to ice Vogt but he floored the guy with his crutch . . .'

'*Crutch?*'

'Yeah. We blew a couple of 'em away, grabbed the kid, beat it. Ran into EnVees, had a tussle, got away. All hell broke loose down here when those choppers arrived. Some jokers were blowing them outta the sky. Hell of a mess. The Reds followed us, but they're tangling with EnVees over there.' He gestured vaguely. 'There's Chinese, EnVees, Russians – Jesus! All shooting at each other. No one knows what's going on!'

'Olsen, Pepper, Vogt?'

'Up the slope.'

'Go get 'em. We'll make for the trees.'

Comeraro said, 'One thing. There's another chopper. It landed intact. The troops jumped out but Olsen and I took out the pilot and crew.'

Hardin didn't hesitate.

'Good man. Let's go.'

Comeraro stared at Hardin's arm.

'I, uh . . . don't think there's anyone else can fly it, Colonel, if you, uh . . . '

'Don't worry,' said Hardin grimly, 'I could fly a fucking tank to get out of this. Oh, and Comeraro . . . '

'Sir?'

'Whatever you do, don't touch me. Or Major Berisovna. Warn the others.'

Comeraro stared at him nervously, then turned and headed for the slope.

Hardin wondered if the choppers were Hoang Van Tho's work. Of course, there had to be another radio shack and when things started to pop the alarm-call would've gone out damn fast. Even so, he had a strong feeling that Hoang would have been waiting, wherever the choppers were stationed. Still, in this confusion . . .

He watched as Comeraro and Olsen supported Vogt past the blazing helicopters at a stumbling run, Garrett, Fuller and the two Russians following, Katarina at their heels. He began to run after them, thinking that those two Reds had done a hell of a job and it wouldn't be his fault if, once they got back south of the DeeEmZee, they managed successfully to vanish when no one was looking.

And then there was Katarina . . .

He was thinking about her, sprinting past the nearest chopper and ducking away from the fierce, searing heat, when he saw Resnovich. Hardin veered towards him. He thought: Let the KGB face the music; that fucker Resnovich deserves everything he's going to get at the hands of the Chinese.

Resnovich, firing at an unseen target, suddenly seemed to sense Hardin's approach. He half-turned, spotted him. His face became demonic, but before he could take the running American out Hardin was on him. He held his left arm stiffly at his side and lunged at Resnovich's guts with his right. Resnovich jack-knifed, dropping his M-16, and Hardin sent in a jolting roundhouse blow to the point of the jaw, socking the Russian over backwards. There was a good chance he'd broken the bastard's jaw.

Hardin ran on, ducking, keeping low, as murderous streams of rounds tore the air around him. The unburned chopper loomed up and he saw that Katarina was standing by the nose.

'Can you fly?'

'Yes, but . . . ' She gestured at her arm.

'We'll both fly the damn thing.'

Hardin flung himself into the pilot's seat. His left arm was starting to throb but this would not affect things too drastically, so long as he could get out fast, get back to Do Thon. The girl ran through an instrument check, quickly and efficiently. Then he heard Comeraro yell from the rear, 'Christ, they spotted us!'

Rounds began to hammer against the bird, rocking it. Tracer flared in long lines, seemingly swerving down towards them. Hardin triggered the switch on the collective, heard the motor whine shrilly.

'They're charging!' bawled Comeraro.

The squad were firing like demented demons out of one side of the chopper, using up mags, jamming more in. Hardin swore as he felt the rotors turning above him; slowly, so slowly. Then he felt something else, a quiver below that had nothing to do with the bird at all, a menacing shudder in the earth itself.

'The plas. It's starting to blow.'

Out of the corner of his eye he caught a vast, soaring gout of fire, so bright it turned the fiercely burning helicopters into mere candle-flames, spouting up into the night-sky; an explosion of roaring dragon's-breath that must have erupted deep out of the bowels of the mountain. He took no notice as he felt the bird becoming light on the skids, nose rising slightly. He corrected, the bellow of the engine deafening, a roar of triumph. The rotors chewed air.

He lifted off, soared free from the holocaust below, rose higher, higher, ever higher . . .